T0348947

IF I COULD GO BACK

Published by Peachtree Teen
An imprint of PEACHTREE PUBLISHING COMPANY INC.
1700 Chattahoochee Avenue
Atlanta, Georgia 30318-2112
PeachtreeBooks.com

Edited by Ashley Hearn
Design and composition by Lily Steele

Printed and bound in March 2025 at Sheridan, Chelsea, MI, USA.
10 9 8 7 6 5 4 3 2 1
First Edition
ISBN: 978-1-68263-775-3

Library of Congress Cataloging-in-Publication Data

Names: Johnson, Briana, author.
Title: If I could go back / Briana Johnson.
Description: First edition. | Atlanta, Georgia : Peachtree Teen, 2025. | Audience term: Teenagers | Audience: Ages 14 and Up. | Audience: Grades 10-12. | Summary: Struggling with anxiety and feelings of abandonment, Aaliyah secretly contacts her parents who left her as a toddler, upsetting her grandfather and the family who has always supported her. Identifiers: LCCN 2024052174 | ISBN 9781682637753 (hardcover) | ISBN 9781682637975 (ebook)
Subjects: CYAC: Family life—Fiction. | Secrets—Fiction. | Anxiety—Fiction. | Abandoned children—Fiction. | African Americans—Fiction. | LCGFT: Novels.
Classification: LCC PZ7.1.J5918 If 2025 | DDC [Fic]—dc23
LC record available at https://lccn.loc.gov/2024052174

EU Authorized Representative: HackettFlynn Ltd., 36 Cloch Choirneal, Balrothery, Co. Dublin, K32 C942, Ireland. EU@walkerpublishinggroup.com

IF I COULD GO BACK

BRIANA JOHNSON

PEACHTREE
Teen

In loving memory of my grandfather,
Willie—losing you inspired me to write
this book.

And my grandmother, Lovie Dell,
who never failed to make me smile.
Without you, life feels meaningless.
I love you and I miss you.

PART ONE
JANUARY

1

Grandpa Joe sends me an ominous text at 8:57 on a random Thursday morning. The message says Come home. We need to talk . . . But I'm thinking he really means *You're in deep shit, kiddo. The next time you're gonna see the light of day is when you're fifty.*

Chlorinated water drips down my face as I stare at the message on my phone. Despite telling my grandpa not to text me anymore because he doesn't understand proper texting etiquette, he keeps on doing it. He drops in an ellipsis at the most inappropriate time along with a vague message and then refuses to elaborate until I get home. It makes me wish my auntie had listened to me and refused to teach him how to text. Instead, she gave him a full tutorial, and now he's a constant menace to my mental health and well-being.

"Aaliyah, why are you staring at your phone like it grew two feet and a tail?" Ivy barely looks up from her phone screen. She's so focused on it that I'm surprised she noticed me having a mini crisis next to her. "Please don't tell me somebody died. I'm not emotionally equipped to deal with something like that."

The logical part of my brain believes Grandpa Joe wants to talk about something insignificant. Like he's upset because I ate the last pint of his favorite ice cream again. The paranoid, guilt-ridden part of my mind insists he knows what I'm planning to do behind his back. "Nobody's dead. Grandpa sent me another weird text, and the vagueness is making my stomach hurt."

"Why are you worrying about your phone? You need to finish your workout so I can leave this humid-ass pool."

Today is one of the rare times where I can't be bothered to focus on my workout. It's been six weeks since I created a Facebook profile specifically to reach out to Lena, but nerves have kept me from messaging her. This should be simple. All I need to do is tell her who I am and what I want.

I don't want her money. Grandpa Joe already has plenty of it from retirement and disability and pensions and all the other adult bull crap I'm supposed to care about later in life. I just want to have lunch with her someday. It's a fair request. She's my mother, for Christ's sake. The least she could do is meet me for a meal after abandoning me as a baby.

"Aaliyah, I know you can hear me," Ivy says.

The urge to tell Ivy about finding Lena on Facebook is at its strongest this morning, but I want to avoid the inevitable fight for as long as I can. The fact I'm even considering messaging Lena will piss her off, so I quickly come up with a way to avoid her question without lying. Ivy and Grandpa Joe tease me by calling me a terrible liar and I can't even catch an attitude because it's true. I'm a pro at finding loopholes though. "Grandpa has been acting weird lately."

Nailed it.

"When isn't he weird?" Ivy asks.

"This isn't his usual weirdness. He's been super aggy, keeps looking off into the distance with a blank stare, and he doesn't talk either. But when he's back to normal and I ask him about it, he says it's nothing and tells me to do my homework."

"We don't have homework. There's still a week of winter break left."

"That's why it's weird. Then he sent me this text with all these dots. I'm about to have a nervous breakdown."

"Let me see." Ivy stops smoothing down her baby hair and takes my phone from me. "It's so obvious what those dots mean when you read between the lines."

I'm skeptical. If it's obvious, I should know, right? "What do they mean?"

"These three dots represent each individual ass whooping Grandpa Joe is gonna give you for eating that last bit of caramel cake he was saving." Ivy cackles when I snatch my phone from her. "RIP. You'll forever be my third-favorite cousin."

Third favorite? *Third?* "Who's above me?"

"Gigi and Rocky on my daddy's side."

"I'm a semi-functioning member of society and they still wet the bed. How are two toddlers beating me?"

"They don't irritate me. They know when to shut up. They actually listen when I tell them something."

"All right. Jesus. You didn't need to make a list," I say, tucking my phone into the side pocket of my Nike bag. "Jerk."

"Don't make me hurt your feelings, Aaliyah."

I wave her off and head back to my pool lane before somebody steals it from me. I'm halfway through my next set of laps when I become antsy. I swim over to Ivy and rest my arms on the pool edge, ignoring her smug little grin. "I probably shouldn't have eaten his cake."

"See, there's no off button with you. And no, you shouldn't have."

"If I go down for this, I'm taking you with me. You ate just as much cake as I did. I'm not gonna feel bad about it either, since I'm your third-favorite cousin."

"Grandpa should've added a fourth dot for the ass whupping I'mma give you if you snitch on me."

"I'm afraid of a lot of things. You aren't one of them."

Her full attention is on me now. Ivy narrows her eyes, shooting one of her infamous "I'll cut you" glares my way. Then she puts her phone down and I know I'm in trouble. I'm a quarter of the way down my lane when Ivy starts chucking pool noodles at me. One clips me on the head, and I go down like a complete drama queen.

"You're lucky you're in the water," Ivy shouts. "I'm—"

Ivy's threat is cut off by a shrill whistle. The lifeguard on duty is this angry-looking dude with a mohawk who clearly takes his job too seriously. "Hey. *Hey!* Out of the pool!"

"Dude, I'm the victim in this situation." I point at Ivy. "She's the one who attacked me. Kick her out."

4

"You see that?" Lifeguard-dude points to the sign on the wall behind him. One of the rules clearly states "No running or horseplay in pool area," and even though I've been coming to the YMCA for years, I act like I don't know what he's talking about. "Quit messing around. I know you can read."

"I'm choosing not to because I'm not done with my workout," I say.

The boy climbs down from his chair, clutching his flotation device in one hand and pointing to the girl's locker room with the other. "Out of the pool before I ban you both."

I don't know what kind of power lifeguards have, but I don't want to push my luck since this is the only public indoor pool in a twenty-mile radius. Everyone still in the water stares at me and Ivy as we leave the area and head back into the locker room with our things.

I punch Ivy in the arm once we're out of sight. "I didn't finish my workout."

"Be for real. You weren't actually working out." Ivy's phone dings, taking her attention away from me yet again. She taps out a response, acrylic nails clicking against the screen at a lightning-fast speed. "Forgot to tell you that you've gotta find somebody else to chill with tonight. I got plans."

"Plans with who?"

"Plans with none of your business, nosy."

"Are you hooking up with somebody?" I dry myself off with a towel and toss it onto the bench when I'm done. "Remember we promised we'd tell each other if we were, even if the person is ugly."

"You need to be worrying about how Grandpa is gonna light you up for trying to link with that bum you call a mama instead of focusing on who I'm spending my time with."

My body temp spikes to a hundred degrees and my pores excrete sweat immediately. If I cursed, this would be the perfect time to drop a fat f-bomb. I haven't told Ivy about my plan to contact Lena. Haven't even hinted at it out of pure fear of her reaction. I'm too afraid to look at her when I ask, "How do you know about that?"

"You left your phone unlocked when you were at my apartment last week. I thought it was weird that you downloaded the Facebook app since you don't have a profile, so I clicked on it and saw Lena's name in your search history. It was pretty shitty of you to keep it a secret from me."

"I swear I wanted to tell you as soon as I had the idea, but I knew you'd be mad. You're loud about your dislike of her."

"Uh, yeah, because she sucks. Why would you even wanna be around that bum after she left you the way she did?"

"Chill. That 'bum' is your auntie."

"And? Family members can be bums. Look at Cousin Ricky on my daddy's side. All he does is beg people for money and ignore his kids. Am I supposed to ignore his bum tendencies because he's blood? No. That's why he's a bum and so is your bum-ass mama."

"Harsh."

"*I'm* harsh?" Oh, God. I got Ivy started. "Lena and that piece of garbage she called her man abandoned you. They pawned you off on Grandma and Grandpa and went on with their lives like you never existed. But yeah, I'm the one that's harsh."

An unnatural heaviness comes over my body and I plop down on the wooden bench situated between two sets of lockers. Ivy's comments bring back all the horrible thoughts I'd shoved into a place where I wouldn't have to ever think about them. Over the years, I've forced myself to believe that Lena didn't give me up because she didn't want me anymore. That something horrible must've happened to keep her away from me for eighteen years. But Ivy blasted through the illusion with her harsh words, and now I'm forced to confront the other possibility—Lena gave me away because she never wanted me, and she hasn't reached out because she's happy I'm gone.

"I'm not gonna let you hurt my feelings because we're in public, but trust that I will cry about it when I'm alone."

"Don't make me out to be the villain because I told the truth."

"You could've kept your truth. I didn't want it."

Ivy's shoes come into view, stopping within inches of mine. I don't look up from the ground and watch as she shuffles her feet around like I'm supposed to know what that means. "I'm sorry, okay? I shouldn't have said it like that, but as much as it sucks to hear, Lena's actions aren't pointing in the direction of caring mother. They're aimed right at deadbeat. And deep down you know that because if she gave half a shit about you, she'd be here right now."

"I refuse to let that be my reality."

"Not to be a bitch, but you sound delusional."

"Better delusional than miserable. You don't get it. Your mom kept you. She loved you enough to stick around even when things were hard, but mine . . ." I dab away the tears building in the corner of my eye before they have a chance to fall. "I know I'm difficult to love sometimes, but that's what moms are supposed to do. They love you in spite of the difficultness. I won't survive knowing my mom was an outlier, so I pretend she's not. I think if I pretend hard enough, I'll manifest it into being true."

"I don't think that's how manifestation works."

"Ivy."

"You can pretend and manifest all you want, but if you're wrong and you link with her, the truth is gonna break you into a million pieces. I won't sit by and let you do that to yourself." Ivy bumps me on the shoulder, and I make room for her on the bench. She tries to wait until I'm looking at her before she says anything else, but I can't hold eye contact for more than a few seconds. "Even if it ends well, it won't end well. Don't do this to yourself or to Grandpa Joe, Aaliyah. Please."

I'm aware of the dangers behind what I'm thinking about doing. Other than pure anxiety, Grandpa Joe is the reason why I still haven't sent a message to Lena in the six weeks since I found her Facebook profile. But I'll never get answers if I don't, and honestly, that's all I've ever wanted. Despite not really wanting to, I say, "I guess you're right."

"Are you gonna pout for the rest of the day?"

"Probably."

"I'm canceling my plans."

"You don't have to."

Ivy sends out a quick message, then tosses me the change of clothes from my Nike bag. "Come on, we'll go back to my place and watch dumb movies all night. It'll take your mind off Lena, and you won't have to answer any of Grandpa Joe's questions when he inevitably asks why you look the way you do."

"He wants me home."

"And you're actually going?"

I shrug. "What else am I gonna do?"

"We'll chill together tonight and you can hit up Tommy's party with me tomorrow. Jen told me you said you'd think about it."

"Be for real. I was never gonna go."

"Fine. Be boring then. You can go home tomorrow, but my daddy's gotta drop you off. Now let's go. It's gross and wet in here."

Grandpa Joe's anger toward Lena and my father, Quincy, especially is extreme more than it's not. He hates them for reasons I don't exactly understand, and we're not able to have a normal discussion about them. The last time I tried to ask him about Lena, it led to him going on a ten-minute rant about how I need to stay away from her because she's no good for me and if I didn't listen, he'd ground me for the rest of my life. Dramatic? Absolutely. But it scared me off from asking anything about her for the next three months.

So, nothing Ivy said was wrong, but it still doesn't feel right. Keeping the peace between me and Grandpa Joe means me feeling incomplete and unworthy of love for the rest of my life. How is it fair that everyone else gets to be happy while I'm forced to be miserable, so I don't make others feel the way I have for eighteen years? It isn't fair. If you ask Grandpa Joe, he'd say that's life. And maybe he's right, but I don't want it to be mine.

2

More than twenty-four hours after receiving Grandpa Joe's vague text, I finally make it home. He isn't in his usual spot on the couch. Tonight he's sitting at the head of the table in the living room playing spades with three of his buddies. He doesn't hear me come in and his friends keep their mouths shut when I press a finger to my lips.

I wrap my arms around him and kiss his cheek. "What's up, Gramps?"

"Don't 'what's up' me." Grandpa Joe doesn't flinch at the contact. It's crazy how hard it is to scare this man. Michael Myers could approach him on the street with a butcher knife aimed at his chest and Grandpa Joe would look Mike right in the eye and tell him to go bother somebody else. "I told you to come home yesterday. It's damn near tomorrow."

"Technically you told me to come home. You never specified a date or time."

"Watch yourself before I specify this belt to your behind."

"That doesn't make any sense." I smile at Grandpa Joe's friends to be polite. "Hey, how y'all doing?"

"Don't answer that. She's up to something." Grandpa Joe twists in his seat and eyes me the way he does when he thinks I'm up to no good. "What had you so busy that you couldn't come home when I asked? I want the truth."

"I told you I was at the Y."

"At the Y with who? You better not have been with that Thomas boy."

I keep telling him I haven't seen Tommy in weeks because Grandpa Joe hates our friends-with-benefits relationship, but he never listens. It's like he's blocking out what I say on purpose because it doesn't fit the nonsense he's made up in his mind. Rather than repeat myself, I take the risk of making him mad and ignore him. "Can I spend the night at Ivy's place this weekend? She said she'll pick me up, so you don't have to take me."

"You and Ivy always talking 'bout spending the night. Then it turns into a spend the week. Next thing I know it's gonna be a spend the month."

"Sounds like you be missing me when I'm gone."

"Deflecting." This big, burly dude named Henry stares at his cards, rearranging them until he's satisfied with the order. "Bad sign, Joe."

The other two guys at the table, Gregory and Pete, nod in unison. Then Pete opens his big mouth and says, "Notice she didn't mention who she was running around the streets of Chicago with."

"Probably was off getting into all kinds of trouble with that boy you don't like," Gregory says.

"You guys are being so not chill right now. I was with Ivy." But it's too late. The damage has been done. Grandpa Joe is looking at me like I'm hiding a Tommy-sized secret from him, and I realize the best thing to do is to remove myself from the situation. "I'm going up to my room, so y'all can stop trying to get me into trouble."

They all crack up.

"Don't go too far, kiddo. We need to talk."

Grandpa Joe doesn't hint at what he wants to talk to me about, and he kind of stops paying attention to me the moment it's his turn in the game.

Upstairs in my room, I start panic-pacing. Due to a moment of carelessness on my part, Ivy found out about my plan to contact Lena. Grandpa Joe could have found out somehow too. Not from Ivy. She might pick on me, but if I tell her a secret, she'll take it to the grave. But he could've seen the app on my phone and got curious the same way Ivy did. It's not that far-fetched. I leave my phone everywhere and it's not always locked. This is bad. Maybe I should come clean. My punishment might not be as severe if I do. I'd be able to finish out the final part of my senior year with a short grounding versus one that lasts months, but if I'm wrong about him knowing, I could screw myself by accident. I really wish my grandpa had told me what he wanted to talk to me about. I wouldn't be sick to my stomach if he had.

I swipe over to Facebook on my phone and click on it. Because I never intended to actually use the app, I only have one friend, Uncle William, who adds everyone, and only one person is in the search—Lena Campbell. Like I have many times over the past six weeks, I click on her profile and scroll down to her posts. I almost drop my phone. It looks different. She's added a picture of her and a guy. I zoom in on him. He's got the bottom half of his face covered by his hand, but those eyes. There's something familiar about them.

I cross my room and grab the only picture I have of my parents together. And there he is. Quincy. My dad. It's the same guy on Facebook, but I don't understand. Grandpa Joe always said he doesn't like Quincy because he abandoned Lena after I was born, which directly led to her leaving me with him and my grandma. But if that was true, why are they together now? And if they are together, why didn't they take me back?

It stings seeing Quincy and Lena together and looking happy. I should be there with them, but they didn't want me. That's never been clearer than it is right now.

Before I have a chance to truly spiral, I receive a FaceTime call from Ivy. She doesn't give me a chance to speak, just says, "I knew something was wrong with you. I felt a shift in the cosmos."

"That doesn't make sense."

"Am I wrong?"

"No. I thought you were going to Tommy's party."

"I'm here now in Jen's room. I wanted to check on you before I started having fun. Grandpa Joe fake grounded you again for eating his cake?"

Grandpa Joe's fake groundings are well known in our little family. He punishes me to keep me from thinking I can get away with anything, but there's no substance behind them. No real anger. He takes my phone and tells me I'm forbidden to leave the house until the grounding is over. Then, thirty minutes later, he's asking if I want to watch a movie or play a card game. Ivy always says he does it this way because if he really grounded me, it would keep me away from him, and he's lonely now that Grandma is gone. It's kind of heartbreaking when you really think about it and knowing that it's mostly true is what's kept me honest over the years. I refuse to break his trust and leave him angry and alone.

"He hasn't brought it up yet 'cause he's playing spades with his friends."

Ivy narrows her eyes the way she does when she sees something she doesn't like. "Then why do you look like that?"

"The way you ask questions is kind of rude sometimes. What if I came up to you and said, 'Look at your face! Why do you look the way you do?'?"

"I hear you. But you trying to change the subject won't work on me. What's wrong?"

"I don't wanna say 'cause you'll yell at me."

There's only one taboo subject we tend not to discuss because of how uncomfortable everyone gets, and Ivy knows that. She disappears from the screen and all of a sudden all I see is Jen's ceiling. Then she groans, uninterrupted, for an outrageous amount of time. To keep her from jumping down my throat, I quickly tell her what I saw. "Lena posted a picture of her and Quincy on Facebook."

Ivy pops back into view. Her irritation is gone, replaced with pure confusion. "Like recently?"

"Yeah. Yesterday."

"But Grandpa Joe said—"

"I know. It's weird, right?"

"A little." Ivy shakes her head when my eyes widen with excitement as she agrees with me, her surroundings on the camera looking like they're practically vibrating around her. "I already know what you're thinking, and I need you to listen to me when I tell you it's a bad idea."

"Even if Grandpa knows the story behind what brought them together again, he won't tell me. He's obsessed with keeping me in the dark about all this. The only way to find out the truth is to—"

"La la la la la la." Ivy has her eyes closed like she's afraid reading my lips will be as bad as listening to the rest of my sentence. She only stops once she's sure I won't be talking anymore. "I don't wanna hear about what crazy plans you're formulating. I need plausible deniability for when Grandpa Joe finds out—and he *will* find out—so he doesn't punish me along with you for doing this dumb thing you're thinking about doing."

"I have to know."

"At least try to ask him before going behind his back. Maybe he'll slip up and drop a nugget of truth amid all the bullshit. That way you get answers without even needing to ask Lena."

"I've already tried. He never tells me anything about her. All he does is trash Quincy, and I've heard enough of that."

"If you let him know how you've been feeling, it could soften him up enough to tell you more. He might be pissed you're asking but imagine how pissed he'll be if you reach out to Lena, and she starts coming around to see you. Grandpa will have a heart attack, and if he ends up in the hospital because you couldn't mind your fucking business—"

"I hear you."

Ivy just stares at me like she's trying to see if I actually under-stand, and I do. Nothing is worth Grandpa Joe's health. But I just don't see it like that. This would be me putting the family back together, and any anger that arises surely is worth it, right?

3

Ivy's strong words have me rethinking my approach with Lena. I decide to follow Ivy's advice and test the waters by telling Grandpa Joe how I've been feeling lately.

A few more hours go by before the guys pack it in for the night. My grandpa's buddies head out the front door with scowls on their faces and promises of sweet revenge at the next spades night. Grandpa Joe, being a sore winner, counts his winnings in front of them. Once they're gone, he stuffs the money in his wallet and cuts off the TV. "I love taking money from those suckers."

"You're so disrespectful." I peep the way my grandpa grimaces on his way to the couch, but I don't comment on it. He hates it when I fuss over him. I part the blinds with my fingers, checking to see if Grandpa Joe's friends are all right as they get into their cars. "What did you wanna talk to me about?"

"Who the hell told you it was okay to eat up all my cake?"

I look at him over my shoulder. "For real? I was losing my mind upstairs! I thought I was in real trouble. Not fake cake trouble."

"And why would you think that?"

"Because I have anxiety. Duh. That's why you're supposed to tell me what you wanna talk about instead of letting my brain come up with all these wild, crazy conclusions. I almost passed out 'cause I was worrying so bad."

"Wanted to make you sweat a little. Now quit eating my shit. This is the sixteenth time this month you done did something like this."

"Grandpa, we're only, like, two days into January. That's not possible."

"It is when I've got your hungry ass living in my house."

I ignore his dramatics and look out the window again. Grandpa Joe's friends are gone, but he doesn't care about them. All that matters is his cake. And all that matters to me is Lena.

"I've been thinking about Lena lately." I spit out my words in a rush, so he doesn't shut me down like he's done in the past. "I know you don't wanna talk about her, and I've tried to respect that but . . . I mean, I'm eighteen now."

"And what? You think that makes you grown?"

"In the eyes of the state . . ." No. I'm not getting into the legality of what being eighteen means. "I should know more about Lena than what I know now, and that isn't much. It's been eighteen years. Isn't it time for me to get the full story?"

"No."

Grandpa Joe sits on the couch with his arms crossed, glowering at me. He'll have an attitude for the rest of the night if I don't sweeten him up somehow. If I hadn't eaten all of his cake, I could've used that. I settle on using a classic—ice cream. I go into the kitchen and come back with two pints. Rocky road for him. Mint chocolate for me. Maybe if I keep calm and let him eat in peace, he'll finally answer some of the questions I have about Lena and all the things I can't remember. Like if she loved me after I was born, even a little, or if that worry deep inside me is right and she never cared at all. If she ever called Grandpa to ask how I was over the years. Or if she ever told him she missed me and asked to see me. Even if it was just in pictures. I let another few minutes pass before attempting to talk to him.

"Feeling better?"

"Little bit." Grandpa Joe sticks his spoon into the ice cream, scooping up a large chunk of rocky road. "Wish I had some cake to go with this ice cream."

"Oh, my God. Are you ever gonna drop that?"

"Never."

"I'll buy you another cake."

"You better get it from the same place I got mine. Angelica's Bakery."

Dang. No wonder why he's so upset about it. They make some of the best cakes in the city. I scrape a sliver of ice cream onto my spoon, wondering how mad Grandpa Joe will get once I continue to press him about my parents. Normally, I'd drop it, but I'm too curious about the picture on Lena's profile. To my knowledge, my parents split up years ago and never got back together. Too much bad blood, but they looked happy together on Facebook. This changes things. "Why don't you ever wanna talk about Lena?"

"Because I don't."

"I don't see what the big deal is. It's not like talking about her is gonna make her materialize out of thin air like the boogie man. And even if she does, what's so bad about that? She's not gonna kidnap me. She didn't want me when I was baby. Doesn't make sense that she'd want me now."

It's meant to be a self-deprecating joke, but it ends up sounding way too depressing because of the way my voice wavers as I say the words.

"Aaliyah—"

"I'm okay. It's just . . . Was something wrong with me? Is that why she left me with you and Grandma?"

Grandpa Joe sets his pint of ice cream on the coffee table and puts mine down next to his. He grasps my hands and looks me right in the eyes when he says, "*No*. You were the most perfect little girl I'd ever laid eyes on, kiddo. Still are. Don't go around thinking it was you, 'cause it wasn't. Never was."

"I had to have done something. She wouldn't have left me if I were as perfect as you say."

"Wasn't nothing you did. It was that damn Quincy." Grandpa Joe throws his hands up. "He got my baby pregnant and left the moment things got too hard. He was no good for her. I always could see him for what he was—a deadbeat."

"I get why you're mad at Quincy—he left when he should've stayed—but what about Lena? What did she do to make you hate her so much you won't talk about her, even to this day?"

"I could never hate Lena. Quincy is a whole 'nother story. That boy ain't brought nothing but chaos to my life and hers ever since she met him. I told her not to get roped up with that knucklehead and what did she do? She didn't listen to me. That's for damn sure." Grandpa Joe grumbles something about how nobody ever listens to him. "All I wanted was for her to find somebody good. Somebody who'd take care of her after I was gone. Somebody reliable."

"And that's not Quincy?"

"The hooptie I got parked in the backyard is more reliable than that boy."

"So, you're mad because Lena didn't listen to you?"

Grandpa Joe points his spoon at me. "Don't make it sound like I'm being petty."

"That's kinda how it sounds," I mumble.

"Whatchu say?"

His tone is so sharp that I don't dare repeat what I actually said. "That's not how I was trying to make it sound. I guess things aren't really adding up."

"Things don't gotta add up. I'm the only one in this house grown enough to add."

I'm well aware that Grandpa Joe never really told me why he refuses to speak to or about Lena. He'll go on all day about how bad of a guy he thinks Quincy is and rant about all the bad things he did, but when it comes to her, the little he does give feels like less than nothing.

Here's what I know—Lena had me at sixteen and with Quincy gone, she had a hard time taking care of me, so she gave me to my grandparents. To me, it's always seemed like he abandoned her for petty reasons. She was with Quincy and because Grandpa Joe didn't approve, he dropped her and never looked back. I can't believe he would do that to his youngest child. I don't want to believe it. Grandpa Joe is a good, caring man. But there's a part of me that suspects it may be true. It's why I keep boys he disapproves of at arm's length. I'd rather be a little unhappy than live my life without my grandpa by my side.

"Gotta promise me something, kiddo. Swear you won't go down this road with Lena. Not now. Not ever."

I quietly eat my ice cream. He doesn't know I'm already on the same road as her, driving down it and hoping to pick her up off the side of the highway like she's a hitchhiker. It's not like I want to hide this from him forever. I'll tell him after we link, so he can't forbid me from contacting her. The entire situation is shady, but Drake said 40's mama told him to ask for forgiveness, not permission. Those are the words of wisdom I've been following for the past six weeks.

I can't stay silent though. He'll become suspicious and I don't need him barging in at the last minute trying to take away what could turn out to be one of the greatest moments of my life. I look at the bottom of the empty ice cream carton and choose to nod rather than saying something that could get me caught in this massive lie.

"Come on and gimme a hug." Grandpa Joe holds out his arms, smiling as I lean into his embrace. "You know I'm just doing what I think is best, right? Wouldn't be keeping you from her if things were different."

"I know."

"All I've ever wanted to do is protect ya, kiddo. Promised your grandma I would a long time ago. That's a promise I plan on keeping."

Grandpa Joe rarely talks about Grandma Dee. He can't even say her name without his eyes watering and his voice catching on the lump in his throat. And even though it's been three years since she got sick and passed away, he acts like it's been no more than a day.

That's how grief works. You never really get over the person who's gone, no matter how much time has passed. It's how we all feel now that Grandma Dee is no longer with us. But there's another kind of grief that no one ever talks about. The kind that comes from a person being missing in your life and knowing you'll never be able to fill that hole. It's something I've had to live with my entire life.

Grandpa Joe busies himself with pulling up Netflix so we can start our weekly movie night. I'm too distracted to help him pick something out because I'm thinking about Lena's picture of Quincy. When was it taken? Recent enough that she decided to post it on Facebook. They must be together again, but when did that happen?

Whenever I've asked about them, Grandpa Joe has always told me that they broke up, but he wasn't there. He doesn't know how things were when it was just me and my mom surviving together. Only Lena knows. I need to talk to her. I need to know the truth.

Everyone who matters is against this and that would normally be enough to dissuade me, but the ever-present urge to learn whatever I can about Lena is too strong to ignore. And despite Grandpa Joe's best efforts to turn me off to her, I can't help but think that growing old and having no memory of the woman who birthed me isn't the way I'm meant to live my life.

I type up a message to Lena in the Facebook Messenger app before I chicken out.

> Hi, this is Aaliyah Campbell. Your daughter. I was wondering if you wanted to meet with me someday? Just to talk. I've been thinking about you a lot lately and figured this was probably the best way to contact you. Sundays are usually good, but I can work around your schedule if you're not free. Um, yeah, so . . . Let me know.

4

It's been three days and Lena hasn't responded or even looked at the message I sent her. Thoughts of her ignoring me on purpose consume me, making me physically ill. I hold on to the last sliver of hope I have that she wants to see me as much as I want to see her because the alternative might kill me.

"Campbell." Coach Barnes's voice snaps me out of my daze. He's on the other side of the weight room making sure the rest of the sprinters are lifting properly, but somehow, he still clocked me slacking off sixty feet away. "Focus up."

Jen Zhu moves above me with her hands out, ready to assist me with the weight bar if I start to struggle. "Fifteen good reps. Coach is still watching."

God. I can't do anything without Coach Barnes breathing down my neck. It's not like I'm slacking during a real practice session. The new semester just started and we're still a month away from the beginning of the indoor season. I can afford to have an off practice or two.

After completing more than half the workout, I'm sweating profusely, breathing heavily, and having some serious regrets about joining the track team freshman year. I push through my last set, grunting with each rep until I hit fifteen. My arms quiver under the weight of the bar and I let out a weak "Help."

Jen grabs the barbell and lowers it onto the rack. "Pathetic. You're gonna die at the first real practice."

"Weren't you struggling to get through a full set of L-sits, like, three minutes ago?"

"Yeah, because it's hard. Duh."

"Bench pressing ninety percent of my body weight ain't easy, Jen."

"Campbell! Zhu!" Coach Barnes hasn't been on our side of the weight room, yet he's still barking orders like a madman. "Too much talking. Not enough lifting."

Ivy shakes her head at us on her way past. "Coach is gonna light y'all up if you keep playing around."

"Better move quick before he ropes you in with us."

Unlike us, Ivy is smart enough to keep her head down during practice to avoid Coach Barnes's wrath and moves on like Jen said. Me? I continue talking because Coach hasn't come our way, meaning we still have a few more minutes of goofing off before he gets serious. "I'm definitely seeing laps in our near future."

"Oh, absolutely." Jen takes my spot on the bench and reclines back, gripping the bar tightly. She pushes up, then lowers it, blowing out puffs of air with each rep. "My brother's been asking about you."

I pretend like I'm not all that interested. "Has he?"

"All he wants to do is talk about you and how you're doing and if you've mentioned him at all. I keep telling him to leave it alone, but you know how he gets with you."

"You sound bothered."

"Let's just say you're really lucky we're friends." Her smile feels off. I can tell she's pissed at me and for once, I don't have to drive myself crazy wondering why—Tommy's her brother. She'll kill to protect him, even if it means killing a close friend. "He's got an attitude 'cause you skipped his party."

"Not sure why anybody thought I'd show up. I hate parties."

"He was hoping you'd make an exception to show you cared."

"I care."

"Do you?"

That "Do you?" strikes me hard in the chest. Has Tommy said something? He must've for her to be talking to me like this. "I'm giving him and his girlfriend some space. Remember, she threw a rock at my head the last time she caught us hanging out. I still have the scar."

"That's part of the reason why he broke up with her."

I'm not sure how to feel about their breakup. They've ended things more times than I can count, and it always goes the same way. He comes back around, and we hook up in secret for a while. Grandpa Joe loses it because he finds out somehow, and I distance myself from Tommy out of fear. Tommy rekindles things with his ex, and we go through another period of not talking to each other until the next breakup.

Jen drops the barbell onto the holder and spins around on the bench to face me. "I can't go into specifics, but I think he'd like hearing from you. He's been different lately. She really messed him up."

He could've called me. Things might be messy between us, but we've been friends since I was twelve and he was thirteen. He's on my list of people to never ignore. It doesn't matter if I'm mad at him or if we haven't spoken in weeks, I'll always answer if it's him. I hate that we've gotten to a point where he feels like that no longer applies.

"In case it wasn't clear, I'm telling you to reach out to him. He'll come around if you do. And obviously, we never had this conversation."

"Right. Obviously."

"Just, when you do . . . Don't be so you this time."

"Excuse me? What does that mean?"

"You know what it means, Aaliyah." Jen drops the topic after she's said her piece, but I'm stuck on it. Don't be so me. I have no idea what that means, but clearly the version of me that spends time with Tommy isn't good enough in her eyes. I have to do better because if I don't, Jen might kick my butt. "Wanna come over after school? My dad went grocery shopping, so we've basically got everything you could ever want in our kitchen."

"Will Tommy be there? Not because I don't wanna see him, I just need time to obsess over exactly what to say before I do."

"He's back at school. Won't be home until the weekend."

Something in the stifled weight-room air shifts. I check over my shoulder, and I'm not surprised to see Coach Barnes standing behind me all red-faced and angry. "Laps?" I ask, resigned to my fate.

"In the small gym," he says.

Jen and I make our way through the weight room, grinning at Ivy and a few other teammates on our way out.

Coach Barnes doesn't let us stop running until practice is over, making the laps we have to run that much more brutal. Once Coach Barnes finishes lecturing us, Jen reminds me to come over to her place later to eat snacks and unwind. I check my phone as we part ways in the parking lot, her to her car and me to Ivy's, hoping desperately there's a message from Lena in my Notification Center. But just as when I checked before practice, and during every passing period, and in the mornings when I woke up, there's nothing.

5

Since my car is acting funky, Ivy had to wait an extra twenty minutes because of the trouble I got into with Jen. She's understandably upset when I meet up with her in the parking lot, and she's quiet on the ride back to her apartment. When I ask if she's mad about me keeping her late after practice, she says no and goes back to being silent.

She showers. Then I shower. She eats and I eat. We study for our precalc exam. And throughout all that, Ivy still doesn't speak to me. Not even when I tell her we need to head to Jen's house soon. Even though her being quiet probably has nothing to do with me, I can't help the way my thoughts spiral, thinking of what I might've done to piss her off. It had to be something. But what?

"Please relax," Ivy says. "I'm not mad at you."

"I'm completely relaxed."

"You are not. You're all fidgety, and I can practically hear your loud-ass thoughts from here. So again, relax. If you did something, I would've told you by now."

Of course I know that, but with the way my brain is set up, sometimes I need a reminder. Ivy has always been good about giving me those. I close my eyes and breathe in and out deeply. One. Two. Three. Four. The count in my head calms my body, and within a few minutes, I'm back to only having a mild nausea instead of feeling like I'm about to spew my guts.

Ivy needs time to soften up. Rather than bugging her endlessly and *actually* pissing her off, I focus on texting Tommy like Jen asked.

> **Me:** Hi.
>
> **Tommy:** look who finally remembered I existed
>
> **Me:** I'm not the only person in this friendship with thumbs, Tommy.
>
> **Tommy:** maybe I was testing you to see how much you cared
>
> **Me:** Clearly, I care a lot since I'm still entertaining this nonsense conversation.
>
> **Me:** Now I've gotta test you to see if you care. It's only right.
>
> **Tommy:** you know I do
>
> **Tommy:** come to my dorm tonight need to see ya

Need, not want. That's new. I don't let myself become invested because there's a reason we're mostly just friends with a few secret benefits and not something more, but the romantic part of me that kind of loves Tommy is clawing its way to the surface after being dormant for months. If this were another day, I'd be tripping over myself to meet up with him in his dorm at the University of Chicago. He's single and I'm single, and we've been apart long enough to keep Grandpa Joe from becoming suspicious of where I'm spending my time. But I take one look at Ivy sitting on her bed with her knees up to her chest and know I can't leave her while she's still upset.

Me: Not tonight but soon. I've been missing you.

As soon as I send the text, I want to die. The reason this thing between us works is because I don't say embarrassing things like I miss him or I like him more than any guy I've ever met, even if it's true. I keep him at arm's length, and maybe that's mean of me, but it's the only way we work. He doesn't immediately reply back, so I stuff my phone into the side pocket of my Nike bag. "Tommy broke up with his girlfriend."

"For how long?"

"Jen made it sound like it was for good this time."

Ivy barely glances at me when I sit at the edge of her bed. "Guess that means you'll be running back to him then?"

"I don't like the way you phrased that."

"I don't think she likes the way you treat her brother." Before I can even ask, Ivy says, "She said something the other day about him being your dirty little secret. I don't know. I didn't listen too hard 'cause it'd make me feel bad for him, and because of solidarity reasons, he gets no sympathy from me as long as Grandpa Joe hates him."

Ivy and Jen are making it sound worse than it is. Like Tommy's the victim and I'm the mean old witch who goes around treating him like crap. They know how Grandpa Joe can be. That's why it has to be this way. Ivy admitted herself that she doesn't want to like Tommy too much because of our grandpa. He's a bit crazy when it comes to the guys I date. It's partly why I want to know more about what happened to Lena. So I don't end up like her. "I'm as nice to him as I possibly can be. Any more and he'll think he can start coming around like it's cool. It's not."

"I get it. I don't wanna get on Grandpa Joe's bad side either, but if you keep this up, you might get on Jen's bad side, and I don't know which is worse."

"I'm trying to find the perfect balance, but it's hard."

"Talk to Tommy about it."

"He doesn't get it. He thinks I'm being dramatic."

Ivy laughs. "He definitely doesn't know Grandpa Joe."

She seems to be in a better mood, so I risk a change in subject. "So, are you gonna tell me what's wrong or am I gonna have to start pouting?"

"You're such a brat."

"A brat that you love and shouldn't keep secrets from because I'm your favorite cousin, despite you trying to pretend like I'm not."

Ivy finally looks at me head-on. I'm expecting irritation, but she just seems kind of sad. It throws me off because Ivy doesn't get sad. She says it's her one strength. "You don't tell me everything."

"Yeah, well, clearly neither do you. Hold on. Did you hear that?" I hold my hand up to my ear like I'm listening to something in the distance. "Oh. Never mind. It was just the ball being smacked back into your court."

"You're really testing my nerves today, huh?"

"I'm being Normal Aaliyah. Normal Ivy would tell her what's wrong."

"Normal Ivy would whup Normal Aaliyah's ass, so don't start with me because I'm not in the mood."

Ivy does her best to beat me in a stare down, but she fails miserably. I wouldn't typically press her like this. She likes to come to me when she's ready, and I've always respected that, but this sad-girl routine of hers is more my thing, not hers. It's kind of freaking me out.

"I wanna help, but I can't do that if you don't tell me what's wrong."

Ivy gives me nothing. No response. No hint that she heard a word I said.

"Come on. I'll cancel with Jen so we can talk about what's wrong and I can spend the rest of the night fixing it."

"You can't."

"At least let me try."

Ivy keeps her gaze trained on the fuzzy comforter on her bed and picks at the material, pulling up pieces of lint. She flicks them onto the floor, and I assume she's ignoring me because she's still not ready to talk. Then, suddenly, she asks, "How do you make everyone love you?"

How do I even respond to a question like that? I could give her some magical answer about me casting a spell on the people in my life to make them love me, but the truth is I don't do anything special and when my paranoia is at its peak, I'm convinced that people hate me, even when I don't have a reason to believe that. But I can't tell Ivy that because she's upset, and I'd be making this about me in a way she might not be comfortable with. "I'm confused. Catch me up to where you are in this conversation, so I can figure out what I should say."

"The girl I like doesn't like me back."

"Oh. She said that?"

"No, but it's obvious she doesn't."

"I'm lost again. How is it obvious?"

"Vibes, Aaliyah. Vibes."

"Maybe don't go off vibes with something like this. The best way to know is to tell her how you feel and give her a chance to tell you whether she feels the same way or not."

"And what if she says she doesn't?"

"She won't."

"How do you know?"

"Because you're awesome and even if you don't think it, everyone loves you. Duh."

A high-pitched chime comes from deep inside my Nike bag. It doesn't sound like a text or an Instagram notification. It's something unfamiliar. I dig my phone out of my bag and stare at the screen. I only have one notification, but it's the one I've been waiting on for three days.

Lena Campbell: You don't know how happy I was to see your message pop into my inbox. Sundays are perfect for me. What day do you wanna meet?

Ivy clocks the shift and darts across her room to steal my phone from me. She gives me a look that I think means "Are you stupid?" after reading the message, then says, "Bitch, are you dumb?" So I was pretty spot on.

"Sometimes. Yeah."

"I feel like I'm losing my mind. Didn't we just talk about why contacting Lena is a bad idea?"

"Yes, and I elected to disregard that talk because I changed my mind. Grandpa Joe didn't tell me anything new, so I had to go straight to the source. I just wanna talk to her. Find out why she and Grandpa fell out, and maybe if it wasn't too bad, I can fix things."

"Aaliyah, you can't fix everything. Sometimes things are unfixed because that's the way they have to be."

"But—"

"This isn't a regular argument. This is years and years of bad blood that's festered under the surface, and neither one has tried to fix it because . . . It. Can't. Be. Fixed. Leave it alone."

"I—"

"Leave it. Alone."

Ivy hands me my phone and walks out of the room, sending a final warning in the form of a sharp glare. I should listen to her to avoid the inevitable argument, but I can't. Getting the full story has the potential to change everything. What if I can fix things between Lena and Grandpa Joe? Find out the truth of why she gave me away as a baby and put to rest all the anxiety I have about not being good enough. I can't pass up an opportunity like this. Not when Lena is as excited to meet me as I am to meet her. Her message proved that.

A debate enters my head the moment I start thinking about Lena's message. Should I say something right away or be cool and take my time like she did? If Ivy weren't vehemently against the idea, I'd go to her for advice, but I'm on my own here. I decide to be cool, even though it physically pains me, and let the message sit in my inbox, unread, for a day. After I finally hit her back, her response is almost immediate, and I nearly cry when I read the message.

> **Lena Campbell:** Meeting up with you on Sunday is gonna be a dream come true for me, Aaliyah baby. I haven't been this excited about seeing someone in a long time. I hope I'm not a disappointment. And if you're comfortable with it, I'd love for this to be the beginning of a relationship between you and me.

6

In less than forty-eight hours, I'll be linking with my mom for the first time. This interaction is important. It'll either make or break our relationship, and the perfectionist in me wants to do whatever I can to turn the dreams I've had of our first meeting into a reality. The anxious mess in me wants to hide under the covers, turn off my phone, and pretend I never contacted Lena.

Grandpa Joe watches as I pace the length of the living room like he thinks I'm about to rob him. "The hell are you so nervous about?"

He's used to me running around like a small child hopped up on too much sugar, so if he's pointing it out, I must be doing too much, even for me. I return to my spot next to him on the couch and sit with my hands in my lap like a well-behaved eighteen-year-old girl. "This is a normal level of anxiety for me."

It's not like he can argue with that. I'm nervous more than I'm not. My hands have a near-constant tremor, and I've always got this weird, sinking feeling in the pit of my stomach like something is going to go terribly wrong. Heart pounding. Hyperventilating. Fainting. It's all normal for me.

But I'd been doing good recently. Most days are better than others. Most days my stomach hasn't felt like it's suffering through a brutal ride on a roller coaster. Most days my hands don't have a tremor at all. Today was supposed to be a continuation of those good days, but I'm sitting on the couch next to Grandpa Joe, and I'm practically rocking the thing with how much I'm shaking. I can't tell him what's wrong with me though. I have to pretend like everything is fine to keep the peace in our house.

"Ivy, get in here," Grandpa Joe calls.

My cousin strolls into the living room with a pizza puff in one hand and her iPhone in the other. "What's wrong? Is Aaliyah being annoying again?"

Any protest I wanted to let out is cut off by Grandpa Joe's disapproving grumbles. "The girl is shaking the couch like a got-damn earthquake. What's she so nervous about? I know you know. Y'all tell each other everything."

I make a quick cutting gesture across my neck, dropping my hands back to my lap when Grandpa Joe looks at me. As soon as he turns to Ivy, I start cutting again.

Ivy takes a bite of her pizza puff, holding off on answering his question because she loves making me sweat. "I think she said something about being excited about a meeting . . ."

All kinds of alarms go off in my head. None of them have to do with somehow forcing Ivy to stop talking. That's something no one can do. The alarms are screaming at me to run before she spills the beans and Grandpa Joe slaps me upside my head for disobeying the one order he's ever given me—stay away from my parents.

"Yeah, she was meeting with someone," Ivy continues. "The name is coming to me. Starts with an R. Or maybe a P?"

Ivy is careful not to use the initials of my parents' first names, Quincy and Lena, but she's still too close for comfort. I send Ivy a nonverbal distress signal that practically screams *Please, shut up.* She ignores it.

Grandpa Joe whips around, eyes lighting up with anger and a bit of concern. "A meeting with who? Aaliyah, you know better than to go meeting up with people without telling me where you're going or who you're gonna be with. Anything could happen to you out there, and I wouldn't have no idea where to look 'cause you keeping secrets."

"No. Wait." Ivy takes another bite of her pizza puff. "It wasn't a meeting. It was a track meet. She's worried about our first track meet of the indoor season. Something about how she hasn't been working hard enough in practice. You know how she gets."

Grandpa Joe is more concerned than angry now, but I'm still afraid. He bumps my thigh with the back of his pockmarked hand. "Why didn't you just say that, kiddo?"

My inability to tell a believable lie prevents me from answering him right away. If I could lie the way Ivy can, I'd tell nothing but lies until the day I die. But since I'm useless, I shrug. The less I talk, the better. "Excuse me, Grandpa. I need to talk to Ivy for a second."

"But you're gonna miss the rest of our show," Grandpa Joe complains. "It's just getting good."

"I can look up spoilers online," I say.

"That's not the same as watching it right here with me." Grandpa Joe points at our pints of ice cream on the coffee table. "All the ice cream's gonna melt, and you're gonna miss the cliff-hanger at the end. Can't you give me a few more minutes of your time, kiddo?"

He doesn't pull the "You're going across the country for college" card, but I can tell he wants to. These seven months before August are going to be all we have left before everything changes. As much as I want to slap the crap out of Ivy for messing with me, I desperately want to spend as much time as possible with Grandpa Joe too.

Being away from him is going to be tough. I won't be waking up to the smell of banana pancakes on Sunday mornings. No more surfing through Netflix for hours only to end up watching the same movie we'd already seen a thousand times. He'll be here, and I'll be at UCLA. And sure, it's a short plane ride, and we'll be spending my breaks together, but that's not the same as living with him.

"All right, but I'm not watching the preview for next week." I take my seat, but not before sending a death glare Ivy's way. She's completely unaffected by it. "They always give too much away."

"That's the best part," Grandpa Joe says. "Ain't that right, Ivy?"

"Sure is, Grandpa," Ivy says.

I split my time between eating my mint chocolate ice cream, watching the final scenes of *Chicago Fire*, and nonverbally telling Ivy that I'm going to kick her butt the second the show is over.

Once the credits start rolling, I hop over Grandpa Joe's legs and make a beeline straight for Ivy, who books it to the stairs.

"Y'all better not break nothing in my house," Grandpa Joe shouts. "If you do, I'm whupping both of y'all's asses."

The one sure thing I have over Ivy is that I'm quicker than her. Even with her head start, I catch up to Ivy and push her in the back to get her off balance. She goes tumbling over the threshold to my room, sending her phone and pizza puff flying through the air.

"You're crazy, Aaliyah! I was still eating."

"This wouldn't have happened if you weren't such a jerk. Why do you always mess with me?"

"Because it's funny and you deserve it for what you did." She picks herself up off the floor and comes closer, her eyes flicking between me and the bedroom door. "I should tell him. He'd stop all this nonsense with that bum you call a mama before it even gets started."

I shove Ivy a little too hard, and she falls onto the bed behind her. "Don't talk about her like that."

Ivy stands and then shoves me back twice as hard and flips me off for good measure. "You're real defensive over a woman who pretends you don't exist three hundred sixty-five days out of the year."

"That was mean."

A minute goes by. Ivy has her arms crossed over her chest, but she doesn't make a move to leave because we've got a rule. Never leave when we're mad. It'll just make things worse. "I wasn't trying to hurt your feelings but . . . I mean, am I wrong? To her, you didn't exist for almost two decades, and now, because you're nice, she's gonna think that shit is cool. Newsflash, it ain't."

Oh. *Oh.* "You care about me. You love me!" I go in for a hug, and Ivy stops me with a hand to the face. "What's up?"

"I've still got an attitude with you."

"Well, then I've got an attitude too."

"Fine."

"Fine."

Because there's nowhere else for us to go, Ivy takes a spot on the end of the bed, and I sit at the head. She picks up her phone and starts typing out a message to whomever. I have someone I can call. I probably should, after his lack of response to my last text, but it'll only create a mess, and I can't have a Tommy mess conflicting with the Lena mess. That's too many messes. Grandpa Joe might actually have a heart attack. But I meant what I said. I do miss Tommy.

I play with the idea of texting him again. It's not an easy decision because I know if I message him a second time, he'll want to link up. The only thing is, I'm kind of restricted with what I can use as an excuse because Ivy's here with me. If I leave without her, Grandpa Joe will become suspicious. I settle on not seeing Tommy. If we're meant to link, it'll happen. No need to force it, especially with Grandpa Joe nosing around the way he always does.

7

Grandpa Joe isn't home when I make it back from a late practice the next day. Ivy had plans with someone else right after, so I took the train home. It wasn't until I arrived that I realized I didn't have my keys. I call him and ask when he'll be home, but he's at Pete's house for their weekly spades night. Because Pete lives in the 'burbs, it'll take nearly an hour for Grandpa to drive back to the city, and I don't want him running back here to rescue me because I was too dumb to make sure I had housekeys when I left before school. I tell him I'll call a friend and end the call after reassuring him I'll be okay.

Things with Ivy still aren't the best; I owe her a pizza puff after accidentally knocking hers to the floor, and she's still pissed about me reaching out to Lena. I tried to get her to see things from my perspective after Lena sent another message talking about how excited she was for Sunday, but Ivy wouldn't budge, so I dropped it. Ivy's approval isn't a necessity. Calling someone and getting them to rescue me from the cold is though.

I FaceTime Jen because she's the most logical choice, and if I can count on anyone to help me out of a tight spot, it'll be her. "What's up?" she says when she answers.

"Can you come pick me up?"

"Like from your house?"

"Yeah. I'm locked out of the house again and can't go to Ivy's apartment because we're in a fight. It's twenty degrees outside, Jen. I'm not built to endure conditions like this."

"Um, I just remembered I'm super busy, so I can't pick you up." Jen hurriedly adds, "But don't leave yet. Stay where you are."

"I'll be honest, if I stay out here, I think I might die, dude."

"Stop being dramatic. It's not that cold."

"Easy for you to say. You're not the one in it."

"Hold on for a little longer."

Jen ends the call, leaving me confused and shivering. Cars speed past me, kicking up slush and salt with their tires. And as my body trembles with each gust of wind, I find myself wishing I knew one of the drivers, even if it was a classmate I didn't like, because at least then I'd be warm while I hold on for the little longer Jen asked for. I pull my coat around me tighter and hang out on the porch in hopes of getting some kind of shelter from the cold, but it doesn't help all that much.

An unwanted answer to my silent prayer comes in the form of Tommy's purple Dodge Challenger. It slides into the only empty spot in front of my house. A range of emotions flutter through me as I try to decide how to behave around him after Jen and Ivy altered the way I feel about how I've been treating him. Most of the time I ignore the things Ivy says to me, especially if she's right, because that'll just bother me endlessly. But if Jen is saying it, and especially if it has to do with Tommy, I feel like I have to listen. Mostly because she could kick my butt if she really wanted to. I take a breath. Be cool.

Tommy walks toward me, eyes dragging up and down my body. When I come down the steps, his toothy grin is on full display. "You look good."

"Thank you for the compliment."

"You know the appropriate thing for you to do would be to give me one back."

"Oh, it would?"

"Yeah. I'm making it real easy for you too. Look at me. Perfect hair. Even perfecter jawline. I'm in the best shape of my life. Plenty of sexiness to use as material for your compliment."

Gassing his inflated ego has never been fun for me, but irritating him by downplaying his attractiveness? That's hysterical. "You a'ight."

"A'ight? *A'ight?*" he repeats. "Please. I'm gorgeous."

"You're also full of yourself."

"Nothing wrong with a little confidence." Tommy does a little hop-skip to close the distance between us, with his gaze more on my lips than my eyes. He leans in for a kiss and groans when I put a hand on his chest to stop him. "The hell is that about?"

"There's a ninety-two percent chance that my grandpa is watching us on his Ring camera. And if he is, there's a one hundred percent chance he'll ground me until I'm dead if you put your lips anywhere near me."

"He still hates me?"

"I think he always will."

"That's all right. I love myself enough for the both of us."

"What are you doing here, Tommy? Remember we talked about you not coming to my house unless it was an emergency?"

"This is an emergency."

"How?"

"You said you missed me. Did ya mean it?" I can't help it. I smile. And then Tommy smiles, laughing and pointing at me as if I'm being embarrassing, like he isn't the one giggling like a nerd. "Look at you. Hahahaha. Dork. You totally missed me. That's so embarrassing for you."

"Shut up."

Tommy's reply is cut off when he catches me trembling after a strong gust of wind blows by. He nods at his car, and I quickly jump into the passenger seat, teeth chattering as my body gets used to the warmth. "Wanna grab a bite to eat? I can tell you're starving by those clothes you've got on."

"And how can you tell that?"

"You've got on your track shit. You're always hungry after practice."

Tommy puts the car in drive and pops a quick U-turn, heading toward our favorite spot—Baba's. We always get the same thing. One crispy Philly cheesesteak with mild sauce on the fries for him. A garden salad and mozzarella sticks for me. A blue raspberry lemonade for him and a cherry one for me. He goes inside to order our food and pays for it without asking me for my half. As we slide into a spot in the local library parking lot, I'm reminded of the old times when we used to do this, what felt like every day. Now we barely hang out at all.

He divvies up the food and smiles when he sees me looking at him. "Whatcha staring at me for? I got a booger or something?"

"Gross. And no. I meant it when I said I missed you."

"That why you spent the last month ignoring me?"

His comment isn't unexpected. All it does is prove that he definitely complained about our situation to Jen, and I understand why. Lapses in our friendship are common now, but it wasn't always like this. I miss when we'd hang out nearly every day and FaceTime or text on the days we didn't. Our friendship changed and things are different now. More complicated. Not because I want them to be. They just are. "I was keeping my distance until you figured out whether you were serious about ending things with your ex or not."

"Me and you hook up on breaks all the time," he says. "What's the problem?"

"I don't wanna deal with any more relationship drama. This thing with you and Sabrina is as messy as things were between me and Daniel last year. It was exhausting then and it's gonna be exhausting now, so I'm nipping the drama in the bud before it morphs into full-blown chaos." I point at the dark mark on the left side of my temple. "And I didn't forget about how your girlfriend threw a rock at my head during your last break because she's possessive and weird. I'm not interested in a repeat of that."

"*Ex*-girlfriend, and if we can't hook up, can we at least be friends again?"

"We never stopped being friends."

"Yes, we did. Back when we were real friends, we hung out all the time. Now I barely see you unless we're hooking up in secret. I don't want that to be all we do anymore." Tommy drops his half-eaten Philly into his to-go carton. He doesn't look at me, even when he starts talking again. "I want things to go back to how they used to be. You're my best friend and I need you. My life is shitty when you're not in it, Aaliyah."

The secrecy. The breaks in us hooking up. Being friends only sometimes. It was all necessary in the past because he had his thing with Sabrina, and I had my thing with Daniel, and then Grandpa Joe's dislike of Tommy got mixed in and it turned into a giant mess. Now Tommy's allegedly done with Sabrina, and my relationship with Daniel ended badly, but Grandpa Joe still hates Tommy, and I don't know what to do about it. Still, it's *Tommy*. Our broken friendship is clearly bothering him, and I don't have the heart to watch him hurt like this without doing something about it.

"I feel like I should hug you. I'm gonna hug you. C'mere." Our embrace is awkward and kind of terrible because we're in a car and we both have food in our laps. I hope it manages to accomplish what I wanted it to, though—making Tommy feel better. "We can hang out for the rest of the night. I'm free until curfew."

"Won't your grandpa be mad if he knows you're out with me?"

"Not if I tell him you dropped me off at your house to hang with Jen 'cause I left my key."

Tommy goes back to eating like nothing was ever wrong. He's good at that. Pretending to be okay, even when he's not. I try to keep munching on my mozzarella sticks, but my appetite is nonexistent now. I can't believe I never realized how upset Tommy was about the state of our friendship. I mean, I figured he wasn't happy about it because I wasn't either, but I didn't know it was this bad.

Grandpa Joe texts me not long after demanding to know why I left with "that Thomas boy," and I'm extremely glad he didn't call. He would have been able to hear the lie in my voice, but through text? Yeah, through text I'm a pro at lying. So I tell him Tommy took me back to his parents' place to hang out with Jen until he makes it home. Then I send one of the many pictures I had Jen take with me for situations like this because after two years of hooking up with Tommy against my grandpa's wishes, I've learned to be sneaky.

8

Today's the day.

I threw up twice before leaving my house, and I've been sitting in the parking lot of the diner for fifteen minutes because I can't bring myself to go inside. With trembling fingers, I scroll through my recent calls and come across Tommy's contact info. Even with how complicated our relationship is and all our problems, I can still count on him to be there for me, so I call him. "I'm having a crisis, Tommy."

"What's wrong?" he asks.

"I'm about to meet Lena and I'm freaking out. Tell me everything's gonna be okay."

Without missing a beat, Tommy says, "Everything's gonna be okay."

I rest my forehead against the steering wheel. "What if I say the wrong thing? I could ruin everything with my big mouth. Tommy, this is my only chance to make a good impression. I can't afford to mess it up."

"You won't. You're making a big deal out of nothing."

"Doesn't feel like nothing to me. It feels like something. A real big something."

"That's because your anxiety is blowing this up in your head like it always does. Keep breathing or you'll start panicking."

I probably shouldn't need a reminder to breathe, but anxiety is weird like that. I'm already feeling better a few breaths in, and I give myself a mental reminder to tell Tommy how much I appreciate him. "I'm breathing."

"Good. You're not gonna ruin anything either."

"How do you know that?"

"Because you're the best person I know. You're sweet and caring and generous, and if Lena doesn't immediately clock how amazing you are, then she's fucking crazy. But even if everything does go to shit, you can't let this moment be the deciding factor on whether or not you're worthy of love. Lena's opinion of you doesn't matter when you've got people like Jen and your grandpa and Ivy around to show you what love really is. And, uh, you know . . . I'm also included in that group, I guess."

"You don't know if you are?"

"I don't know shit, Aaliyah. Never have. Never will."

"You seemed pretty wise to me just now."

"Weed makes me sound more smarter than I am. I think it's wearing off though, 'cause I feel dumb again."

"I'm trying really hard not to laugh because I don't wanna hurt your feelings."

"I appreciate that. Don't worry so much about this thing with Lena, all right? Everything will go down the way it was meant to, and whether the outcome's good or bad doesn't really matter so much. You put in the effort. That's what counts."

"I'm glad I called."

"Me too. Let me know how it goes."

"I will. And Tommy?"

"Yeah?"

"You're a really good friend."

"The best?"

"Hands down."

I end up sitting in Ivy's car for another few minutes to build enough courage to walk inside the diner. It's one of those places where you seat yourself, and once I finally make it inside, I head toward a booth in the back corner when I don't see Lena. I figure we'll need some privacy for this reunion. I'm a hundred percent sure I'll end up bursting into tears the second she walks through the door.

"Don't panic. This is just a regular lunch with the mother you've never met. No big deal. You can do this. When she arrives, just say, 'Hey, I'm Aaliyah. It's nice to meet you.'"

An older woman with kind eyes approaches my table, holding a notepad in her hand. "You here by yourself, honey?"

"Yeah. I mean, no. I'm meeting someone here, but I guess I'm a little early." I check the time on my phone. I'm about fifteen minutes early. Thirty if you count the time I spent hyperventilating in Ivy's car. "Can I have a glass of water?"

"Of course." The woman easily navigates through the sea of tables and chairs, returning with my water a minute later. She sets a pitcher near me in case I want a refill. "Do you wanna order now or wait for the person you're meeting?"

"I'll wait. She should be here soon."

"All right, well my name is Louise. Flag me down if you need anything in the meantime."

"Thanks."

I set my phone on the table with the screen up, so I can see if Lena sends me a text. I'm so nervous, my entire body is shaking, and I remind myself to take slow, deep breaths. Lena can't see me like this. She might think something's wrong with me, and being anything less than perfect isn't an option. Not with so much riding on our first meeting.

The minutes creep by, moving at a snail's pace until it's finally noon. Lena should be here any second now.

I sit up with my hands folded on the table. Too uptight. I move them to my lap, smoothing out the creases in my pants. At half past twelve, I send Lena a message. Did you hit traffic? Accidents are always popping up all over the city.

Ten minutes go by without a word from her. I debate the consequences of calling. It could make me seem thirsty, but I don't think those same rules apply when it comes to your mom. I pull up Lena's contact info, thumb hovering over the call button for a few seconds. My thumb is trembling so badly it hits the button before I'm ready. "Oh, crap. Crap. Crap. Crap."

But all my panic is for nothing because she doesn't pick up. I call her again. And again. On the third call, I start to worry. That worry lasts until the tenth call. It goes straight to voicemail.

My body buzzes with . . . something. Whether it's anger or embarrassment or a mixture of both, I'm not sure, but it's so bad that I have to set my phone back on the table to keep it from flying out of my hand.

After another thirty minutes with no word from Lena, I admit the truth to myself—she isn't coming. She stood me up, and I was stupid enough to believe all the lies she told me about how excited she was to see me in the follow-up messages she sent me on Facebook.

I should've listened to Ivy. Sure, she's bitter and pessimistic, but she's also right a lot more than she's wrong. Maybe if I hadn't been so naively optimistic, I could've saved myself from all of this—the ache in my heart, the pitying look Louise gives me as she checks on me again, the pain of knowing that the person who should love me more than anyone else on the planet doesn't think I'm worth the two seconds it takes to text me and say she can't make it.

I slide out of the booth and slap a ten-dollar bill on the table with a quick apology to Louise for wasting her time. She tells me she's sorry the person I was waiting for didn't show up, and I say, "Me too."

Deep down, I think I knew she wouldn't.

9

I park Ivy's car in front of my house. Despite her telling me not to run to her if Lena played me, I do it anyway. She always acts tough, but she's never had the heart to turn me away. Not even when we're mad. Today is no exception. That and a stream of tears from me is why she let me use her car even though she disagrees with me.

She's in my room and has a bunch of my pillows propped up against the headboard behind her with an ankle perched on her thigh. Her fingers tap quickly against her phone screen as she has a completely different conversation with someone through her AirPods. "I don't wanna go there. It sounds boring."

"Hi," I say in my most pitiful voice.

"Let me call you back. Aaliyah's crying again." Ivy ends the call and sets her phone down next to her. "Not to sound like a bitch, but if you're looking all sorry because what I think happened actually happened, I told you not to give that bum a chance. She didn't deserve one."

I slump against the wall, sliding down until I end up on the floor. The floor is perfect for my current mood. I wouldn't mind staying here forever. No one can ever hurt me if I never move from this spot. "I thought . . . I guess I was hoping she really meant it when she said she was excited to see me. But she didn't show up and never even told me she needed to reschedule. I sat there by myself looking like a loser, waiting for somebody who clearly doesn't give a crap about me."

"Aaliyah—"

"You don't need to say anything." I pull my knees into my chest and lower my head to hide the tears dripping down my cheeks. Now that I'm away from prying eyes, I let out everything I've been feeling since the moment I realized what Lena had done. All the anger and disappointment and embarrassment comes rushing out until all that's left is an empty void where those emotions should be. "I really wanted it to be a special moment for us."

Suddenly, Ivy is right next to me, bumping against me as she gets settled on the floor. She doesn't put an arm around me, but she lets me rest my head on her shoulder and holds my hand to keep it from shaking too much. "I did too. Had to be low-key about it though."

"You did?"

"Girl, just 'cause I had, like, negative faith that Lena miraculously wouldn't turn out to be a massive piece of shit doesn't mean I actually wanted her to hurt your feelings."

I wrap Ivy up in a tight hug, ignoring her dramatic protests. I'm glad Ivy didn't leave me to deal with this on my own like she said she would. At least now I can look back on this awful moment with the knowledge that someone loves me enough to stick around. My parents couldn't do it, despite having an obligation to love me and protect me and take care of me. Last year, my ex, Daniel, dipped out on me, even though he told me he loved me too much to ever leave. But Ivy has been a constant in my life for longer than I can remember. I can always count on her to be there for me when I need her.

10

Grandpa Joe makes it home earlier than I expect him to. I'm still on the floor with Ivy when he pops his head into my room, no doubt to complain about something, but he pauses with the complaint still on the tip of his tongue. It's an unusual scene. Not the part with me looking like I just spent an hour and a half crying—that's nothing new for me. But cuddling up to Ivy is surprising because this kind of thing doesn't happen with us unless something is really wrong.

"Who hurt you?" he asks. "Do I need to mess somebody up?"

Ivy laughs. "Grandpa, you're sixty-three. The only thing you're gonna mess up is your hip."

"Watch it, missy," Grandpa Joe says. "Aaliyah, what happened?"

There's no way I can keep hiding the truth from him. I'm fully prepared to take whatever cruel words come out of his mouth; I went into this knowing he'd be angry about what I'd done, especially once I swore I wouldn't go down this road.

I push myself off the floor, groaning as my joints crack and pop like bang snaps hitting the pavement. "I need to tell you something, but before I start, you have to know I was the one who reached out. So if you wanna be mad at someone, it should be at me."

"Aaliyah." Grandpa Joe growls out my name this time. "Spit it out."

Ivy stands behind me, close enough that I can feel her body heat on me. She doesn't complain when I reach back and grab her hand for an extra bit of confidence.

"I reached out to my—" It feels weird referring to Lena as my mom. A mom wouldn't have left me or stood me up the way she did. Or at least a good one wouldn't. A good one would be like Ivy's mom—Auntie Yolanda. Or Jen and Tommy's. Supportive. Someone who never lets their kid down. Someone who puts their kid's needs over everything and everyone. Someone a kid can count on to be there when they need them. So, in other words, the exact opposite of mine. "I reached out to Lena. I thought maybe she never came to see me because . . . Well, because she was afraid of what you'd say when she got here. I know you told me to stay away from my parents, but after I saw her post a picture with Quincy, I couldn't stop thinking about them. I had to talk to at least one of them. Even if it was just for a moment."

Telling Grandpa Joe the truth about meeting with Lena, or attempting to, was never going to be easy. The history between him and my parents is messy and complicated and kind of unknown because he refuses to tell me what happened, but I guess I thought my grandpa would forgive her in time if he was forced to interact with her. It might have worked if Lena hadn't stood me up.

Grandpa Joe's mouth moves a lot, but no words come out. I can only imagine what he's thinking. Maybe he's wondering why, after all this time, he's still not enough for me.

I want to tell him that I've been secretly wondering the same thing about Lena and Quincy. That even though our feelings are directed at different people, they're the same. And I desperately want Grandpa Joe to know that he is enough for me. That just because I have this deep longing to know Quincy and Lena, it doesn't erase any of the feelings or appreciation I have for him.

"You knew about this, didn't you?" Even though Grandpa Joe asked Ivy a direct question, he doesn't let her get a word in. "'Course ya did. All y'all do is talk. Always in cahoots with each other."

"Nobody can change Aaliyah's mind once she's set on doing something," Ivy says. "You know that better than anyone."

Grandpa heads down to the first floor without uttering another word. He sways a bit, bumping his elbow against the banister a few times. That's normal for him. It's the pause that catches me off guard though. He stands at the bottom of the staircase and grips the banister so tight that the veins in his hand pop out.

"Grandpa?" I run downstairs as quickly as I can without tripping over my feet. "Hey, what's wrong?"

"Ain't nothing wrong with me." Grandpa Joe shakes me off and sits on the couch with his arms folded over his chest. He isn't staring at anything in particular, but I don't think he cares what he's looking at as long as it isn't me. "You swore, Aaliyah. You looked me right in the damn eye and lied to my face. Didn't even have the decency to come clean about it when I asked."

"I know and I'm so sorry about that, but I thought it'd be easier for you to accept if you found out after I did it. But look, this is the first and only time I'll try to meet up with Lena." I show him my phone as I delete everything to do with Lena—her phone number, the text conversations I had with her, the call logs, Facebook messages—everything. It's dramatic because I could find her again if I wanted to, but I don't. I put myself out there and she rejected me. "I'm done, okay? I swear."

"You already did that, remember? Don't mean much to me now." He takes a long, shuddering breath and releases it in a broken gasp, sounding like he's on the brink of tears. But he doesn't cry. He never does. And when I reach for him, he yanks his arm away from me. "Don't."

His rejection hurts more than anything Lena could do to me. "Grandpa, don't be like this. I said I was sorry."

I might as well have not said a word for how thoroughly he ignores me. Even though I had a strong feeling this would happen, I still sort of hoped that it wouldn't. I hoped our relationship was strong enough to handle what me reaching out to Lena could do to it. I was wrong, and I see that now, but in the moment, I thought it was a risk I had to take. I thought if it ended with our family being back together again it would be worth it. I never believed Lena would stand me up and that because of my decision, Grandpa Joe would ignore me as thoroughly as he has. I give him his space because he doesn't give me a choice but hope that tomorrow he'll be more understanding.

The next day, Grandpa Joe makes the executive decision to ground me for the remainder of January as punishment for going against his wishes. I'm not sure how upset I'm allowed to be. I was the stubborn one who didn't listen to Grandpa Joe because, in his words, I thought I knew better than him. But that's not it at all. I wanted so badly to believe that Lena wanted to meet me. That she loved me the way I've always hoped she did. Our failed meeting told me that she doesn't, and I'm sick to my stomach over it. Things shouldn't be this way. I should be happy right now, planning a meeting to smooth things over with her and Grandpa Joe. Instead, I'm in bed crying myself to sleep.

PART TWO
FEBRUARY

1

The tension between me and Grandpa Joe doesn't fade with time. All the anger he normally aims at Lena and Quincy is now directed at me, and it's seeping into every crevice of our lives like poison. He does his best to pretend I don't exist until he has no choice but to talk to me, and when he does, he doesn't say more than two words at a time. After he's finished cooking, he says, "Dinner" or "Breakfast." When he wants me to do chores, he says, "Clean up." He doesn't ask me to watch TV shows or movies on Netflix. We don't eat pints of ice cream in the evenings as a treat after I finish my homework. He barely blinks when his buddies ask me more questions about college during the next spades night. Despite how broken I was after Lena stood me up, the slow deterioration of the bond my grandpa and I formed while he took care of me for all these years hurts me the most.

I spend my first day of freedom in my room with a hot face and stinging eyes because Grandpa Joe barely glanced at me when he returned my phone. Tears trickle onto the collar of the long-sleeve shirt my grandpa bought me at our UCLA campus visit last summer, staining the gray fabric with each thick drop. I'm deep in a depression session when my phone rings. Ivy's name pops up, and I answer it even though I don't really feel like talking to anyone.

"Girl, where the hell are you?" Ivy asks. "I can't see you with the mountain of covers on your head."

I peek my head out from under the covers and immediately want to hide again. The skin on my lips is cracked. My face is puffy. The whites in my eyes are all red. I look horrible, and to top it all off, my hair is a tangled mess. I pull the comforter back over my head until only my eyes are visible.

"I'm gonna be nice and not comment on how you look," Ivy says.

"I appreciate that," I say.

"Grandpa still isn't talking to you?"

"No. I apologized like a million times and didn't even complain about my punishment. We should be on our way to being good again, but he's not budging, and I don't know what else to do."

"You know how he is when he's got an attitude. He thinks everybody's an asshole until he gets over it. Give him some space and let him come to you."

"There's no such thing as space when you live with somebody. My entire existence serves as a reminder of how badly I screwed up. I think he hates me."

"I don't wanna say I told you so."

"So don't."

"Fine, but I'm thinking it."

Ivy isn't in the frame anymore. Her surroundings blur as she moves around her room like everything is fine. Everything for her is normal. Normal life. Normal parents. Normal apartment. I've always wanted that and never could have it. I thought I was getting close to it when Lena agreed to meet with me, but that wasn't real. It was just what I deluded myself into believing I could have.

"Pack a bag and tell Grandpa Joe you'll be staying with me for the next week," Ivy says. "He'll be so bored that by the time you get home, he'll be begging for you to hang out with him."

For the first time in almost three weeks, there's a light at the end of the tunnel. Ivy just gave me an actionable plan that'll almost definitely work. The one thing I can always count on from Grandpa Joe is that when I'm gone, he misses me no matter how mad he is. In normal circumstances, it would only take a few hours, but this is an emergency situation. A week without me will force him to remember the good times we've had and will hopefully get him to forget the bad from last month. The most important thing to do is to completely scrub Lena from my life. It's been close to a month, and she hasn't attempted to contact me to explain why she never showed, and it's taken this long for me to realize she never will. I get cleaned up and tell myself I'm okay, but the pain is still there, pulsing like a heartbeat.

2

Grandpa Joe sends a text three days later asking when I'll be back. He doesn't respond when I tell him I'll be home in a few days, and I guess I should be a little worried about that, but I can't crack now. It hasn't been enough time.

Ivy suggests we head over to Jen's house to take my mind off Grandpa Joe. We drive in silence because I prefer it more than talking these days. Once Ivy parks in Jen's driveway, her hand wraps around my forearm, preventing me from getting out of her car. "We never really talked about what happened. I know you're not okay, but are you gonna be?"

"No."

She nods like she understands but she doesn't. No one does. Maybe one day it won't hurt as bad to think about what happened with Lena. For now, the pain is endless and excruciating. It's not just a part of me that aches. There's a tear in my soul, and when the soul rips and the feeling of emptiness becomes vast like the ocean, there's no repairing that.

"I know she's my auntie, but I wish I could beat her up," Ivy says. "I'd obviously let you get a couple hits in, so you can get your lick back."

"I don't wanna hit her."

"It might make you feel better."

"Can we not talk about her anymore? This is making me feel depressed again, and I don't wanna be that anymore. It's exhausting."

Ivy drops the Lena topic and releases my arm. I follow her in silence and at a distance to keep from having to answer more questions about dumb stuff like feelings and the status of my mental health.

Jen lets me remove my coat and kick off my boots at her front door but stops me from going farther into her house. I begin to dread coming out tonight. If I'd known everyone was going to bring up the worst moment of my life, I would've stayed at Ivy's place.

"Real quick, I may have told Tommy you were coming over," Jen says. "And I may have also told him you were outside like three seconds after Ivy texted me. And he may be waiting for you in the kitchen."

"So, all those things are clearly true."

"They are. Tommy is upset too," Jen says. "Maybe you can make each other feel better."

Tommy is in the kitchen eating a dipped Italian beef with sweet and hot peppers. He looks kind of beautiful tonight. His skin is perfect and smooth with no blemishes and looks dewy the way it always does when he steals Jen's skincare products. He's got on a backward baseball cap with his fluffy black hair poking through the hole and a Chicago Bulls jersey that accentuates his biceps. The sight of him makes me smile, even though I know I need to be cold toward him. I've never been good at being cold to him though.

"Shouldn't you be at a house party somewhere?" I ask. "It's a Saturday night."

"I was three drinks deep when Jen told me you were coming over," he says.

Dropping everything to see me isn't something he's done before, and I can't help getting a little curious as to why he's switched up like this. "So you decided to leave the party to come see me?"

"Yeah." Tommy squints and leans over the countertop between us. It's weird. The more I back up, the closer he moves and he just . . . stares. "I'm glad I skipped the party. Your spark is gone."

"Excuse me?"

"The one in your eye. It's not there anymore." He sets down his sandwich, washes his hands at the sink, then pulls out a bunch of veggies and a stalk of lettuce from the fridge. "Talk to me, and don't say it's nothing 'cause I can tell it's something."

"What are you doing?"

"Making you a salad."

Standing here with him and talking about my feelings is far from what I actually want to do. I don't want to talk at all. I never wanted to come here in the first place, but Ivy made me because she said it's not good for me to sulk and isolate myself when I'm feeling blue. Now I'm thinking she set me up with Jen's help and they arranged this little meeting with Tommy.

"Come on," he presses. "I'm listening."

"It's a lot."

"I can handle a lot."

Tommy's right here asking me to talk to him like the old days when things were simple, and we were just friends. He doesn't make any inappropriate jokes. Doesn't mention wanting to kiss me or touch me. All he wants to do is talk, and I can't lie; I missed doing that with him. And just because we can't hook up doesn't mean we can't be friends again, right? "I'm in a fight with my grandpa. Or I guess he's in one with me."

"Because of Lena?"

"Yeah. Hiding it from him didn't feel right, but I'm kinda wishing I didn't say anything at all because now he's so pissed he won't even talk to me." I push myself onto the countertop opposite the island he's chopping veggies on. "Now everything's all screwed up and I can't even live in my own house anymore."

Tommy finishes chopping up the rinsed lettuce and veggies and throws everything into a bowl with croutons and red vinaigrette dressing on top. "You two are gonna be okay. Always are."

"You didn't see the way he looked when I told him the truth. It feels different this time. I think I broke him."

"Can you blame him for being upset? He's probably feeling like you tried linking with Lena 'cause you wanted to get your real parents back."

"But that's not what I was trying to do."

"Paranoia doesn't make sense, Aaliyah. You know that better than anyone." Tommy hands me the bowl with a fork and joins me on the countertop, munching on the rest of his Italian beef.

"I bet he's got all sorts of thoughts floating around in his head. You might've had him feeling unappreciated and whatever. Disrespected. I mean, you've gotta see how this looks. You're creeping around, making secret meetings with Lena to get lunch. You could've really hurt his feelings, but he doesn't wanna tell you 'cause he thinks he'll look soft."

"I didn't mean to hurt his feelings."

"Nobody means to hurt somebody's feelings unless they're an asshole."

"I don't know what to do. I'm doing Ivy's plan, but I don't know if it'll work because he's never been this pissed at me before, and if it doesn't . . . I can't think about that. I'll drive myself crazy, and Auntie Yolanda will try to have me committed."

Tommy catches my free hand and runs his thumb along my knuckles until the tremor is only minimal. The act calms me enough that I can eat the salad he made me without it falling back into the bowl. "I'd tell you not to stress about it, but I know you're gonna do that anyway. So I'll just say this—you weren't wrong for wanting to learn more about Lena and what happened to you back then. One day Joe will understand why you felt you had to do things the way you did, and even though it doesn't feel like it right now, all this pain you're feeling will fade. Just gotta give it some time."

"And if it doesn't?"

"It will."

Things are better now that Tommy has said his piece. I still can't go home because Grandpa Joe isn't talking to me. I can't go back to the past and stop myself from reaching out to Lena. But

I love Tommy for doing what he does best and talking me down from the ledge. I breathe a little easier. "That was good advice. Have you been getting tips from Auntie Yolanda?"

"I had a whole month to think about what I wanted to say. Jen's been keeping me updated on the situation."

"I haven't talked to Jen about this."

"She said Ivy told her."

Odd. It's always been me and Jen and me and Ivy and the three of us kind of come together because we're on the same relay team, but Jen and Ivy aren't the kind of friends who talk about personal issues like this. I guess things changed while I was grounded. I let my hand slip from Tommy's grasp and pick up a few more pieces of lettuce, along with some bits of tomato and bell peppers. "Jen said you were upset too. What's wrong?"

"My ex became a stalker over winter break. She called me fifteen times yesterday."

"Is she all right? Like mentally?"

"Obviously not. Her antics are really starting to bum me out. I can't do shit without her badgering me about getting back together." Tommy hunches his shoulders and tosses the rest of his Italian beef back into the wrapper. His phone dings in his back pocket, and I swear he flinches. "Fuck it. I'm throwing it in the toilet."

He's halfway to the bathroom when I realize he's actually intending to flush his phone down the toilet. I hurry to catch up and slip around him, pressing both hands to his chest to stop him from doing something he'll regret in about three seconds. "Hey, maybe cut your phone off for a while instead."

"Tried that. Doesn't work. She'll show up wherever I am and start yelling at me."

Tommy and I haven't spoken much about his relationship lately, but I don't remember things being this bad with him and Sabrina. Something had to have changed. Or he's finally being open about his relationship. Either way, I don't like what I'm hearing. "Have you told anyone about her?"

"Just you and Jen."

"Someone else should know. Like an adult someone who can actually help."

"I don't wanna tell anyone. I'm handling it."

He's got his eyes trained on the floor and it's really none of my business, but it doesn't seem like he's handling it well. I can't push Tommy to do something he doesn't want to do. If he wants to deal with his ex on his own, that's his right. All I can do is be a friend and support him. I hold out my arms for a hug, and this time he definitely flinches. I'm sure of it. "Tommy, what's going on?"

"Nothing."

His nothing sounds a lot like something but it's clear he doesn't want to go into specific details. If he did, he would've done it by now. He hugs me after a moment, pressing his body close to mine. His muscles tense under my hold, then the tension slowly seeps out of him. It's so quick that I feel like I imagined it and I end up not commenting on it even though I really want to.

"I'm worried about you," I say.

"That's good," he says. "Means you'll come around more."

"If you wanted to see me, you could've asked. We're still friends."

"Are we?"

"Of course."

Tommy pushes my arms up and around his neck when my grip loosens. He moves his arms to my waist, and this begins to feel less platonic and more like something else. I'm not surprised that things have shifted as quickly as they have. Self-control has never been our strong suit. It's the reason why we fell into a friends-with-benefits situation in the first place, but I meant what I said about not wanting to further ruin things between me and Grandpa Joe. With my eyes on his lips and a lump in my throat, I say, "I should get down to the basement."

"Can I come?"

"You never wanna hang out with us."

"I'd rather be alone with you, but I'll take what I can get. Sort of feels like if I don't take advantage of tonight, I won't get another chance to see you for a while."

Tommy has always been able to tell when things shift with us, even when I deny it. I should've anticipated him clocking me and my plan to distance myself from him. But after finding out about him and his ex, I'm not sure if that's the best move anymore. He needs me now more than ever, and even my grandpa would understand that being a good friend to him means not pushing him away—and setting clear boundaries with our friendship.

3

When Ivy drops me off at home eleven days later, an unfamiliar car is idling on the opposite side of the street. The driver hops out of his car once I get out of Ivy's, but I don't pay him any mind. Ivy doesn't pull off until I'm inside my house. I catch a glimpse of the stranger as I shut the door. He doesn't head toward anyone's home, and no one comes out to meet him. He gets back into his car and continues to idle.

"Finally decided to come home, huh?" Grandpa Joe asks.

"Sounds like I was missed," I say.

He's quiet as he watches TV, cracking peanuts with his back molar and tossing the shells into the plastic bag near his foot. He pops the nut in his mouth, scowling at a car driving by blaring its music. "Could be doing something useful instead of standing around. Pick up a broom. Mop something."

"You definitely missed me."

Grandpa Joe runs a finger along the coffee table in the center of the room and shows it to me. "Look at this. Filthy."

"There's literally nothing on your finger, but I could be persuaded to clean a dish if you talk to me."

"Talk about what?"

"Lena."

"No."

"You kind of don't have an option, so . . ."

He cracks another peanut. Splinters of the shell stick to his bottom lip as he spits them into the bag. "Better not be planning on reaching out to her again."

"I should've listened to you, but I thought I knew better. I didn't wanna believe Lena could do something to hurt me and I figured if I could just talk to her and get her side of things, I could be the one who fixed everything. I'd get you two talking again, and we'd all be a family. Ivy said I was delusional. That Lena didn't care about me and that's why she left me with you. I refused to believe that, but she was right, and I feel so much worse now and I just wish none of this had ever happened. I wanna go back to the way things were when me and you were good, and we didn't have this hanging over us. Can we do that?"

Grandpa Joe's silence is loud, and for a moment, I think he's back to ignoring me. He's got his face all turned up and he's looking past me the way he did during my grounding. What if I didn't spend enough time away? What if this isn't something he can ever really get over? My cheeks burn and my body temp rises as I feel the stomach pains I'm so familiar with start to creep up. What if this is what changes everything for us?

"Wouldn't mind hearing another apology," he says.

I release a breath and all the tension and nerves that'd been building during his silence. "I'm sorry, Grandpa. You don't have to forgive me right away, but I hope you can eventually. I couldn't take it if you were mad at me forever. I've only got like four real friends, and I'm related to two of them."

Grandpa Joe's smile is small, but it's there. I take a chance and sit next to him on the couch. For the first time in a long time, he doesn't move away.

"Lena was a lot like your grandma," he says. "Fickle. On the move all the time. Trying to tie them down was like trying to hold water."

I don't know what to say and I'm too scared to interrupt him because this might be the only time he'll talk about Lena this openly. It's certainly the first.

"She loved you in her own little way, but a little love ain't nearly enough when you've got somebody that relies on you. When she had you, it was like all the fun was over because she had a baby. She didn't know how to deal with it. And it wasn't like she could ignore you. You always needed something. You needed to be fed, bathed, loved. Some of those were things she couldn't provide, so your grandma said we should take you. And when she passed, I stepped up and did what needed to be done. I took care of you and protected you and made sure you had everything you needed. I did my best to raise you right because I knew what kinda life you would've had with Lena, and I wasn't gonna let no grandbaby of mine live like that. So I kept you from her, and I'mma keep on doing that until my last breath."

Grandpa Joe's demeanor flips and he's back to his regular grumpy self. "Irresponsible. That's what she's always been. And I don't wanna hear another word about that girl from here on out, you hear me?"

Our conversation about Lena was short, but it reinforced a belief that's always been at the back of my mind. Lena was never going to keep me. Whether she gave me to her parents or to some stranger at an adoption agency, I was never going to have her in my life. And with what Grandpa Joe told me, that's a good thing. He's taken care of me better than she ever could, and I should be grateful to have him. Grateful that he dropped everything to watch over me even after Grandma Dee was gone and protected me from the bad life I would've had with Lena.

"I hear you, Grandpa."

"Help me up. I'm hungry."

I do what he says. "Are you okay?"

"Been having some dizzy spells lately. Nothing serious."

"Sounds pretty serious to me. You should go to the doctor."

"Ain't going to no doctor, so you can get that little idea out of your head. I'm fine."

I'm tempted to push the subject, but I just got back on his good side. "How about instead of cooking dinner tonight, we order pizza? We can add our own stuff like we used to."

Back before the arthritis set in, Grandpa Joe would make his own crust from scratch. I think the only reason we don't still do it is because he doesn't trust me to knead the dough right.

"Want mine with extra cheese." Grandpa Joe touches the wall as he walks down the hallway toward the kitchen. "Extra, extra cheese."

"Cheese isn't good for your cholesterol. It's already too high."

"Ain't that why they got me taking all those pills? Should be able to eat what I damn well please."

"You don't take your medicine like you're supposed to. Don't make me tell them to skip the cheese completely because I totally will."

Grandpa Joe waves me off and tells me he wants to walk into the kitchen on his own. He's slower and more careful than I can ever remember him being and groans with each step. Again, I don't comment on it. "Sometimes I think you forget who's the granddaughter and who's the grandpa."

"I know what our roles are. I'm obviously the grandpa."

Grandpa Joe lets out a chuckle that's cut off by a sharp gasp. His head hangs low as he leans against the wall for support, but when I put my arms around him, he shakes his head. "I'm all right. I'm all right."

I keep my hands out in case I need to catch him. I don't mean to worry about him like this, but he refuses to take care of himself the way he should. He's giving me no choice. "Maybe we should have salads instead of pizza. Dressing on the side."

"Ain't having no salad unless it's secretly a pizza."

"At least take your medicine, so I don't spend the rest of the night freaking out. Please?"

He begrudgingly agrees to the deal, but it doesn't make me feel better because tomorrow he'll be back to not taking his pills at all. I consider calling my auntie after I put in our pizza order. She's good at getting him to do stuff he doesn't really want to do. She could come over tomorrow and force him to take his medication. Maybe even make him an appointment to see his doctor for a check-up But Grandpa Joe is hovering, so I end up sending a text instead.

> **Me:** Hi, auntie. I think something's wrong with grandpa. He said he's been having dizzy spells. Can you take him to the doctor? He's not listening to me.
>
> **Auntie Yolanda:** Send me a list of symptoms you've noticed. I'll schedule an appointment and hopefully his doctor can give us some answers.
>
> **Auntie Yolanda:** Are you okay?

The answer is no but that sounds dramatic through text, so I just say yes. Forty-five minutes later, I step outside to grab the pizza from the delivery person. I spot the same car from earlier, still idling across the street. The stranger is now leaning against the driver's-side door with what looks like a lit cigarette pinched between his middle and forefinger. He raises his free hand as I tip the delivery person and waves like he's beckoning someone over to him. Not just someone. Me. Does he know me somehow? I'm sure I don't know him, so I go back inside the house.

"There was some weird dude waving at me out there," I say. "He's been there since I got home."

"Let me see." Grandpa Joe bumps me out of the way, nearly knocking the pizza out of my hands, and peeks through the blinds. He lets out an odd noise. Almost like a growl. "Gimme my bat."

"Maybe don't immediately go to a violent place. He might have a gun."

Grandpa Joe pretends like he can't hear me and grabs the bat on his own. He swings the front door wide open, stepping onto the porch with his bat clutched in his hand. "Hey! Didn't I tell you to stay away from here?"

"She's eighteen, Joe," says the man. "You can't keep her away from me anymore."

"Yes, the hell I can," says Grandpa Joe. "Get back in the house, Aaliyah."

The guy crosses the street and stops right in front of our gate. With him being closer and the light from the streetlamp illuminating his features, I finally realize who this man is. He looks exactly like he did in the picture I saw on Lena's Facebook. He's Quincy. My dad. "If you wanna talk to me, I'm here, and I'll keep being here until you tell me to go. It's up to you, Aaliyah. Not him."

Quincy is the parent I never wanted to meet. From the stories Grandpa Joe told, he's no good and he abandoned me and Lena only a few weeks after I was born. He's a deadbeat and now he's here because what? All the hard stuff is done, and he thinks he can slip in like nothing ever happened? No freaking way. "I don't wanna talk to you."

I follow Grandpa Joe back into the house and he slams the door shut. Then he goes around and closes all the blinds and locks every window like he thinks Quincy is going to sneak into the house later on tonight. By the time I make it to the living room window, Quincy is already back in his car, and unlike before, he actually drives away this time.

In a way, I'm glad he showed up tonight because it allowed me to prove my loyalty to Grandpa Joe. But I'm also confused. Why did he come? The Quincy Grandpa Joe told me about would never waste time coming to see me. Not for the first time, I wonder if my grandpa has told me the whole story or if he's withholding bits of critical information that would make the full picture make sense. I don't dare question him about it, though. We're finally on our way to being good again, so I forget about Quincy and Lena and focus on me and him. That's what's important.

4

Things go back to normal for the most part. Grandpa Joe still isn't very talkative, and he's suspicious of me whenever I leave the house, but he doesn't ignore me. It means things are on the mend. This is what I wanted. I should be happy, but I'm not and I don't know why.

Downstairs in the living room, Grandpa Joe is propped up on the couch. I tell him Ivy will be here soon and start making my way over to the kitchen when something stops me. It's an internal something. A slight tug in my gut and a voice in my head telling me not to leave him just yet.

It takes a second for me to realize why. The TV isn't on. The TV is always on. I stand in front of him, and he only looks at me for a second before his eyes drift down to his right arm. I squat to stay in his line of sight. "Is something wrong?"

Grandpa Joe pushes himself off the couch and I think for a moment, he'll wave me off and say he's fine and to quit fussing over him. It's what he'd usually do. He doesn't this time though. He turns his back on me.

"Grandpa—"

He stumbles into the coffee table on the way to the kitchen, letting out a loud grunt when his knee catches the edge of the glass. His breaths come out shaky and much too quick, like he ran a race that he wasn't prepared for.

"Hey, maybe you should sit back down."

Grandpa Joe sways unsteadily on the balls of his feet. His gaze is transfixed on something over my shoulder, but I'm too worried about him to check. His eyes glaze over as he scans the room. "Where is this?"

"The living room." I support as much of his weight as I can, doing my absolute best to stay calm. Having a panic attack right now wouldn't do him any good. "I got you, Grandpa."

He didn't make it too far from the couch, so I lead him back there, somehow managing not to collapse under his weight. He might only be having a dizzy spell, but I don't feel comfortable leaving him like this. "I'm gonna call Auntie Yolanda and have her come over and check on you. Sound good?"

He doesn't say yes, but he doesn't say no either, so I assume it's okay.

The toe of Grandpa Joe's house shoe catches on the edge of the rug, throwing him off balance. He slumps against me without warning, and I go crashing into the coffee table.

Pain erupts around my elbow as sharp glass slices into my skin. I bite down on my lip hard enough to draw blood. The coppery substance drips down my chin, mixing with the thick tears now running down my cheeks. I gasp out, "Okay . . . Okay . . . Okay . . ."

A ragged sob slips through my lips, and I shut my eyes to block out the pain. Breathe. Breathe. Breathe. Don't lose yourself to the pain, Aaliyah.

One of my arms is pinned under him, but I manage to maneuver around to get a better view of him and stare, shocked and frightened by what I see when I pop open my eyes. "Grandpa? Oh, no. Your face . . . It's . . ."

I don't know what it's doing or what's wrong or what I'm supposed to do in a situation like this. All I can think about is pain. Sharp, severe, mind-bending pain. And his face. His face.

Grandpa Joe's eyes slide to the left, slightly unfocused, as though there's more than one of me and he's not sure which me he should be looking at. He opens his mouth, but the words come out unclear and incoherent as he slowly loses all ability to support himself on his own.

And his face.

One half looks fine. Normal, even. But the other side looks like it's melting. He finally focuses on me and stares, eyes wide and filled with terror as he moves his mouth, desperately trying to make me understand. But his words aren't clicking in my head.

He needs help. I know he does. And I know I need it too, but I'm frozen in place, unable to move or think or do anything useful. Why can't I move?

I stick my bloodied arm out, wincing as the glass shards stuck in my elbow split the skin even wider. Tiny, shattered pieces dig into the lines in my hand, but I try not to think about the pain. I lay my grandpa down as gently as possible and run back upstairs to my room. "Phone. Where'd I put my phone?"

It's deep in one of the side pockets of my Nike bag. I pull it out with trembling hands and dial 9-1-1, stumbling back downstairs to find him slumped on the floor.

"Nine-one-one, what's your emergency?" the dispatcher asks.

"My grandpa . . . Something's wrong with him. His face is . . . It's melting. I don't—I don't know what to do or—I don't know. He can't speak. He isn't talking at all."

"Is your grandfather breathing?"

I check with a finger under his nostrils. "He is. Yeah."

"I'm going to have you do a test on your grandpa, okay?"

"Okay. What do I do?"

"I need you to ask him to smile."

I don't question her. "He can't."

"Ask him to lift his arms."

"Can you lift your arms, Grandpa? Just a little. He isn't . . . He didn't do it. He can't move his right arm. Only the left one."

"Only the left. Okay. Now ask him to repeat this: 'You can't teach an old dog new tricks.'"

This time Grandpa Joe doesn't react. Not even when I repeat the phrase the dispatcher asks me to say.

"Are you able to tell me what happened?" the dispatcher asks.

"Um, I was talking to him, but he wasn't talking back. He kept staring at his arm. His right arm. It was the right." I cover my eyes with a hand and focus on what happened to him before I called 9-1-1. "He tried to get up. Then he fell. He fell on me."

"Are you hurt, ma'am?"

"I'm bleeding. Glass in my arm."

"You have glass in your arm?"

"Yeah. There's blood everywhere."

"Is your grandpa bleeding as well?"

I do a careful search, lifting Grandpa Joe's bloody shirt to see if there are any marks underneath. It's all mine. None of it is his. "No. Just me."

"Is there anyone else in the house with you? A parent?"

"No. My grandpa is my parent." The pain in my arm is starting to spread to my neck and the room begins to tilt, so I shut my eyes again. *Don't pass out. Please don't pass out.* "Is the ambulance gonna be here soon?"

"They will be. Yes."

I do what I can to prepare for the EMTs, so they don't have as many obstacles in their way. I open the front door because screw the cold and the fact that we're in a not-so-good neighborhood. I sit poised to move away from Grandpa Joe as quickly as possible to give them easy room. I stroke his droopy cheek, smearing blood into the salty tears sticking to his skin. "You'll be okay. Trust me."

The EMTs transport of my grandpa is smooth, and I want to believe that I had something to do with it. That I helped. At least a little. Even the most minuscule thing would be enough to stop the constant flow of tears and the thoughts of how useless I am from plaguing me.

One of the EMTs catches my attention as he's helping roll my grandpa through our yard in a stretcher. "Hey. Hey, kid. What's your name?"

"Aaliyah."

"How old are you, Aaliyah? Can you drive yourself to the hospital?"

"I—" My eyes land on my beat-up car parked on the curb as I stumble after the EMTs. The freaking thing isn't working. Hasn't been for weeks. "I—I—Eighteen. I'm eighteen."

"Don't panic on me, Aaliyah. You've been doing good so far, okay? Now, can you drive?"

A midnight-blue Camry with rusted paint chipping off the hood rolls up behind the ambulance, completely blocking the street. I start crying harder, mostly out of relief because it's Ivy. She'll make everything better by simply being here.

"That's my cousin!" I point at the car. "I can ride with her."

"Good. Okay." I stare at Grandpa Joe on the stretcher as the EMT helps his partner lift him into the back of the ambulance. "Focus on my words. Not on what I'm doing, Aaliyah."

"Aaliyah!"

I snap my head around at the sound of Ivy's voice.

"Aaliyah—" The EMT's voice cuts through the noise, Ivy, and everything else. It's like all I hear now is him. "I need you to remember this—we're going to the university. Not Jackson Park. Repeat that for me."

"The university. Not Jackson Park."

"Call an adult, someone who knows a lot about your grandpa's health and can give the doctors all the information they need. Do you have someone like that?"

I mean, me. But I'll be no good. I'm barely holding on as it is. "Yes. My auntie. She takes care of everything."

"Call her and tell her to meet you at the university. When you get there, go to the front desk and give your grandpa's name to the secretary. Make sure somebody takes a look at your arm too. The health team will handle everything. You just need to get there, okay?"

I nod over and over because I think it's all I can do now. *Nod. Nod. Nod.*

"This is important, so listen up." The EMT jumps into the back of the ambulance with grandpa while his partner rounds the front of the truck. "We're gonna be flying down the street. Don't try to keep up. Tell your cousin that. Take your time. Get to the hospital safely."

Nod. Nod. Nod.

The EMT grabs the door handle and swings it almost all the way shut before he hesitates. "You did good, Aaliyah."

Suddenly the EMT has been replaced with Ivy. Wide-eyed, confused Ivy. "What the hell is going on with Grandpa? What happened to your arm?"

"The university. They're taking him to the university."

5

Ivy has driven like a NASCAR racer since the day she got her license. The only reason why she drove safely prior to that was because she wouldn't have passed her test otherwise. But she hits a new level of recklessness as she speeds down the streets of Chicago in an effort to keep up with our grandpa's ambulance.

"Slow down, Ivy," I say. "We're gonna crash."

"I know what I'm doing." Ivy cuts a sharp right, sliding into the turning lane of the opposite side of the road. "Call my mama again."

I do what Ivy says. The line rings and rings and rings before going to voicemail. "You've reached Dr. Yolanda Sullivan. Please leave a message and I'll return your call at my earliest convenience."

"Auntie Yolanda, you need to call me back. Grandpa Joe is . . . I don't really know what happened to him, but it's bad. It's really, really bad. I had to call nine-one-one. He's in an ambulance now and they're taking him to . . . Um . . ."

"The University of Chicago," Ivy says.

"Yeah, they're taking him to the University of Chicago." The numbness in my right arm persists, despite my doing everything I can to keep the limb operational. "I know I keep repeating myself in every message, but I don't know which one you're gonna check first. I'll try again once me and Ivy make it to the hospital."

"Watch your arm," Ivy says. You're getting blood all over my car."

Blood seeps through the makeshift bandage I created using torn pieces of my shirt. I rip off another strip of cloth and wrap it around my injured forearm. Stupid coffee table. Grandpa Joe said it was tempered glass when we bought it, but it seemed real untempered when I crashed through it twenty minutes ago. "This stupid shirt isn't thick enough, and I can only rip off a little bit of it. Long sleeves or not, it's too cold to be wearing a crop top."

"Here." Ivy swerves into another lane while reaching over to open the glove box. "My mama put a bunch of napkins in here from when we went to Chipotle a few weeks ago."

"I'll find them. Focus on the road."

The next traffic light switches from green to yellow in a split second. Grandpa Joe's ambulance blows through the intersection, but with how far behind we are, there's no way we're going to make the light before it turns red.

"Don't do it, Ivy," I say. "You already got clocked by a speed camera a mile back. You really wanna add a red-light camera ticket to that?"

Ivy slams her foot on the gas. The light turns red as she crosses the white line. She doesn't stop. "Fuck a ticket. Grandpa needs us."

Chipotle napkins flutter around me when I spin in my seat to check out the car we passed. It's a white SUV with a blue stripe along the side of the vehicle and CHICAGO POLICE spelled out in red lettering. "We can't help him if we get pulled over, crazy."

Ivy slows enough to keep the cop off our backs, but she hits the gas once the SUV turns a corner. "Happy?"

"Not really." The UChicago emergency room comes into focus up ahead. Ivy continues barreling down the road, forcing me to grab hold of her bicep when she comes dangerously close to missing her turn. "Slow! Slow! Slow! The turn is right there."

Ivy manages to find a decent spot in a parking garage on Maryland Ave. It takes what feels like a lifetime to power walk across the bridge connecting the garage to the hospital. The waiting room is bright and packed with people who have a variety of illnesses, some visible and some not. I dodge a woman coughing her lungs up and get a few weird looks from a small group of people huddled in a corner because of the Chipotle napkins hanging off my bloody arm. I'm taken to the back to be seen because I look like the protagonist at the end of a horror movie while Ivy tries to find out Grandpa Joe's status.

Once I'm all fixed up, I find Ivy sitting off by herself at the far end of the waiting room. She doesn't meet my eye when I approach her, but she clears a seat for me by removing her coat from the back of the chair. "What happened? When can we see Grandpa?"

"It'll be a while," Ivy says. "A nurse came out to talk to me, but everything she said was hypothetical because he hasn't been seen by anyone here yet. She told me stroke victims are usually given some kind of medication to dissolve the blood clots. But because it took a while for him to get here, she's not sure if it'll even work."

As the paramedics rushed Grandpa Joe out of the house and into the ambulance, they told me he probably had a stroke. I wanted to ask more questions at the time, but everything was going so fast, and they kept telling me I'd get updates at the hospital. But I'm here now and I haven't been told anything new. Scratch that. I have been told something new. Earlier I'd assumed Grandpa would be okay once he got to the hospital. Now I know there's no guarantee of that. "Do they at least know if he's gonna be okay?"

"All they know is that he had a stroke, and it was bad," Ivy says. "They're gonna call my mama, though, since she's his emergency contact. I'mma call my daddy, too, just in case."

"I thought he was out of town."

"He is, but he can still pick up a phone. Maybe his call will be the one she answers." Ivy's phone is dead, so she takes mine from me. "Once they run some tests, we'll know how severe the stroke was. I don't know how long it'll take. Or what we're supposed to do while we wait. I'm freaking the fuck out, Aaliyah."

"Please don't. If you freak out, then who's gonna calm me down when I spiral into a panic attack?"

With her eyes closed, Ivy practices the breathing techniques her mom taught us after the first time I had a panic attack and the first time Ivy fought someone at school. "I'm good."

"You sure?" I ask.

"I said I was." I don't think she is, but I'm not going to argue with her about it. Ivy stands and pulls on her coat. "I'm gonna step outside."

The second Ivy leaves, the reality of the situation crushes me. Grandpa Joe may never be the same, and if he isn't, I won't have any idea how to help. My medical knowledge starts and ends with the basic physical therapy I learned to help out with any injuries Ivy, Jen, Tommy, and I sustained over the years. So I'm the furthest thing from a stroke expert. I'm not an expert on anything. I'm useless.

6

Buzz. *Buzz. Buzz.*

I let my phone ring in my coat pocket the way it has since Auntie Yolanda showed up at the hospital about an hour ago. Talking isn't something I'm up for at the moment, and I wish the person calling would realize that instead of continuing to bother me.

"Aaliyah," says Ivy, carefully nudging me on my injured side.

I ended up needing stitches. Three near my elbow, five on my forearm, and two on my palm. The doctor told me most of the injuries would heal fine, but I may have a couple scars. I don't mind though. I've been getting banged up since I was three. These new scars will fit right in with the ones I already have.

Another nudge from Ivy, this time a bit harder. "Answer your phone. My mama is trying to sleep."

I take the phone out of my pocket and slide my thumb across the screen to answer Tommy's call. "Why do you keep calling me?"

"Because I wanna talk to you. Duh."

"Did you ever think that maybe I don't wanna talk to you?"

"Nope, 'cause I'm great."

Ivy's sharp glare forces me to relocate to avoid waking her mom up. Neither I nor Ivy has any real responsibilities other than school and track, but my auntie already had a long day of therapizing her patients. Now she's up late at the ER waiting to learn if her dad will make it through the night. She needs rest.

"Come hang out," Tommy says.

"I can't," I say.

"But I haven't seen you in forever. I had to hang out with the worst people while you were ignoring me."

"Who?"

"My friends."

I'm way too exhausted and irritated to have this conversation, but I'm in it now. I sit on the waiting room floor with my back against the wall and my eyes mostly closed. "I'm not in the mood for whatever this is, Tommy."

"It's a platonic booty call, obviously."

"Those don't exist. Look, I get that you've been missing me—"

"I never said that."

"It was implied. I'm at the hospital right now, and I don't know when I'll be leaving. I don't have time to hang out."

"What the hell? Why didn't anybody tell me?"

"Me and Ivy haven't told anyone yet. I'm not hurt or anything. Well, actually I am, but it's nothing major. Just needed some stitches."

"Since when are stitches no big deal?"

"Since half your body is covered in them because of all the dumb stuff you do with your friends."

"Yeah, but that's me and this is you. It's different. Why'd you need 'em, anyway?"

"I was trying to help my grandpa walk to the couch earlier, but he collapsed on the way. I needed stitches because I fell into the coffee table." I slide my knees up to my chest. "The doctors are saying he had a stroke, but we don't know much more than that. I'm thinking it was a bad one though, because we got here, like, four hours ago, and no one's given us updates."

"Fuck. How's everyone handling the news?"

I look over to where my auntie and cousin are sitting. Auntie Yolanda is curled up in her seat with her head on Ivy's lap. Ivy is awake and keeps wiping her eyes. I haven't acknowledged the fact she's crying because it'll only make her feel worse. "Exactly as well as you'd think."

"And you?"

With how chaotic tonight has been, I haven't stopped to reflect on how I feel, and I don't know if I want to. I've done my best to stop myself from thinking about all the horrible possibilities because I know once I open the floodgates, I'll never be able to close them. "I'm a mess. I don't really know how to react. Like should I cry? Or scream? Or stay quiet forever? My brain is confused 'cause it can't figure out what to do."

"I'm sure you'll hit all of the above eventually."

"That sounds exhausting." I smooth out the wrinkles in my sweatpants, making my hand buzz from the friction. "I should probably make it clear that I do wanna see you. I just don't have time right now."

"I get it."

"Am I allowed to say that I wish you were here? I feel like this whole thing would be easier to deal with if you were sitting next to me."

"Wait until I tell Jen you like me more than her. She's gonna be pissed."

"That's not what I said."

"It was implied," Tommy says.

Tommy has a knack for being irritating in the cutest way. Tonight is no different and despite that I'm going through something terrible, his teasing makes me smile just a little.

"Don't mock me. It's mean." Grandpa Joe's doctor, Dr. Hernandez, exits through a door marked with a sign that says it's for authorized personnel only. She scans the waiting room, then heads toward Ivy and Auntie Yolanda when she locks onto them. I jump up, but I only make it one step before the room spins. "Jesus."

"What happened?" Tommy asks.

"I got dizzy."

"You stood up too fast, huh? I told you to stop doing that."

"I know, but my grandpa's doctor finally has news for us. I mean, I'm assuming."

"See what's going on with Joe. We can talk later."

"Okay. Yeah." I don't know what else to say, so I end the call and rush over to Ivy and Auntie Yolanda, careful not to trip over the outstretched feet of the other patients and visitors sleeping in their seats. Both Ivy and her mom are more alert than they've been all night, but it's clear from their anxious expressions that the doctor hasn't given them any news yet. "How is he?"

"He's stable," says Dr. Hernandez. "Based on his prior medical history and what the three of you told us about the symptoms he's been experiencing, we believe he has had several TIAs over the last month that led to his stroke this evening."

"TIA?" Ivy frowns. "What is that?"

"TIAs are transient ischemic attacks. They're more commonly known as 'ministrokes,' although that name isn't entirely accurate. These attacks often have the same symptoms as a stroke, but they don't damage a person's brain cells the way a stroke does. Though a TIA doesn't have long-lasting effects, we still encourage our patients to seek immediate medical care following an attack, no matter how mild; often, the risk of having a stroke is much higher once they've experienced a TIA."

"I don't understand why he wouldn't tell us," I say. "We could've gotten him help."

"I don't think Joe understood what was happening to him," Dr. Hernandez says. "Confusion is one of the symptoms of a TIA as well as a stroke. He may have wanted to ask for help but couldn't find the proper words to describe what he needed. It's also possible that the changes in behavior you noticed were caused by his health issues."

All this time I assumed Grandpa Joe was being stubborn and petty when he'd ignore me. And maybe it was partly that, but maybe he'd been suffering in silence and I just didn't realize it.

"I do have a bit of good news," says the doctor while looking at me. "Because of your quick response, we were able to administer a medication that dissolved the blood clot forming in his brain before it caused irreversible damage. You very well may have saved his life."

Ivy's entire body stiffens next to me and without hesitating, I grab her hand. She relaxes a little, still appearing tense, until her mom kisses her temple.

"When can he go home?" Auntie Yolanda asks.

The doctor's expression grows grave. "With something like this—multiple TIAs over a short period of time and the stroke, along with his other health issues—I think it's best if you admit Joe to a rehabilitation center for the duration of his recovery."

"I thought you said Aaliyah helped," Ivy says.

"She did, but—"

"But?" Ivy interrupts. "But what?"

"But the truth is, Joe had a major stroke," the doctor continues. "He'll need speech and physical therapy if you want to ensure he has a full recovery. Or as close as he can possibly get given the situation."

"Hold up," I say. "He can't talk? Or move?"

"He's having some difficulty with both," the doctor says. "But I'm confident that with the proper care, he'll be back on his feet in no time. What he needs from you now is support; the first month is often the most difficult for patients who have recently had a stroke."

Grandpa Joe is going to be in the hospital for at least a month. Maybe longer depending on how long it takes for him to relearn basic things like speaking and walking. I had hoped to never hear anything like that. The words don't even sound real. "That's— how does something like this happen without us knowing?"

"Joe hasn't been to his primary care doctor in quite some time, which led to a blockage in an artery going undiscovered until it was too late. Then there are the risk factors, such as high cholesterol and high blood pressure—"

I want to kick myself for not forcing Grandpa Joe to take his medicine like it was prescribed. If I had done a better job of taking care of him, we could be at home right now, eating ice cream together and watching terrible movies on Netflix.

"—TIAs as I mentioned before, age, gender, a high consumption of tobacco or alcohol, even stress can contribute to a higher risk of a stroke," the doctor says. "It's difficult to determine what combination of risk factors led to Joe's stroke, but after looking through his chart, I can see some possible warning signs that he may not have noticed or taken seriously enough."

The doctor keeps talking, but the world slows around me when she mentions stress. All I've done is stress Grandpa Joe out with this whole Lena debacle. If anybody's to blame for his stroke, it's me. I did this to him.

7

Shouting in the hallway jolts me awake sometime in the late afternoon the next day. Grandpa Joe isn't in the room anymore. Because I'm an anxious, paranoid mess, I jump to the worst-case scenario and spend the next few minutes forcing myself to chill out. If something bad happened to my grandpa, Auntie Yolanda wouldn't have let me sleep through it. Logically, I know that's the case, but logic and the explanations my brain comes up with don't always line up.

I wrap a thick hospital blanket around my shoulders and tiptoe across the cold floor to see what's going on outside Grandpa Joe's room. There are two people standing near the door. Both are angry, but only one of them should be here. That one is Auntie Yolanda. The unwelcome visitor is Lena Campbell.

"Why'd you even bother telling me what happened if you were gonna yell at me the entire time?" Lena asks. "Like, I would've stayed home if I knew you'd pull this shit."

"I called you because you deserved to know what happened to our father." Auntie Yolanda lowers her voice after a passing nurse shushes them. "But I'm not going to act like I'm not angry at you for what you did to Aaliyah."

Lena's icy glare falters for a moment. I might've been convinced she felt bad about standing me up if she didn't go right back to looking unbothered. "Something came up."

"Oh, bull. What could've possibly been more important than seeing your daughter after all these years?" They share a weird look, and Auntie Yolanda nods like she understands. Of all things to understand, I feel like this situation shouldn't be one of them. "It was because of him, wasn't it?"

"He had an accident," Lena says. "What was I supposed to do? Tell him sorry, but I already have plans? Text me when the doctors fix you up and I'll meet you at home? He's my man."

If Quincy's injury was bad enough to get him admitted to the hospital, then I kind of get why Lena didn't show up for lunch. She should've told me that, though, so we could reschedule, and yeah, maybe I would've been disappointed, but I'd rather be disappointed than devastated because my own mother ghosted me.

"It was your responsibility to tell Aaliyah that instead of leaving her to wonder if she'd done something wrong," Auntie Yolanda says. "She thinks you hate her so much that you can't stand to be around her."

Lena frowns like she can't imagine why I would ever believe something that ridiculous. "I could never hate Aaliyah. She means the world to me."

"If she means that much to you then you should've gone to see her sometime," Auntie Yolanda says.

"Dad wouldn't—"

"You are her mother!" Auntie Yolanda slaps her palms together as the anger she's kept at bay for all this time boils to the surface. "You should've been at his house every damn day. Even if she was angry at you or she wasn't ready yet, she still would've known you cared because you were trying. This disappearing act you've been pulling is and always has been unacceptable."

Lena rolls her eyes. "I don't need you acting like my mama."

"I wouldn't need to act like your mother if you were acting like one yourself." Auntie Yolanda lets out a heavy breath like she knows she needs to stay calm or that nurse might try to kick her out of the hospital if she keeps on hollering like she has been. "If you truly want a relationship with Aaliyah, then you're going to need to work your ass off to make up for all the time you've missed. For the hurt you've caused. For everything."

"I know."

"She's right behind that door, catching up on some sleep, but I think she'd be okay if you were the person who woke her up." Auntie Yolanda gestures at the room, and I duck behind the door to avoid being seen by either of them. "Dad won't be back for another hour or so because they're running more tests. This is your chance to explain everything."

I poke my head around the door. Lena takes a few steps back, and that simple action hits me deep in the gut. She's moving away from the hospital room. She's moving away from me.

This hurts so much more than her not responding to my calls or texts or not showing up at all when she promised she would, because she's here, standing less than ten feet away, and she still doesn't want to see me. I wish I was enough for her. I wish I'd been born better. More lovable. Cuter. Funnier. Anything to make me less me. Maybe then Lena would love me.

"It's too late," Lena says.

"It's never too late," Auntie Yolanda says.

"Why are you pushing so hard for this?" Lena asks. "I thought you didn't want her around us at all."

"Dad is the one who wanted to keep you all apart, and since he's her primary caretaker, I respected his wishes, but that doesn't mean I agreed with him. Aaliyah wants to know you. And despite the positive, perky attitude she puts on, your absence is weighing on her. She needs you now more than ever." Auntie Yolanda lowers her voice even further, causing me to strain to hear her over the noise in the hallway. "Dad is probably the most important person in Aaliyah's life besides Ivy, and now he's in the hospital. Ivy still has me and her dad to help her through this. Aaliyah just has herself."

"A'ight. Damn." Lena presses her fingers to her temple. "I'mma come back later. I need to handle some business first."

"Lena . . ."

It's a warning, but Auntie Yolanda shouldn't have bothered with one because I'm not starting a relationship with Lena or Quincy after what happened to Grandpa Joe. I stressed him out so much that he had a stroke, and I hadn't even officially met them yet. Finding out I let Lena into my life could actually kill him. It isn't worth the risk.

I quietly close the door and quickly brush my teeth in the bathroom, then grab the bag of clothes Auntie Yolanda brought for me. All I need to do is leave before Auntie Yolanda and Lena try to corner me. In the hallway, Lena is the first to spot me. Her lips part like she wants to say something, but I avert my gaze. I don't have anything to say to her.

Auntie Yolanda spins at the sound of my gym shoes squeaking on the linoleum. "Hey, sweet pea. Are you feeling all right?"

"Not really. I'm probably gonna call Jen and have her pick me up if that's okay?"

"Of course it is. But maybe you should hold off on that. I think Lena has something she'd like to say to you. Lena?"

"Auntie . . ." I'm having trouble coming up with something to say without being completely disrespectful toward her. She's done so much for me, things that go far beyond auntie duties, and I'd never want to hurt her. But I'd rather stick my hand into a garbage disposal than listen to anything Lena has to say. "I know what you're trying to do, and I appreciate the effort you're putting in, but the only way I'm having that talk is if I'm forced. Are you ordering me to listen to her?"

"You know I wouldn't do that," Auntie Yolanda says.

I shrug as I walk backward down the unit. *Don't look at Lena. Don't look at Lena.* "Then I guess I'm done here."

Don't look at Lena. Don't look at Lena. Don't look at Lena.

Despite me repeating the words in my head like a mantra, I do exactly what I told myself not to do. Lena is so pretty up close that it's shocking. Her eyes are big and brown the way a Disney princess's would be, and her skin is an even brown complexion. I bet she's never had a blemish a day in her life.

Something deep inside me pulls me to her. I almost take back what I said, but I snap out of it when I remember where we are and why we're here. "I need to go. I can't be here right now."

I book it to the elevator and dart inside as the doors begin to close. Finally. No more Lena. Everything will go back to normal eventually, and this will be one of those things that we remember but never really talk about. That's something I'm okay with.

8

I exit through the hospital's revolving doors, checking behind me to see if either of them followed me down to the main waiting area. Nothing. I'm good for now. I don't know where I'll go or how I'll get there since Jen texted me on the elevator ride down here and said she was too busy to pick me up, but it's important that I'm as far from here as possible.

A tall man pinching a Backwood between his thumb and pointer finger materializes seemingly out of thin air, and I almost bump into him in my rush to leave the building. The near collision is clearly my fault. I should've been watching the front of me as much as the back of me. An apology is on the tip of my tongue, right up until I get a good look at him. He's my dad. Quincy Matthews.

Jesus Christ. I go eighteen years without seeing either of my parents and in the span of ten minutes, I run into both of them. The universe is messing with me. Has to be.

Quincy has the same unimpressed expression he had in the picture I saw of him on Lena's Facebook. Full lips turned down.

Eyes low. He's wearing what might be the same dumb hat he had on in that picture too. The only differences are the age lines on his forehead and the heavy bags under his eyes.

"Excuse me," I say when he doesn't move out of the way.

"You good." Quincy blows a cloud of smoke from the corner of his mouth. There's probably a law about not smoking in or around a public establishment, but I'm not going to be the one who tells him to stop. If it's a real problem, hospital security will tell him to cut it out. "Figured I might see you around here soon."

My irritation and lack of interest in having a conversation with him is overridden by my desperate need to have the last word. "That's how you decided to start this unwelcome conversation?"

"Fuck am I supposed to do? Give you a hug?"

A hug from Quincy would simultaneously be the best and worst thing to ever happen to me. I do want one though. Just to see what it's like. Just to see what I've been missing out on for all these years. "I'd rather you didn't."

"Yeah." He sticks his free hand in his coat pocket to keep it from freezing like the other one. "Joe doing all right?"

"How about you stop smoking weed and go see for yourself? I'm not a messenger girl."

"All Yolanda and Lena do is argue when they get around each other. Bet they up there arguing right now."

"They were."

"I'mma pass on that headache." Quincy offers me his blunt like it's normal. Like he didn't miss the past eighteen years of my life and we're close the way we might've been if I'd grown up with him. "You smoke?"

"I don't think you're supposed to encourage your estranged teenaged daughter to use drugs."

"It's legal. You eighteen."

"Pretty sure you have to be twenty-one to smoke."

"Pretty sure don't nobody follow that rule."

I ignore his mocking the same way he ignored my slight dig at him. Quincy's bandaged arm poking out of the sleeve of his coat catches my attention. That arm is the reason why Lena stood me up. I can't tell what's wrong with it by just looking, so I'm forced to ask. "What happened?"

Quincy looks at his arm like he has no idea what I'm talking about. He must be stupid high to not remember what must've been a horrific accident to cause Lena to forget about our plans. He slides up the sleeve and shows it off. The white bandage covers the entire limb, and it's wrapped around his arm like a cast. "Work accident. Ripped the skin and muscle off. You could see down to the bone."

"Gross, dude."

"I'm not no dude."

"Everybody's a dude to me, dude. But, uh, it kinda feels like we're done here, so I'm gonna go. Have a nice life."

"Where you going?"

His sudden interest in me catches me off guard. He hasn't bothered to show any emotion—positive or negative—about how he feels seeing me all grown up, but now that I'm about to walk away forever, he's putting in effort to come off as a caring father rather than what he really is—an uninvolved and dismissive one.

"I don't know," I say. "Haven't gotten that far in the plan yet."

"I could take you somewhere."

"You should probably wait for Lena."

"She's gonna be in there arguing with Yolanda for another two hours." Quincy puts out the butt of his blunt using the bottom of his lighter. He tucks the blunt behind his ear and sticks the lighter in the same pocket he gets his keys from. "Let me give you a ride."

I need to be resilient. No contact. No favors. Not even something as simple as a ride. But then Tommy texts me saying he's too busy to come get me because he's visiting his grandparents with Jen. Ivy still hasn't responded to my text, and a cold blast of air sends an icy chill through my entire body. It's like the universe is pushing me to accept this ride from Quincy because it has some plan for me I can't see yet.

Quincy walks off, and I follow him because what else am I going to do? Stand outside on one of the coldest days of the year so far? Hard pass.

The car ride is awkwardly quiet. He doesn't know what to say to me, and I have nothing else to say to him, so he cuts on his music to drown out the silence. I'm content with not talking at all, but halfway through the drive, he starts prying. Over the heavy bass of a King Von song, Quincy asks, "Where am I taking you? Yolanda's crib?"

"Mine," I say.

"Don't you need somebody in there with you?"

"I can invite a friend over."

"Like a real friend or a boyfriend?" Quincy checks his mirror before switching lanes. "You got one of those? A boyfriend."

I should have walked home. Sure, I might've lost a few toes and fingers in the process, but at least I wouldn't have to sit through this outrageous conversation.

"Girlfriend?" he asks.

"*Dude*. For real?"

"Man, I don't fucking know. You're the one who had your face all turned up. What was I supposed to think?"

"I turned up my face because you're asking about my love life like we're cool."

"I ain't say nothing about love. You're too young for that."

"Says the guy who had a baby at fifteen."

"I was sixteen and that's how I know you're not ready. I been through it."

I'm so not interested in having this conversation with Quincy. For starters, he's four years too late. Grandpa Joe had "The Talk" with me when I was a freshman because I told him I had a crush on this guy from school—Daniel. We ended up dating on and off for three years. But I don't tell Quincy any of that because it's none of his business.

Because I have some manners, I thank Quincy for giving me a ride once he pulls up in front of my house. Our interaction should end there, but he calls my name when I get to my porch and jogs over to meet me.

"Wanna do lunch or something?" he asks. "I promise I won't almost lose my arm again."

"I'm kind of busy with track and homework and stuff."

"Yeah, no doubt." Quincy swipes under his nose to mask his disappointment. "If you ever get unbusy, let me know."

"Sure."

I think Quincy knows I won't reach out no matter how "unbusy" I get. Yet, in spite of that, he gives me his number and tells me to call him if I ever need anything. I say I will to be polite, and that's the end of it. He's gone.

The house is a mess. Evidence of Grandpa Joe's stroke is everywhere I look. In the furniture I pushed to the corner of the living room in anticipation of the paramedics who helped save my grandpa's life, and in the coffee table that's completely shattered. Glass litters the floor. Blood stains everything. My chest tightens as tears flood my eyes. The room spins, slanting as I feel my way up the steps and stumble into my bed.

9

Time is weird. The speed at which it passes is entirely dependent on how terrible your life is at that particular moment. When things are good, the days pass so quickly that you can't even enjoy them, but when things are bad, you're forced to suffer in what feels like a never-ending day of suck. I'm in that suck right now.

"We've been looking for you, sweet pea."

The sudden appearance of my auntie in my bedroom would have normally spooked me, but I'm so numb that it doesn't faze me at all. I spent nearly three days sulking and neglecting my basic needs while researching strokes to make myself feel useful. It didn't work.

"Ivy said you haven't been in school for the past few days." Auntie Yolanda crouches next to me with a hand on my forehead. I can't really see any of her features through the built-up crust in my eyes, but I'm sure she looks concerned. "I didn't expect you to come here after what happened."

"I don't have anywhere else to go," I mumble, voice hoarse from lack of use. "And I'm not going back to school."

"You have to. It's important to keep up a routine to prevent yourself from sinking into a depression too deep for you to climb out of."

"Too late."

"Come on." Auntie Yolanda helps me to my feet and guides me toward the bathroom. She runs a bath and turns to leave, but she hesitates in the doorway. "I'm bringing you home with me. Clean yourself up and make sure you change those bandages. I'll let your school know you'll be missing another couple of days."

Auntie Yolanda is at the kitchen table when I head down after my shower. She has her head in her hands, and the sobs coming from her are so violent that she has trouble catching her breath.

I don't say anything to alert her to my presence. I wouldn't know what to say anyway. I'm not used to seeing her cry like this. Or at all. She's always been such a strong person, resilient no matter what the issue is. Back when Grandma Dee was diagnosed with cancer, Auntie Yolanda held it together and took on the bulk of responsibilities of care. She accompanied Grandma to her appointments and picked up all the medications she needed from the pharmacy. She was at our house every day, brought over meals for us to eat, and made sure Grandpa Joe and I had everything we needed while still working and taking care of her own family. She never complained once. I thought it'd be the same this time around, but today she looks broken. She looks like me.

The stitches in my side feel like they're being ripped out as I try to move fast enough to leave before my auntie notices. My attempt at a quiet exit is ruined because I run into the door by accident. "Sorry. I didn't mean to disturb you."

She quickly dries her tears and forces out a smile. "You could never do that. Come sit down."

I shuffle over to her and take a seat at the table with my eyes cast down. "I don't know if I'll be ready to go to school in a couple days."

"How much longer do you think you'll need?"

Coming up with an approximate time of when I'll be ready to interact with people again is tough. How much time off would be enough? A week? A month? "I don't know. I guess I can try Friday."

"Take the weekend instead and start fresh on Monday."

"I can do that?" I ask.

"Of course. Lord only knows how I would've reacted if this had happened when I was your age. I might not have ever gone back to school, especially not after . . ." Auntie Yolanda swipes the back of her hand over her nose. She keeps her eyes on the letters lying on the table. "I finally received Dad's test results, and his doctor gave a general timeframe for how long it could take for him to recover."

"It's not good, is it?"

"The odds of him fully recovering, even with the rehab, are slim. He'll need to use a wheelchair or a walker to get around, and he'll have to stay in the hospital for at least three months to be half as mobile as he was."

Three months? I was hoping for three days. Maybe three weeks if he was really unlucky, but months? That's the rest of the school year. He's going to miss more than my track meets. He'll miss State. Prom. Maybe even graduation. "When did you find out?"

"About fifteen minutes before you came down." Auntie Yolanda gathers the envelopes splayed out on the table. That's why she was crying. She'd just gotten terrible, overwhelming news and couldn't hold in her emotions any longer. "I understand this is a lot for you to take in, considering you're in your last semester of high school and you have a lot of things planned for the rest of the year. This really couldn't have happened at a worse time."

I'm not really sure what to say, so I don't say anything.

"Your uncle and I discussed it, and we both agreed that it would be best for you to stay with us until after graduation. We don't have a lot of room, so it'll be a tight fit, but we can make it work."

She doesn't mention money, but I know the cost of an extra mouth to feed will put a strain on their finances. Ivy and her parents aren't poor by any means. They don't have to scramble for cash every month, but they aren't rich either. They're getting by because there's three of them. I'm going to throw everything off, so instead of being happy that I won't have to live alone for months on end, I feel even worse because my mess is negatively impacting the people I care about the most.

"I have some birthday money saved—"

"No. Absolutely not." Auntie Yolanda rests her hands on top of mine and squeezes until I look her in the eye. "That money is for college. Save it. For books or for your dorm—whatever you decide. But make sure it's for school, okay?"

When I don't respond, she presses me a little harder. "Okay?"

"Yeah. Okay." But it's not okay. Not even a little bit. "I don't wanna be a burden. I think things are tough with the economy, probably. We might've just got out of a recession or maybe we're still in one. I don't know. I feel like I should be doing more to help."

Auntie Yolanda sighs like she's got the weight of the world on her shoulders. Maybe she does. Maybe we all do. "I don't want you worrying about our finances, Aaliyah. We'll be okay. Focus on school and track."

It's clear Auntie Yolanda is stressed and trying to pretend like she's not. I kind of feel terrible for not thinking about how I'm not the only one affected by what's going on with Grandpa Joe. I guess I should've been trying to make things easier for her instead of worrying about how uncomfortable I'd be. "I'll do it."

"Do what, sweet pea?" Auntie Yolanda asks.

"I'll go to school tomorrow. And stay there. Maybe not the whole day, but like half?"

Her brows lift in surprise. "Really? What changed your mind?"

"I figured it's good to do what I would normally do. Keep up a routine like you said, to keep from losing my grip on reality." I smile, but it's not really a happy one. "Plus, if I cut school again, Coach Barnes is gonna flip. Captains aren't supposed to skip practices, and I can only be absent a few days before it starts turning into a truant problem."

Auntie Yolanda smiles, too, but it seems forced. It's then I realize we're kind of in the same boat emotionally. Both of us are struggling to deal with Grandpa Joe's stroke. Both of us lived with him for years. Both of us were raised by him.

The only other person who could possibly get what we're going through is Lena. I shouldn't care about that, but things are different now that Grandpa Joe had a stroke. If she hadn't walked away from me at the hospital, I think it would have been nice to have a moment with her to talk about him and how she feels about him being in the hospital. I could've asked if she's worried about him or if she stopped doing that a long time ago. But again, she failed to do the bare minimum when it comes to me, so a talk like that is out of the question.

"Why did you tell Lena about Grandpa if they haven't talked in years?"

"It doesn't matter how long they go without talking. She'll always care about him, and I thought she deserved to have an opportunity to see him if she wanted to."

"Did she see him?"

"She did. She wanted to see you too."

"Well, I didn't wanna see her."

"Because you didn't want to or because you think Dad doesn't want you to?"

"It's best to forget about her to keep the peace."

"Don't let Dad dictate your life like this. You're eighteen now, and you need to start making your own choices based on what you want. Not on what he thinks is acceptable."

Deep down I know she's right, but the last time I used the "I'm eighteen now" excuse to learn more about Lena, it nearly ruined my relationship with my grandpa. I refuse to let anything get in the way of our making-up process, no matter how badly I may want to know the truth about what happened all those years ago. It's not worth the trouble it would cause.

10

I haven't spoken to Ivy about anything other than track since the night of Grandpa Joe's stroke. We usually never go more than a few hours without sending at least a text, but now that I'm officially living with her full-time, it's like we're on two different planets.

Maybe she's upset because I haven't gone to see Grandpa Joe since they moved him over to the rehab center. I feel bad that I haven't, but that's the thing about a depressive episode. It doesn't matter how bad you feel about not doing what others think you're supposed to do. You can't do it until you're ready. And as of now, I'm not ready.

Jen eclipses my view of the high jump mat and waves her hand in my face, dark brown eyes widening with concern. "Aaliyah. Hello! You're supposed to be warming up."

"Huh?" I ask. "For what?"

"For your next race. Duh."

We're in the small gym where all our indoor meets are held. It's kind of dusty, and the lighting casts a creepy yellow glow on everything, but it's nice if you ignore those things. I swallow thickly and make my way through the packed gym without waiting to see if Jen's behind me.

Tonight's the first meet of the indoor season, and the one person who should be here isn't. Grandpa Joe is supposed to be cheering me and Ivy on from the stands. Not cooped up in some rehab room by himself. His absence is weighing on me. I feel like a ghost wandering aimlessly throughout the gym, and I know I should be focused on my next race, but my mind keeps going back to Grandpa Joe.

Tommy grabs my hand as I pass him on the bleachers. I hadn't even noticed he was here. What the heck is wrong with me? "Hey. Are you all right? You look sick."

"I'm fine."

"Right. Well, I'm recording the meet on my phone for Joe. Just you and Ivy. I'm gonna send the videos tonight, so you can show him the next time you see him."

It's kind of unbelievably sweet that he recognized I'd miss Grandpa Joe being at my meet and as taking it upon himself to record the entire thing without me having to ask. "Thank you."

"I just wanna help." His entire demeanor shifts, but not the way it would when he's putting on his tough guy act. He shrinks into himself and frowns at something over my shoulder. "My ex is here. Was kinda hoping she didn't love her brother enough to come to this track meet. But hey, at least he runs for a different school. I shouldn't have to see her at one of these again."

"Does Jen know?"

"She's keeping her eye on me."

"I will too."

"Come over tonight?" Tommy can't meet my eye for longer than a second at a time. "I've, uh, kinda been missing you lately. It'd be nice to clock in some friendship hours or whatever."

I don't understand why he gets so awkward when he's being vulnerable. Jen once told me she loved me because I killed a spider for her. Even their parents are open with their emotions. It's weird that he isn't. "Kinda missing me?"

"Fuck off."

"You're the only person I know who can make profanity sound affectionate."

"I'm a skilled guy. So, you'll come over?"

"Sure."

Jen gives me a weird look, mixed with worry and curiosity when I make it over to the corner where the rest of our team-mates are hanging out. "You and Tommy kissed and made up, huh?"

"We were never in a fight."

"But you and Ivy are? I can tell something's off."

"And how could you possibly know that?"

"Because if things were cool between you two, she'd be the one over here checking on you."

It's true that Ivy has kept her distance from me since that first night at the hospital. But it doesn't necessarily mean she's mad at me. I'd say there's a 50 percent chance she is and a 50 percent chance she's in her head because she's worried about Grandpa Joe.

"I'm not trying to start anything, but if something is going on and you need a place to crash for a while, you can stay in our guest room," Jen says. "My mom and dad already set it up for a just-in-case scenario."

"Your parents are ridiculously nice." I bounce on the balls of my feet, hoping it'll shake me out of the funk I'm in. "I think I'll be okay though. Ivy is in a mood. She'll be her normal self soon."

"If you say so."

Before I can ask Jen why she said "if you say so" the way she did, Coach Barnes yells my name from across the gym. His wave is aggressive enough for me to clock that he's extremely stressed and that I shouldn't test his patience by taking my time getting to him.

On the way over, I pass by a pretty cool dude on the team I only kind of know named Kendall. He's right next to Ivy, who either doesn't notice me or is doing her best to ignore my presence. And when I stop a few feet behind her, she gets up and heads in the direction I came from to go sit with Jen. I look at Jen and she looks at me, and it's almost like she knows something I don't.

I'm thinking Coach Barnes will give me his usual quick tips about what I should do before my next race, but when I make it over to him, he tells me he wants to talk in private. Since the gym and the hallway are both filled with people, there isn't much privacy to be had, so he takes me to the quietest place he can find—the swimming pool bleachers. I really wish he'd picked a cooler place. It feels like it's August up here. Hot and humid. Terrible.

Coach Barnes takes a seat on the highest section of bleachers near the entrance. I remain standing to prevent myself from getting too tense after my warm-up. Keep moving. Gotta keep moving. "Where's your head at, Campbell?"

It's the last thing I expect him to ask, and I freeze. "Uh, it's here. At the meet."

Coach studies me for a moment. "Tell the truth."

Of course he clocks my lie immediately. I roll my shoulders back as the tension I'd tried to keep at bay comes back, but it's no use. Coach Barnes is right to question me. I'm off my game today, and it's obvious that Grandpa Joe not being here is a big reason why. "Life is weird right now. Everything's changing, and it's throwing me off."

"Enough to knock you off course?"

He means before State in May. I'm going for another state championship like last year and the year before. First place in the hundred-meter dash and 4x100-meter relay. If I keep up with practices and push it during my meets, I think I can do it again. "I'm focused."

"I hope so. I can only do so much to help you with your goals. You need to be here, physically and mentally. Not to mention that your team is counting on you to be a real leader."

"I'm a real leader," I say, offended that he's implying I'm not.

"Then prove it. Get your head out of the clouds and onto the track. I don't wanna have to ask Sullivan to reel you in again."

The 50 percent chance that Ivy is mad at me is now a 100 percent chance. If Coach asked her to talk to me and she told Jen to do it instead, it means she didn't want to be around me for some reason. Jen must know more than she let on. Why else would she have her parents set up the guest room before I knew I needed it myself?

"Think about the example you're setting for the under-classmen," Coach says. "If they see you and Zhu and Sullivan and the rest of the upperclassmen taking this sport seriously, they will too. If they see you winning, consistently at that, they'll want a taste of victory for themselves. It'll push them to work harder to match you all. Understand?"

"I do. Yeah." The energy that's usually coursing through my body comes back full force. I can't stop moving. "I'm gonna be focused. I promise."

Don't think about Ivy. Don't think about Ivy. Don't think about Ivy.

"Good. You've got two more events left. I expect you to win both. And if you don't, you better be right on Zhu's heels."

"Uh, hold up. Two? I only have one. The 4x-200-meter relay."

"I'm tossing you into the four-hundred-meter dash."

I groan. "Those are practically back-to-back."

Coach ignores my complaints. He always says he doesn't want to hear a peep unless we're hurt or are going to pass out. We all complain anyway. "And just so you know, the whole team is doing universals at some point. Distance, sprinters, fielders. Everybody."

I collapse against the tile wall, letting out a dramatic sob. Universals are literal torture. Definitely the worst workout next to the stairs. "I thought you liked us!

"I'm making you tougher. You'll miss me when you start running for a college team and realize how bad you've really got it." Coach Barnes stands and heads for the stairs leading out of the pool balcony. "I want you and Zhu at the front of the line during the workout. If either of you falls behind, I'm adding another lap."

That sounds unimaginably horrible. No. I can imagine it because it's happened before. Coach Barnes loves making us do universals. It must make him happy to see a bunch of teenagers cry.

"Don't think that because I want you at a hundred percent, I don't care about what you and Sullivan are going through. I'll tell you exactly what I told her. Take your time to fully deal with your family problems and don't hesitate to talk to me or the other coaches if you're feeling overwhelmed by it all. We're giving you both a lot of leniency, and there's no time limit on that. That being said, I don't want either of you to use this as an excuse to slack off."

"I understand."

"Got your time in the fifty-five-meter dash," Coach Barnes adds. "Good race tonight."

"Thanks, Coach."

"Could've been faster."

"Yep."

I should've seen that coming. Coach never gives a compliment without tacking on a complaint about how you can do better. He's the king of making you feel good and then crushing you moments later.

11

oach Barnes's words spark something inside me, and as I prepare for the next race, I zero in on the most important part of what he said. I want to win, and to do that, I need to focus. No more distractions. I join the rest of my relay team in the center of the gym, and each of them—Chloe, Jen, and Ivy—looks like they know something I don't.

Jen is the one who breaks the news to me. She's discreet and says into my ear, "Ivy wants to switch."

Chloe. Jen. Ivy. Me. That's the usual lineup, and it's what I'm most used to. There are times when we do switch, but there's always a reason. I don't get one this time, and the race starts before I have a chance to ask about it. Not that I would. It's not hard to guess that Ivy wants to switch because she's angry with me.

Chloe steps onto the track with the silver baton in her hand. She bends over, knees shaking as she puts her feet into the blocks. Nerves. They'll either help you or hurt you. With Chloe, they usually hurt. That's why she goes first. The rest of us are fast enough to make up for the lost time if she messes up her start, and we can capitalize off her lead if she doesn't.

The gun goes off, echoing over the screams in the crowd. Chloe messes up her start and Coach Barnes goes ballistic. "Go, Watts! Go!"

Before Ivy moves onto the track, Jen touches her hand. It's so quick that if you weren't looking, you'd miss it, but I caught it. That isn't the weird part though. It's Ivy's reaction. Her smile. The soft way she looks at Jen before going back to being visibly irritated.

As the girls round the final bend, Ivy points at Jen, shouting over the crowd. "Be ready!"

Chloe is in third place by the time she reaches Ivy, whose hand is outstretched. The second the baton connects with her hand, Ivy takes off the way Chloe should have. Fast and hard.

Coach Barnes's face is red as he runs around the sidelines, shouting encouraging words at Ivy as she pulls ahead to second place. Ivy's handoff to Jen is smooth like butter. Coach Barnes's face is still red, but it doesn't look like he's going to pop a vein any time soon.

As I watch Jen and the rest of the girls in her leg, a now-familiar guy in the crowd catches my eye. He's taller than most of the people around him, and unlike the others, he isn't shouting and jumping around. He's standing still. Standing still and looking right at me. Beard. Beanie. Same hooded eyes that pierced into me outside the hospital.

I hit the track with the rest of the anchors, wondering why Quincy of all people is here and how he even knew where to find me.

"Let's go, Aaliyah!" Chloe shouts.

I glance behind me, shaken out of my staring contest with Quincy. Jen is coming up right on the lead girl's heels, pumping her arms as fast as they'll go. Like me, Ivy, and Chloe, she's all legs, perfect for running track.

When Jen hits the acceleration zone, I take off with my hand behind me. The metal connects with my palm a few seconds later. Every girl in my leg falls behind one another in the first lane, but I'm looking to pass the person in front of me. She's quick. Long legs like mine with big strides, but she's got zero stamina. The moment she hits the second bend, she starts to slow down.

I blow past her, silently begging my body to keep this speed up for a little while longer. The finish line looms in front of me. There are people on both sides—teammates, the opposition, and friends and family—all cheering for the person they want to win. I block them out and run until there's nowhere left to go.

The girl I passed crosses the finish line not even a full second after me. She was a little too close for comfort. If I had messed up, we would've lost. That's unacceptable.

My teammates congratulate me, and the other girls on our win, but I'm back to being distracted now that the race is over. I lose Ivy in the crowd, and in my search for her, I notice Quincy leaving the gym. As much as I want to ask Ivy what's wrong, I want to know why Quincy is here a little bit more. I do another quick check around the small gym for Ivy, and when I don't find her, I grab my sweats and hoodie and follow Quincy out into the cold.

"Hey!" Putting on sweatpants while walking and still wearing shoes is made even harder by the moving cars I have to dodge as I cross the parking lot. "Quincy!"

He stops once he's at his car. We're far enough away from the school no one can tell it's us, and knowing Ivy won't see me with him makes this talk a lot easier. The last thing I need is for her to run to Grandpa Joe and tell him about this before I have a chance to explain things. He had a stroke because I tried linking with Lena. Finding out I had a conversation with Quincy might kill him. That thought gives me pause. What am I doing? I shouldn't have come out here. No good can come from this. I should go back inside and forget about Quincy. But as much as I know that's what I should do, I don't move. I have to know how he knew where to find me and what he's doing here. I think it's okay to be curious about that.

"Relax," Quincy says. "I wasn't gonna run away."

"How did you find out what school I go to?"

"Yolanda let it slip at the hospital."

"And you're here because . . . ?"

"Figured you'd need somebody supporting you since Joe's not around."

"That's weirdly considerate."

"I can't be considerate?"

"From what I know about you and the brief conversation we had, no. I don't think you can." I pull my hoodie over my head and stick my arms through the sleeves. It doesn't do much to protect me from the cold, but it's better than wearing short sleeves. "Even when you showed up at my house, you left without a fight."

He sticks his hands in his coat pocket and shrugs, gaze falling on everything in the lot except me. "What did you want me to do? Run into your crib and take you with me? Jump up and down like a little kid on their birthday?"

"No. Some enthusiasm would be nice though."

Quincy smacks his lips. "I want you around. Good?"

"Minimum effort. D+ at best."

"Don't be an asshole."

"Maybe that's all I know how to be."

"Then we got that in common. Here." Quincy digs around in his back pocket and hands me a card with my name on it in what essentially looks like chicken scratch. "That's from both of us. Me and Lena. Mostly her though. She's better at words than I am."

It looks like a birthday card, but my birthday was back in October. I guess I shouldn't be surprised they don't remember when my actual birthday is. They never bothered to send a card.

I open the pink envelope and pull out a cute little card with a golden flower on the front. On the inside is a short message from the card company that's the equivalent of them saying "Congratulations or whatever."

But it's the handwritten note that catches my attention. It fills up the entire left side of the card. The writing is loopy and neat, clearly written by someone other than the person who wrote my name on the envelope. Not to sound mean, but I'm pretty sure that was Quincy.

"Lena wanted you to know how she—we—really feel about you," Quincy says. "It's all in the card. Well, as much as she could fit."

Aaliyah baby,

I know you have a lot of questions for me, like why I never showed up for lunch and why I didn't say anything when I first saw you and why Quincy and I never came around. The truth is that he and I don't have reasons for why we've done things the way we have. At least not good ones.

I want to try to explain everything in person, but I'll understand if you don't want to hear from me. I kinda came off as a bitch and I guess I am sometimes. I don't want you to think that of me though.

It may seem like I don't care, and I understand why you might think something like that. But that's nowhere close to being true. I think about you every day you're gone from me. I love you. I have always loved you. I hope you can forgive me.

Love, Lena (Mama)

Tears prick my eyes, and I dab them away before Quincy notices. There's so much to unpack in this little note, I don't know where to begin. I don't really want to have a full conversation with Quincy about it, and even if I did, I don't have time, but there is one thing I desperately need to know. "Why didn't she come tonight?"

Quincy doesn't give a single thing away with his expression or body language. It doesn't seem like anything can faze him. Not even my questions or any mean thing I can think to say about him and Lena. "She's at work. They couldn't get a tech to replace her, so she stayed late."

"She's a tech? Like in a hospital?"

"Yeah."

I finally flip over the extra sheet in the card and pick up the folded cash. It's all one-hundred-dollar bills, and there's five total. I quickly tuck them back into place, looking around to make sure nobody saw. I'd hate to get robbed outside my own school. "There's money in here."

"I know. I'm the one who put it in the card."

I peek at the bills again. There's still five of them. They still total five hundred dollars. "I think you gave me too much money."

Quincy laughs for the first time. I kind of like his laugh. "I didn't."

I stare at the money-filled card in my hand. What the heck am I supposed to do with five hundred dollars? "I don't really know what this is for."

"You going off to college in August or some shit, right? It's for that. Buy some stuff for your dorm. Get one of those expensive-ass textbooks they sell." Quincy approaches me tentatively like he thinks I'll run if he comes at me too fast. "I get that you don't fuck with us. But if you need money for whatever, let me know. I got you."

"I can't take this from you."

"You don't have a choice 'cause I'm not taking it back."

"This is . . ." Words like *unacceptable* and *unwanted* pop into my head, quickly followed by an explosion of anger. "You can't pop back into my life with a ninety-nine-cent card and bribe money. That's not how this works. That's not what being a parent is about."

"Fuck. We're trying. That don't mean nothing?"

"Not when your attempts are whatever this is." I place the card and the money on the hood of his car. "I don't want it."

"Take the damn money and quit being so stubborn."

"No."

"You're a fuckin' brat, you know that?"

"Maybe if you were around, you could've raised me to be less of one."

Whatever snippy remark Quincy had ready never comes, and the way he drops his head makes me second-guess what I said. It isn't fair that I have to make him feel better when I'm the one who's hurt. But Grandpa Joe would tell me to respect my elders or whatever, and even though I don't know if Quincy and Lena are included in that, disrespecting them doesn't feel right. I take the card and the money and put them into the front pocket of my hoodie. "Your attempts at trying to smooth things over with me suck. Respectfully."

"I had already made a good attempt. You shut me down." Quincy rests his arms on the roof of his car. "I'mma text you sometime. Cool?"

"I guess."

"Get back inside before you get sick. I don't need Joe coming up with another reason to hate me."

I hesitate. "Are you really gonna text me?"

"Said I would."

He hops into his car and drives off. For the rest of the meet, I find myself going back and forth when it comes to Quincy—him not keeping his word lines up more with the image I have of him, but it would be nice to be wrong. That way I'd have at least one parent who actually cared about me and my feelings.

12

The next morning, I manage to sneak out of the apartment without Ivy knowing. I'm not avoiding her or anything, but I also don't want to talk about what her problem is with me yet. After our track meet last night, she left without speaking to me and ignored me once Tommy dropped me off back at her place. There's a fight incoming and I know it'll happen soon, but I'd rather push it off until it's either inevitable or she forgets she's mad and everything goes back to normal.

Grandpa Joe is sitting up in bed with the TV on when I enter his room. He watches as I drag a chair across the room to be closer to him, but he doesn't say anything.

"I'm sorry I disappeared again," I say. "I wanted to see you, but I couldn't really get out of bed. That's what I like to tell myself anyway. I think I also kind of figured staying gone would be better since you may not have wanted to see me. Because of this thing with my parents and because your doctor kept talking about all these risk factors. She said no one thing contributed to it. That argument we had couldn't have helped, but the real issue is that I wasn't there for you because of it."

"Don't. Blame. You."

He says it like he's fighting something internally that's preventing him from getting his words out. I give myself a mental reminder to only ask yes or no questions to make things easier.

"Are we okay?"

"Yes."

Hearing him say he doesn't blame me doesn't erase the guilt I feel for abandoning him the way I did and what happened to him as a result of that. But it's nice to know he isn't mad about it. "I have some cool footage of me and Ivy's track meet yesterday. Wanna see?"

"Yes."

"Full disclosure, because I know you'll wanna know why Jen is in the videos as much as us, Tommy's the one who recorded them."

"Tommy? Boooo."

For once I'm kind of happy Grandpa Joe doesn't like Tommy. Booing him might be rude, especially after he was so thoughtful, but it's the most Grandpa Joe thing he's done since the stroke. That boo makes me smile because it means he isn't completely gone. There's a part of him that's still him; it's just buried beneath the surface.

"Oh, hush," I say. "Just watch and be happy Tommy did this for you."

Grandpa Joe focuses on the phone in my hand like it's showing a gripping action scene from a movie instead of me, Ivy, and Jen running around in circles for twenty minutes. He's much quieter than he usually is when he watches us run, but he still grunts his approval and smiles with the left side of his face when Ivy breaks a school record in the fifty-five-meter hurdles. "Oh, wow."

"She broke it by point-two seconds," I say.

Grandpa Joe has me replay the videos because he wants to rewatch his favorite parts. But every clip contains a moment he loves, so we end up rewatching the videos about four or five more times, just not in the same order.

"Wow," he says again.

"Want me to bring in more stuff like this?"

"Yes."

"Just so you know, we're only watching them, like, twice max. I can't hold my arm up that long again." He can't complain about it, so he's kind of forced to agree to my rule. "I didn't think you'd be talking this much so soon. The speech therapist is helping a lot more than I thought they would."

"Working overtime."

It's sweet that he's working hard to not miss the back half of my and Ivy's senior year, but I don't want him overexerting himself and making things worse. I drop a hand onto his. "Don't rush it. We can work around the rehab so you're there for the important moments. And if you can't come, it's okay. Tommy can record everything for you."

Grandpa Joe doesn't *say* he's dissatisfied, but I can tell he is because of the stank eye he gives me. He's back to being my favorite grumpy old man. "Thought he had school."

"He's been coming around more."

"Go away."

"I'm obviously not gonna tell him you said that."

"You together?"

"If you mean romantically, then no. I think he wants to be something. Like more than friends. He keeps asking me to hang out, but I know how you feel about him, so I'm keeping as much distance between us as I can. It's just hard 'cause he's going through this thing with his ex, and I'm worried because he won't tell me what's going on. I feel like it's bad though. He's different now."

"Want to be with him?"

"Not if you don't want me to be."

"Want you to be happy."

It's hard to know what he's saying because he can't really say what he wants to. Is he telling me it's okay to be with Tommy? That I can finally do what I want without worrying about how he'll react? I'm not sure, but without full reassurance, I still don't want to risk it.

"You okay?" Grandpa Joe asks.

He must see something in me that's making him believe I'm not okay. I'm not, but I don't like that he's noticed. "I've been feeling kind of lonely. You're not around and obviously I don't have parents to pick up the slack. Now Ivy's not really talking to me, and she spends so much time with Jen I don't get too many moments with her anymore. I'm sad a lot and trying not to be."

"You need me."

I don't look at him when I lie. "I'll be okay."

"Don't believe you."

I figured that would be the case. It's pretty unchill of him to call me out though. As much as I want to tell him he's right—that I do, in fact, need him, and I'm drowning in guilt and loneliness; that the depression that's kept almost entirely at bay by his and Ivy's presence in my life is smothering me—I don't. Because improving his physical health is more important than my failing mental health. So I put on a smile and say, "Don't worry about me. Let's focus on you right now."

13

wo weeks have gone by since the start of the indoor season. About two seconds after he left the school parking lot, I gave up on Quincy keeping his word to contact me. Then, on a random Saturday afternoon, and to my utter disbelief, I wake up from my daily evening nap to a text from him. He's as blunt as he was when I first met him.

Unknown: It's Quincy. Let's grab dinner sometime.

I toss my phone back into the mess of covers and finish the homework I neglected to do the night before, but my mind keeps drifting back to Quincy's text. Despite every part of me screaming to toss my phone in the closet, I pick it up and take it into Jen's kitchen with me.

The last time I agreed to meet up with a parent, it ended with me in Ivy's lap, sobbing and genuinely believing I wasn't loved. Something tells me she won't be as empathetic if this blows up in my face a second time. But I'm curious about Quincy and why he's acting so unlike the man Grandpa Joe told me about. Maybe he's different now that he's older. That happens. People change all the time. Is it really fair to keep holding on to the person they used to be instead of finding out who they are now?

Jen taps me on the shoulder. Judging by her worried expression, she'd already tapped me few times before. "What's got you all frowny faced?"

"Nothing."

"Y'all need more toilet paper in your bathroom," Ivy says.

"I'll do it later," Jen says. "You sure you're okay, Aaliyah?"

There's no way I'm going to bring Quincy up while Ivy is here, but I don't want to be rude to Jen since she was cool enough to let me stay at her place after our track invitational earlier today. I slide my phone over to Jen, who lifts a brow in response. I press my lips together. For us, that is an entire conversation.

"So, y'all just gon' act like I don't exist?" Ivy asks.

"Isn't that what you've been doing to me for, like, three weeks?" I shoot back.

Jen rushes over to Ivy's side of the island and puts her hands on her shoulders to keep her from coming at me. "Okay. Let's all chill out and agree to stop ignoring each other. Our relay team is suffering because of all the drama."

Ivy's dark eyes are steady on me with a glare cold enough to cut glass. "I saw that piece of shit at our meet. You already let Lena fuck everything up. Now you wanna give Quincy a chance to do the same thing?"

"He hasn't done anything wrong."

"Right. Other than ignore your existence for the last eighteen years. I'm so sick of this bullshit with you and them. There's a reason why Grandpa Joe doesn't want them around you. It's because they can't be trusted to do their fucking job and parent you right. But that's not getting through your thick-ass skull because you're delusional when it comes to them. They don't care about you. When are you gonna accept that?"

"Why should I have to? Why can't Grandpa Joe be wrong and I be right?" I hold up my phone with Quincy's text displayed on the screen. "I've got proof right here that Quincy wants to see me. He texted me. Not the other way around. He came to see me. He wants to spend time with me, and I didn't have to beg or force him to do it. That's gotta mean something."

"It doesn't mean shit. He's gonna drop you once something better comes along."

"Just because you feel that way doesn't mean it's true."

Ivy smacks her lips and rolls her eyes. "Oh, my God? I can't believe you're gonna let another one of your bum-ass parents torpedo our lives with their existence."

"I haven't decided—"

"Don't lie. The minute I turn my back, you're gonna convince yourself there's no harm in linking with him. That nothing bad will happen. But you know what? Something bad has already happened. Grandpa Joe is laid up in the hospital right now. He can barely talk. Can't walk. Can't lift his arm and pick up a glass. He can't do anything he used to, and it's your fault."

"I didn't mean to—"

"*Grandpa almost died,*" Ivy snaps, stepping to me with a rage in her eyes that I haven't seen directed at me before. She jabs her finger at my chest and her nail leaves a stinging mark in my skin. "I don't give a damn what you didn't mean to do. You still did it. We almost lost him because of you. Because you wouldn't fucking listen when we told you to drop this thing with Lena."

"Ivy, come on," Jen says.

"Stay out of it, Jen," Ivy says.

"I'm sorry," I say. "I wasn't trying to hurt him. I just—"

"Keep your sorry. It's not good enough."

Her words hurt like a knife to the chest. I can't bear to look her in the eye, so I keep my tear-filled gaze trained on her feet. She just voiced the same thoughts I had after I found out Grandpa Joe had had a stroke.

Ivy is right. I nearly killed my grandpa.

There's no way she'll ever forgive me for that.

PART THREE
MARCH

1

I manage to convince Auntie Yolanda to let me stay with Jen the week before spring break to give me time to think about what I want to do about Quincy. As hard as I try to ignore his text and stand strong with Ivy and Grandpa Joe, part of me just wants to say eff it and join him for dinner. I want to know if what Grandpa Joe said about him is true. This would be the perfect way to figure that out.

Tommy makes an effort to spend as much time with me as possible. We're in the guest room right now, studying for my history quiz and his poli-sci test, but honestly, I wish I'd told him I was busy because I so don't want to do this. I toss my notebook onto the bed with a huff. "Tommy, this is boring."

"We've gotta at least pretend. My mom is gonna kick me out if I'm just chilling in here with you for no reason." Tommy doesn't take his eyes off his book. He's acting like such a nerd tonight. "And you said you wanted to study. That's why we're doing this."

"Yeah, but now that I'm doing it, I'm realizing I don't actually wanna do this. I've been studying all week. I'm too exhausted. I just wanna lay in bed and do nothing all day."

He glances at me from his chair, smiling the way he's taken to doing these days. It's soft and makes me feel like I'm not annoying him, despite being a big baby. "Fine. Tell me about your fight with Ivy."

I hide my face in a pillow. "I take it back. I wanna study."

"Jen said it was a bad one. She's worried the drama between you two will fuck with your relay, and you'll end up losing at State because of it."

"That's a very valid fear. It's something I'm also worried about. But Ivy is pissed at me for hurting our grandpa, and talking about it won't help because you can't talk your way through almost killing a family member. That's, like, a very serious, unforgivable thing, Tommy."

"Blaming you for that is kinda harsh though. From what Jen told me, she said some pretty fucked up shit to you. Ivy's not always right."

"She pretty much is."

"Not this time."

"Tommy."

"Yeah?"

"I don't wanna talk about this anymore." In the quiet, I hear the soft buzz of his phone. It's been going off all night, and by now, I know who's on the other line. I slide the pillow off my face and stare at Tommy as he ignores the call from his ex. "I think it might be time to get a new number."

"I can't. I'd have to tell my mom why I wanna change it, and it's gonna turn into a whole thing. I don't wanna deal with that. It sounds exhausting."

"Right. But, like, it kind of needs to be turned into a whole thing because it's starting to turn into something a little more concerning. Not to alarm you or anything, but you're being harassed. I'm pretty sure that's illegal. Tell your dad and he can work his lawyer magic to make sure she never bothers you again."

"I'm not being harassed. I'm being stalked."

"I'm, like, eighty percent sure stalking is a form of harassment."

"No way."

"Way, dude."

"Would it be horrible if I start dating her again just to get her off my back? I mean, she's twice as mean when we're together and I was miserable every second I was with her, but at least she wasn't a stalker. That feels significant."

The *no* is on the tip of my tongue before I even fully register what he's saying to me. Under no circumstances should he ever rekindle his relationship with his ex. But if I say that, with our history, it'll make it seem like I want him to myself. That's not what this is. I just want him to be safe and happy, and being with Sabrina won't give him that. "I think you'll regret jumping back into a relationship with her. If you do, you'd be playing into her hands, and I feel like if you go back to her, she'll never let you go. Is that what you want? To be with her forever?"

"No, but I don't wanna be stalked forever either."

"Then tell someone who isn't me or Jen about it." I toss the pillow I had clutched in my arms and swing my legs over the edge of the bed. Tommy slides back in his chair, but when I reach out to take his hand in mine, he flinches so hard he nearly falls out of his seat. I keep my hands to myself after that and rest them on the bed. "What was that about?"

"I thought you were gonna hit me," Tommy says quietly.

"Why did you think that?"

"Because you came at me too quick. It freaked me out."

I've never put my hands on him in an attempt to hurt him because I'm not that kind of person. But clearly someone has messed with him, and I'm pretty positive it was Sabrina. "Did someone do something to you?"

"I don't wanna talk about it."

"Now or ever?"

"Now."

I don't press him, and he doesn't offer up any more information, but the pieces are starting to come together the more he tells me about Sabrina. I'm nowhere near equipped to deal with whatever's going on between them, and I don't want to ignore his wishes by going over his head to his parents, so I decide to talk to the next best person—Jen.

2

Jen is in the kitchen fixing herself a meal when I come downstairs the next day. She acknowledges me with a nod, then goes back to making her sandwich. Something must be wrong. She's never this quiet around me. Did I do something to her? Maybe it was Tommy. They tell each other everything. She probably knows about the talk we had last night.

"When are we gonna talk about what happened between you and Ivy?" Jen asks.

My appetite goes flying out the window and crashes onto the street in a million pieces. I set down the banana I was about to eat and take a seat at her island. "Never. I was hoping we could talk about Tommy instead."

"Fine. Tommy first, then Ivy. Did he tell you?"

"About Sabrina stalking him? Yes. I mean, kind of. He won't go into specifics. Look, I don't wanna jump to conclusions, and it's probably none of my business, but I think she hurt him and he's refusing to talk to an adult. I felt like I should come to you because you two are close and it'd be easier for you to convince him to do it."

"I've been trying to convince him to tell our parents for months and he won't listen. I'd tell them myself, but if they confront him, he'll know I snitched, and he might not come to me for help anymore. Right now, I'm the only person he trusts enough to be honest with because he's embarrassed and thinks everyone else will make fun of him."

"Even me?"

"Especially you. He cares about your opinion the most." Jen slices her veggie sandwich right down the middle and slides half of it to me. "I'm glad you sort of know what's going on. It's been hard dealing with this alone."

"How long have you known?"

"Four months. I'm pretty sure it's been going on for longer. That's just when he decided to tell me."

It's not easy hearing about how long Tommy has been hurt by Sabrina and especially that he thinks it's better I don't know about it. But that's not what this is about. Tommy's trauma and pain isn't about me and how I feel. I need to remember that. "I wanna help. What can I do?"

"Help me beat up Sabrina. He finally gave me permission after she basically kidnapped him at our first track meet, and I've been looking for an opportunity ever since."

I'm not much of a fighter, and not because I can't fight— Grandpa Joe taught me how to hold my own, so it's definitely a skill I have—but he also told me not to jump straight to beating up on another person just because I can. He wanted me to protect myself without becoming a bully. But what do I do when someone is hurting one of my friends? I don't remember him giving that lesson. "How bad is it?"

"Bad. He won't admit it, but he's afraid of her."

"And you're sure fighting her won't make things worse? Because it seems like it might."

"Sabrina talks tough, but she's a punk at the end of the day. The only reason why she's treating him like this is because she knows he's too nice to hit her back. But if we hit her, it'll make her think twice about messing with him again. It's foolproof."

It's the first time someone has admitted what's true—Sabrina is hitting Tommy. Jen doesn't seem to notice her slipup, and I don't bring attention to it because I don't want to mess with the trust she's built with him. He needs her more than he needs me. "So, what's the plan?"

"Tommy's throwing a party here next week, and she'll show up like she did the last time because she's a literal stalker. We can jump her then." Jen takes a big bite of her sandwich. "Speaking of jumping . . . Ivy will be there, and you can jump into a conversation with her and squash this shit between you two."

"Terrible segue. One of your worst."

"Come on, don't you think this has gone on long enough? It's time to move past."

"Can we not talk about it? I don't wanna be reminded of our fight. It completely sucked for me."

"I think you know avoiding it's not really an option. And squashing this thing with Ivy will make you feel better."

I take a few bites of the sandwich Jen gave me. "This is good."

"Aaliyah."

"What do you want me to do?"

"A mutual apology would smooth things over real nice."

"Me, apologize? She's the one who was a jerk. I already feel bad enough about what happened to our grandpa. I didn't need her chipping in and making me feel worse. And it's not like I meant for any of this to happen, you know? I didn't go into this situation thinking, 'Oh man, I hope something awful happens to my grandpa as a result of my actions.' It was an accident. I didn't—I mean, I knew something was wrong, but how was I supposed to know he would get this bad? He'd never had a stroke before. That wasn't even in the realm of possibilities in my mind. I just thought he'd be mad, and he'd get over it. But he let it fester and—"

I drop the sandwich and rest my chin on my hands. "It's tearing me up, Jen. It's eating me from the inside out, and I feel so bad all the time because I know it's my fault, and I don't know what to do about it. And now Ivy's even more pissed at me for something I haven't even done yet."

"I don't think it's fair of you or Ivy to blame yourself for what happened. It's like you said, you didn't mean for him to have a stroke."

"Just because I didn't mean for it to happen doesn't mean it's not my fault. And now Ivy is double mad because she thinks I'm gonna link with Quincy. I don't know what to do, Jen."

"I guess the first thing to decide is if you're gonna prove Ivy right and link with Quincy."

"No. It'd cause too much chaos."

"If you're worried about the fallout, nobody has to know."

I'm suspicious of Jen's motives. She's had no interest in either of my parents, like ever, and now what? Suddenly she's in love with the idea of me linking with Quincy? Please. "Why are you pushing so hard for this? It's just gonna cause more problems with Ivy."

"Because resolving this thing with your dad will clear your head, and we need you to be locked in if we stand a chance in our relay this season. Ivy being mad is manageable. She won't let her mood affect her run times. But you're different."

"It kinda sounds like you're calling me soft."

"I'm saying I know you."

It still kinda sounds like she's calling me soft, but I understand what she means. Ivy can push past her emotions to do what she needs to do on the track, but I can't. It's something everyone knows about me, and it's why Coach Barnes checked in to see how I was doing after Grandpa Joe's stroke. I let my feelings cloud my mind, and I'm not always strong enough to shake those bad thoughts away. Jen is doing her best to make sure I don't fall into one of my bad habits.

"But Ivy—"

"Doesn't have to know about this right now," Jen continues. "Hearing what he has to say will ease your mind, and if you don't like how it goes with him, you can delete his texts and pretend like it never happened."

"He won't show up, Jen. Something more important is gonna happen, and he'll ghost me the same way Lena did. I can't survive being stood up by both my parents in the same year. I'll have a mental breakdown for real."

"Let's make sure that doesn't happen then." Jen picks up my phone and scrolls through my messages until she finds the thread with Quincy. When she's done tapping out some words, she sets it back down in front of me. "I told him how you felt. See what he says and decide based off that."

My phone vibrates across the countertop. An unknown number with a 7-7-3 area code flashes across the screen, and I assume it must be Quincy since his is the one number not saved in my contact list. I don't answer the call until Jen gives me an encouraging nod. "Hello?"

"I'll show up," Quincy says. "You've got my word."

"Your word doesn't mean much," I say. "I don't know you."

"That's why you gotta come. Can't get to know me if you don't spend some time with me. Right?"

"Sure."

"Let's do it today. I can be at the diner in a couple minutes."

I don't let myself feel anything other than a growing sense of unease. But the temptation is too strong for me to outright refuse, especially with Jen actively pushing for me to meet with him. "It's gonna take me a while to get there. My car is being weird."

"I'm on medical leave from work. I ain't got nowhere to be."

"Okay. I guess I'll see you soon then."

Jen is already on the move after I end the call. She grabs her keys, winter coat, and a pair of boots. "Go get dressed. I'll warm the car up."

I feel bad about making Jen wait for me, so I quickly put together an outfit and head out the door. We arrive at the diner in no time to my immense displeasure, but I don't get out of the car yet. I'm still not sure Quincy will actually be here. It would be so much easier if I could pick out his car in the crowded lot. All I can remember about it is that it was either blue or black and had nice rims. That describes half the cars around me right now.

"I can't see his car," I say.

"I'm sure it's here somewhere." No offense to Jen, but I really wish Ivy were here. She wouldn't be nice about it, but she'd force me to confront my fears, even if she disagreed with what I was doing. "Quit stalling and go inside the restaurant. You've been sitting in my car for, like, twenty minutes."

"What if he's not in there?" I ask.

"Then I'll come in and we can eat together."

The walk to the front door of the diner is much slower than it needs to be. I lie to myself and blame it on the ice coating every inch of the concrete, but ice has never slowed me down before. This is all me and the dread building inside of me that I'll have to suffer through a repeat of the Lena debacle. And to top it all off, the same waitress is here and unfortunately, she remembers me. This is terrible. I want to jump off a cliff.

"Back for round two, honey?" the waitress asks.

"I'm meeting a different person this time," I say. "He said he was already here."

"What does he look like? I can point him out to you."

"Um, he's tall. Dark skin. Probably wearing a dumb hat. He's got a bandage wrapped around his arm. Oh, he's rude too."

That last thing isn't a physical description, but it's accurate, and I felt like it was necessary to add.

"Oh." I mentally prepare myself to be disappointed. But the waitress points to the back of the diner and says, "Quincy said you'd be showing up. He's right there in the corner."

3

I almost turn on my heel and head back to Jen's car, prepared to tell a blatant lie about Quincy not being there. She wouldn't question it, and I could continue to move on with my life without further upsetting the people I love. Grandpa Joe could heal in peace without worrying about who I'm spending my time with, and I wouldn't have to lie to him.

Quincy isn't facing me. Hasn't even seen me yet. I could do to him what Lena did to me, but then I remember the pain I experienced when she didn't show. I remember how broken I was and how I cried for hours and hours until my eyes were puffy, and my voice was hoarse. I wouldn't wish that kind of pain on my worst enemy, so I take a deep breath and approach him. "Hi."

That's all I say. No rambling. No tripping over my words. Just a quick and simple greeting. Thank God I practiced this with Jen on the drive over. I would've been a mess if I hadn't.

"Hey," Quincy says. "Got you water 'cause I wasn't sure what you wanted to drink, but you took a minute to get here, so I drank it."

There is one empty cup on the table. Another contains a dark, fizzy drink. If he's anything like my family, then it's Pepsi, which is considered superior to Coke. "I'll just have water."

"That's all? No juice? Pop?"

"Not during the track season. I stick with Powerade and water mostly. Stuff with electrolytes."

"Well, I've got an extra side of biscuits and gravy right here." Quincy nudges the plate toward me. "Go crazy."

"I don't eat meat."

"Why not?"

I scan the restaurant from our booth. I'm afraid someone my grandpa knows will pop up on me and it's making my stomach hurt. "My grandpa had some health problems before the stroke, so his doctor told him to eat healthier, but he'd complain whenever he saw me eating meat. I stopped eating it eventually."

"That was nice of you."

"Not really. I only did it because I wanted him to shut up."

Quincy laughs. "You gonna stick with it after you graduate or nah?"

"Maybe. It depends on how good the food is in LA."

"What's over there?"

"UCLA, my dream school. I applied early because I want to run for their track team and made a verbal commitment to run for them in the fall."

That was the plan before, but now things are different. More complicated. I wouldn't be comfortable leaving Grandpa Joe while he's still recovering. He's going to need me when he's finally allowed back home. I just don't know how I'll be able to help him if I'm not even in the same state.

"LA's pretty far. You didn't apply to no schools in Illinois?"

"Yeah, I have a few backups. University of Illinois. Loyola. University of Chicago."

"I like those better."

"Are you saying that objectively or because you don't want me to go to California?"

"The second one. What's your major gonna be?"

I'm kind of tripped up by how readily he admitted that he didn't want me to leave the state for college. He isn't a factor in my decision, but if he keeps popping up like he has been, he might have to be. "I don't know. My high school made me do some dumb project about what I wanna do for a career, so I chose engineering and threw a bunch of crap together. I'm hoping I'll get to school and, like, stumble into something great that I love though."

"You don't wanna go into engineering?"

"I don't even know what engineering is."

"You're the one who picked it."

"Yeah, but I didn't retain any information. I zoned out and paraphrased the Wikipedia page."

Quincy laughs again. I can't help but look at the door when it swings open and breathe a sigh of relief as a couple of strangers walk in. He checks over his shoulder and is frowning when his gaze returns to me. "You all right?"

"Not really. Being here with you is kind of freaking me out."

"How come?"

"Um, well, the last time I tried meeting with a parent, it caused my grandpa to have a stroke that nearly killed him and ruined my relationship with my cousin, so I'm a little concerned about somebody seeing us." I try to shake out the tremors in my hands, but it's no use. I can't even pick up the glass of water the waitress dropped off for me without spilling the liquid all over the table. "Sorry. I'm trying to be chill about this whole thing, but I don't really know how. I'm a very unchill person."

"Should've told me that. We could've met somewhere private."

"I didn't think it'd be this bad."

"If it makes you feel better, I come here all the time and nobody that's cool with Joe knows about this place."

"How could you possibly know that?"

"Joe's had the same friends since I've known him. He don't like to branch out and neither do they. If they'd come here, I would've seen 'em. You don't gotta worry about nothing while you're here."

Quincy's admittance relaxes me ever so slightly. My shoulders drop and I stop focusing on the people in the restaurant and focus solely on him. I realize this whole time he's been learning all this stuff about me, and I still don't know anything about him. That's the whole reason I'm here. "Will you tell me something about you?"

"I'm a goon. You don't need to know about me."

"That's funny, 'cause I heard you were scary."

"Who the hell told you that?"

"My grandpa. He doesn't talk about you much, but when he does, he makes sure to make you look bad. He said you abandoned Lena when she got pregnant because you couldn't handle the responsibility."

A dangerous glint flashes in Quincy's eyes when I mention my grandpa. "That's a fucking lie. I hid from him 'cause he said he was gonna kill me, and I liked being alive at the time. But I was there every time Lena needed me. I went to all the doctor visits. Made sure she had whatever vitamins and shit they told her to take. I didn't dip out on her like he said I did."

That doesn't make a lick of sense. All my life Grandpa Joe made it clear that the reason why Lena had such a hard time taking care of me was because she didn't have help from Quincy. That Quincy left because things got too hard and he couldn't hack it. It's like Quincy knew I wouldn't believe him, because he pulls out his phone and shows me picture after picture of him and Lena together while she was pregnant. There are even pictures of me with them after I was born.

They look so young. Way too young to be taking care of a baby, and yet there they are, holding me and kissing me and loving me. I finally look away because I can't take any more of this. Grandpa Joe lied to me. The proof is right there on Quincy's phone.

I shut my eyes tight and breathe. It'd be so embarrassing to finally meet one of my parents and mess it up by spiraling out of control. There has to be a good reason for why Grandpa Joe lied to me. I can't believe he'd want to hurt me, but I am hurt. All this time I thought Quincy wanted me even less than Lena did, and to find out this? It makes me wonder what other lies my grandpa told me.

"He said you were a deadbeat," I say quietly. "He told me you were no good."

"Joe hated me from the moment Lena brought me home to meet him. He didn't think I was good enough for her. I was a bum, in his mind, with no purpose in life. Didn't have no goals. No aspirations."

Quincy lists all the reasons why Grandpa Joe hates Tommy. But it makes me hopeful that instead of losing Tommy forever, I can turn him into someone my grandpa loves. I just need to convince him that Tommy is good enough for me.

"I didn't wanna let you go," Quincy says.

"Then why did you?" I ask.

"The prebirth stuff was easy, but when you got here, things wasn't simple anymore. It got hard, and we didn't know what to do."

"Was I too much? Like did I need too much attention, or did I cry a lot?"

"You didn't do nothing wrong. We're the ones who fucked it all up." Quincy rubs the back of his neck and keeps his eyes on the table. I think he might be too scared to look at me. I know I would be if I were in his shoes. "I wish I could go back, you know? I think I could get it right if I had the chance. But sometimes I feel like it's good that Joe and Dee did what they did, 'cause I was nowhere near ready for a baby. If I keep it a buck, I'm still not."

I have so many questions for Quincy, and I have no clue where to begin. He's being more open than I thought he'd be, but his story is still too vague. I need more. "How come you never came to see me? You never wrote. I never got a birthday card or a call or even a text asking how I was. You disappeared and now you're here and that's great, but where were you then?"

"I tried. Came around a lot those first few years you were gone, but the more I showed up, the more pissed Joe got. He told me you didn't need me 'cause you had him, and he was gonna treat you better than I ever could. It took a while, but I finally realized he was right. Figured with him in your ear, you wouldn't wanna see me, so I stayed away like he asked."

"I mean, you're not wrong. I always thought you left Lena 'cause that's what my grandpa told me, and I didn't wanna see you because of that. Even after you showed up at my house and at my track meet, I still wasn't sure about you. But being with you now, hearing your part of the story, it makes me glad that I came today. This was nice."

"We could do it again if you want."

All I've ever heard about Quincy was that he was no good. Unreliable. Immature. Not worth my time. But I'm sitting here with him now after having a real conversation, and he doesn't seem so bad. Maybe the version of him that my grandpa knew doesn't exist anymore. "Will you tell me more about when I was with you and what happened after? I only know what my grandpa told me, and it isn't much."

Quincy's smile falls immediately. He doesn't seem mad though. He looks more embarrassed than anything. "You gotta swear you won't be pissed at me if I tell you the truth. Can you do that?"

"No."

4

Refusing to promise I won't be upset with Quincy if he tells me the truth is a risky move. He could decide that me hating him forever isn't worth the risk. For the rest of lunch, he kind of skirts around my prying questions, and I sort of understand. He already lost me once. He might not be eager to go through that again. Besides, no one wants to tell a story that's going to make them look bad.

I could join ranks with Grandpa Joe and Ivy and pretend he and Lena don't exist, but a completely different possibility pops into my head later, while I'm overthinking in Jen's guest room: What if Lena and Quincy, somehow, aren't the bad guys in this situation? What if it's Grandpa Joe? What if that's why he's told me to stay away from them for all these years and why he lied about Quincy abandoning Lena? Because he knew if I found out the truth, it could change everything between us.

No. No freaking way. Grandpa Joe would never hurt me like that. It's not who he is. Grandpa Joe can't be the bad guy. He must've lied to protect me for some unknown reason. Maybe Quincy did something unforgivable back then and that's why he's so nervous to talk about the past?

Before I can even think about whether or not I want to see Quincy again, I need to come clean with Grandpa Joe and find out why he lied to me. I learned my lesson from last time and don't want to keep secrets from him. Especially not about this.

Today Grandpa Joe is in the recliner next to the window. He's got the TV on, and if we weren't where we are, it would almost be like things were normal and we were at home. I pull up a chair next to him, and this time he watches me. Half his face is still drooping, but the other half has what looks like an almost smile.

"Hi," I say. "How are you feeling today?"

"Good," he says.

Despite knowing I have to, I'm hesitant to bring up Quincy because it's sure to piss him off, and I don't want to ruin any progress he's made so far. I want him home, so things can go back to normal.

"Something's wrong," he says.

"I wanna talk to you about something, but I don't want you to stress yourself out like before. The last thing you need is to have another stroke when you're just now getting over the last one. But it's important, and I won't feel good if I leave without bringing it up."

"Tell me."

I take his hand in mine, noticing how he's not able to put any pressure into the handhold. I hate that I did this to him. It literally breaks my heart that he's going through this and I'm the reason for it. Even though I know he wouldn't want me to blame myself, the fact that Ivy blames me lets me know that it *is* my fault. "It's about Quincy."

The side of my grandpa's face that can still twitch does. His good eye narrows and his chest starts moving up and down at a faster pace, his breath coming out heavy and labored.

"Grandpa, please relax. He didn't hurt me or anything, but I spent some time with him just talking about the past and he told me something. He said he didn't leave Lena like you told me he did. He said he stuck with her throughout the entire pregnancy and took her to all of her appointments and made sure she had her medicine. Is that true?"

It takes Grandpa Joe a moment before he says, "Yes."

The yes hits me like a truck. I deflate under it. I was hoping he'd say he didn't know what the truth was and told me what he thought was right. An admittance of the lie hurts more than the belief. "Why'd you lie about it?"

There's no way to know what he's thinking, and with how much trouble he has forming sentences still, I'm not sure I'll ever get a proper answer. Instead of trying to speak, he points at the whiteboard on the desk beside his bed. He waits until I hand him a marker with the cap popped off and writes on the board as I hold it steady for him. He writes:

fudged it

didn't want you thinking he was a good man

they weren't together when we took you

I'm sick of being given half-truths about the circumstances that led to me being raised by my grandparents. Quincy only told me what would make him look good. Grandpa Joe fudged the truth because he wanted Quincy to look bad. I understand that he thought he was doing what was best, but he really should have told me the truth—especially when I started asking about it.

"You really hate him so much that you'd lie about his involvement in Lena's pregnancy?"

"Yes."

"Jesus. You're crazy, you know that, right?"

love ya, kiddo

"I love you too." A combination of him telling me he loves me and the fact that I don't want to stress him out while he's in recovery softens me. I kiss the back of his hand. "I know you don't wanna hear this, but I think I might wanna spend time with Quincy."

"No."

"I wasn't asking for permission. I'm eighteen now, and Auntie Yolanda said I need to be the one to decide if I want him and Lena in my life. I know you wanna protect me from them and I get why, but you can't make these kinds of decisions for me anymore. It has to be me, and you have to trust that you raised me to be strong enough to take care of myself. I have so much love and respect for you, and I'll always be grateful to you for taking care of me. I know it couldn't have been easy. And I want you to know they could never replace who you are to me. But the stuff that happened in the past was just that—in the past—and Quincy seems different now. You might end up liking him if you gave him a chance."

Grandpa Joe musters up the energy to send a nasty stink eye my way, but he doesn't tell me no again. It's the closest I'll ever get to a blessing, and I decide to run with it before he has a chance to change his mind. I'm going to see Quincy again, and I won't let my feelings get in the way of us having a good moment.

5

I don't leave Grandpa Joe until visiting hours are over. He's far from happy I've decided to give Quincy a chance at redeeming himself, but I think he realized he can't stop me. I'm no longer reliant on him. I can't be, and he doesn't have the same power over me while he's in the hospital. I have more freedom than I've ever had before. I should be taking advantage of that like Tommy said, but I won't because I need my grandpa's blessing, and I won't be at peace with myself until I get it.

Tommy moseys into the guest room sometime after his parents fall asleep. His mouth parts, no doubt about to say something outrageous, but it never comes. "You look off. What's wrong?"

"I think I'm starting to make myself sick. I keep typing and deleting texts to Quincy to tell him I wanna see him again, but nothing feels right."

"You're in your head again, huh?"

I sit up in the bed and bend over with my head between my legs, clutching at my gut. "If I do what my grandpa and Ivy want me to, I'll make them happy, and that's what I should be aiming for. I need to fix what I broke."

"Aaliyah, no. You need to say fuck them and do what's best for you."

"I'm obviously not gonna say that."

"Then I will. Fuck 'em. Send that text to Quincy. Tell him you wanna see him again if that's what you're feeling."

Tommy's one of the few people who can get me out of a funk once I'm in one. I lift my head, and his goofy smile makes me smile too, but then I realize he shouldn't be here to cheer me up. It's a weeknight. He has class tomorrow. He should be sleeping at his dorm. "Can I ask you something? Why aren't you ever at school anymore? You're always here."

"Because you're here and I wanna see you."

It's cute of him to stick around because of me, but I still don't understand how he's able to keep up with his work if he's never at school. That just doesn't sound right. "How was your poli-sci test?"

"Skipped it."

"Is everything okay?"

"Yes."

"Tell the truth."

He rolls his eyes, but he sits on the bed when I pat the spot in front of me. I make sure to keep my hands to myself this time, and he doesn't seem as on edge. Focusing on him instead of myself makes me feel a lot better too. "Nothing makes sense in my classes and they're boring. I wanna drop out."

"Isn't it too late to drop a class?"

"I meant out of school. The only reason why I haven't done it already is because everybody's gonna think I'm an idiot."

"Doubt it."

"Sabrina will."

"Her opinion matters to you?"

"Yeah. Not in the way you're thinking though. I wanna prove her wrong. She used to tell me I'd be a loser with a bunch of kids working at White Castle to pay the bills, and it really fucking hurt 'cause I know I could at least get a job at a fancier fast-food place like Five Guys. Maybe even Potbelly."

"That's not funny."

Tommy scoots closer to me. He looks so sad and broken, and all I want to do is give him a hug, but I can't be the one to initiate. It has to come from him. "Can I be real with you for a minute?"

"Of course."

"Sometimes I wish I was more like you and Jen. You guys have, like, goals and plans for the future. That's the kinda thing that'll make people proud, and I don't have that. I don't know what I wanna do, and the only thing I was ever good at was wrestling. That's not a reliable life plan."

"All of my life plans are sort of falling apart right now, so I don't know if you should lump me in with Jen." The thoughts I had while telling Quincy about my college plans come back full force, and I wonder again how I'll be able to take care of Grandpa Joe two thousand miles away. Deep down I've known the answer since I first asked myself the question. I can't. "Don't tell anyone, but I'm thinking about not going to school in the fall."

"I thought going to UCLA was your dream."

"It is. Or it was, at least."

I've wanted to go to UCLA ever since I started running for Coach Barnes my freshman year. He told me their head coach worked with track athletes in the last two Olympics, and that if I wanted to aim high, I needed to go to a school that could help me achieve my goals. But now Grandpa Joe is sick, and I can't imagine being more than two thousand miles away from him if something else happened. The only good thing about this is that me staying in Chicago would make Quincy happy. I don't think too hard and send a quick text to Quincy like Tommy suggested.

> **Me:** Scale of 1 to 10, how happy would you be if I changed my mind and didn't go to UCLA in the fall?
>
> **Quincy:** Off the charts.
>
> **Quincy:** Something happen?
>
> **Me:** Just thinking about my options

"If I change my mind later on, school will still be there when I'm ready. I'll just have to let go of my dream of running at UCLA. Being here with my grandpa is more important than that."

"That's heavy." Tommy doesn't try to tell me that I'm wrong or try to pressure me into going to UCLA anyway. He just lets me sit with it the reality of the situation I'm in, and he hugs me when I ask him to. "At least we can be college dropouts together."

"If I never go, I can't be classified as a dropout, but I don't think you should quit school just yet."

"No?"

"You haven't even been at school for a full year yet. Give it a little more time and see what happens. Maybe you'll take an elective that helps you decide what your dream job is, or you'll realize school really isn't for you—and that's okay too. It's your life. You've gotta do what makes you feel good."

"Oh, really." Tommy taps his chin. "Sounds like that's advice you should be giving yourself."

"Hush."

"Just saying you sound like a hypocrite."

"And you sound like a shut up."

Tommy just smiles at me. The warmth and emotion in his eyes when his meet mine shock me. I can't remember a time when he's ever looked at me like this—like I'm the only person on earth who matters to him. I want to ask him about it, but I'm afraid of what he'll say. "If I make a move, will it ruin the good thing we've got going?" he asks.

"A move?"

"Like if I kissed you, would you be mad?"

"No. But I don't think we should."

"Because of your grandpa?"

"Yeah. He still hates you and that's a big deal for me."

"He doesn't have to know."

There's a burning sensation in the pit of my stomach, like it's warning me not to jump back into a situationship with Tommy, who's clearly still having problems with his ex, whether he wants to be with her or not. But I'm weak and it's kind of shocking I lasted this long. I've never really been good at saying no to him.

I tell him it's okay. It's just a kiss. Nothing bad has ever happened because of a kiss. I lie to myself and say that's all we'll do. But then his mouth is on mine, and I forget everything—all the reasons why this is a bad idea, the lies I told myself—they're all gone, replaced with the immense pleasure I feel when he touches me and the warmth of his breath on my skin as he kisses my neck.

6

Grandpa Joe tells Auntie Yolanda to bring me to the rehab facility a few days after I hook up with Tommy, and it's hard not to spiral. Tommy must've told Jen, who told Ivy, and of course Ivy would tell our grandpa because she wants to ruin my life. But when I walk into my grandpa's room, he's sitting up in bed and Auntie Yolanda is in the chair next to him. I don't think she would be involved in a talk about Tommy, so this must be about something else.

"Am I in trouble?" I ask. "Because if I am, I'd like to remind you that I'm, like, three months away from graduating, and I'd appreciate it if you made my punishment brief."

"You're not in trouble, Aaliyah," Auntie Yolanda says. No nickname? Kind of feels like I'm in trouble. "As I told you before, you're eighteen and therefore, it really is up to you to decide whether or not you want to have a relationship with your parents. But Dad has concerns and has asked me to help him tell you the full story before you make that decision."

I'm immediately suspicious of Grandpa Joe's motives. He's never once wanted to tell me anything about my parents, and now he's offering that information voluntarily? That's sus. "You're hoping if you tell me what happened, it'll make me not wanna see them."

"Damn straight," Grandpa Joe says.

"Dad, please," Auntie Yolanda says.

"Let's hear it then," I say. "What did they do?"

"Before we start, I need you to understand that what happened back then wasn't malicious," Auntie Yolanda says. "I don't want you to vilify Lena for something she couldn't control, the way Dad has."

"Did she get sick or something?" I ask.

"She suffered from postpartum depression shortly after you were born. I had it too with Ivy, and as much as I loved her, as perfect as I thought she was, I couldn't do the things I needed to do. Taking care of my own basic needs, like showering and eating, felt impossible. Being a good mother to an infant was like climbing a mountain every single day. I'd never been swallowed whole by my feelings before, but after I had Ivy, it was like I couldn't control myself. The rage I felt was so intense, I thought I might hurt my baby girl."

Auntie Yolanda's voice cracks as she speaks. She wipes away her tears, and I want to reach out and take some of her pain. She's the nicest person I've ever known. She doesn't deserve this.

"I love Ivy more than I love myself, yet for five months after I gave birth, I couldn't stand to be around her. The only reason why things didn't end horrifically is because your uncle and his family stepped up and kept me afloat while I worked through my issues with a therapist. Lena didn't have the same support system."

"How bad was it for her?"

"In all my years working as a psychologist, I still haven't seen anything like it. Mine lasted five months. Hers went on for two years. I tried to help, but she'd already started pulling away from me. Her inability to care for you became more apparent as the months went by and her depression continued to worsen until she couldn't shake it off anymore. That's when Mom and Dad decided to intervene."

"Place was a mess. Trash everywhere. Dirty dishes piled up. You was screaming your head off. It was filthy. Quincy was nowhere to be found. Lena was in the bed under a pile of clothes." A tear falls down my grandpa's cheek. He uses his strong hand to wipe it away. "You was just a baby. Didn't deserve to go through that. And she didn't care. She was happy we took you. Didn't put up a fight or nothing. Now they wanna barge in sixteen years later. After all the hard stuff's done. After I did all the work. They don't get to do that."

It's the most he's said since the stroke. His sentences aren't complete the way they used to be, but he's talking more and that's a win in my mind. I recognize he's improving because of how much help he's getting in the rehab facility. Help. It's something Lena never had, and I don't understand why.

"I'm confused," I say. "Why was Lena alone?"

"She and Quincy were on a break at the time you were taken," Auntie Yolanda says.

"I meant family. Grandma was still alive, and Grandpa, you were still in contact with Lena, right? Her being by herself doesn't make sense."

Auntie Yolanda shifts in her seat. "Mom and Dad were of the opinion that if you were old enough to make a baby, you were old enough to take care of one. It was tough love. I went through the same thing, but your uncle's family took me in. Quincy and Lena had no one."

There's a nasty, bitter taste in my mouth. Lena was only sixteen, and sure it was irresponsible of her to have a baby at that age, but she was too young to handle that responsibility alone. He should've helped her. "Grandpa, that's . . . How could you do that to Lena? To me?"

"Didn't do nothing but help you," he says.

"You let me believe my parents didn't love me. You lied to me about everything for years. Every time I asked you about them, you never once told me the truth. You made it seem like they were terrible parents who couldn't be trusted to handle the responsibility of raising a child when you did nothing to make sure they'd be able to do that. I went to bed every night believing your lies. Believing you would never hurt me when you were doing just that for sixteen *years*. That's nothing to you?"

"Aaliyah—"

I don't let my auntie get in a word. This isn't about her. This is between me and Grandpa Joe. "I thought they didn't want me because something was wrong with me. And maybe that's true. Maybe taking care of a kid was too much for them and I made it even harder by being me. It still would've been nice to have them in my life, even if it was from a distance, but you took that option from me without bothering to see what I thought."

"Did what I thought was best for you," Grandpa Joe says. "Not gonna take it back now."

I scoff. Of course he won't admit when he's wrong. He never has. "It's not just about me though. You taught me to be kind to everyone no matter who they were or what they'd done. You said it was important to help people in need, not because you wanted something in return, but because it was the right thing to do. You told me to never turn my back on family. But you went against all of that and abandoned Lena when she needed you. What you did was cruel, and you couldn't even man up and tell me the truth. You hid everything from me because you knew I'd be angry and didn't wanna deal with the consequences of your own actions."

Grandpa Joe leans back against the headboard, stone-faced, with his eyes forward as I rise out of my seat. I hope he feels shame for treating Lena the way he did and for lying to me all this time.

"Aaliyah, where are you going?" Auntie Yolanda asks.

I'm halfway across the room when I turn back to my grandpa. "You keep saying you did what you thought was best, but I don't agree. You made a bad call."

I storm out of the rehab center with tears in my eyes, unsure of where to go. This whole time I've been so worried about Grandpa Joe and what he thinks of me and the things I do and the people I spend my time with. I've built my life around him and did things according to what he would or wouldn't like because I loved him like a father, and I didn't want to risk losing the only dad I ever had. I thought he respected and loved me just the same, but he doesn't. He only cares about himself.

7

I don't attempt to speak to Grandpa Joe after learning the truth about what he did to Lena, and he doesn't tell Auntie Yolanda to ask me to come back to the rehab center in the days following our disagreement. I should be leaving Jen's house because I'm sure I've overstayed my welcome, but I just can't be in my auntie's apartment right now. Especially with me and Ivy still having issues. She'll no doubt be on Grandpa Joe's side, and I don't want to fight both of them. I just want them to see things from my perspective. I want them to understand why I'm so angry. Not only did he lie to me, he also abandoned Lena when she needed him the most. Talk about hypocrisy.

Because I currently don't have my grandpa, I've been leaning more on Quincy, and he's taken on the light increase in responsibility well. He responds to my texts and answers my calls and says all the right things. I'm not naive. I know he's being this way so he can impress me and get on my good side, but it's nice to have family care about me now that things with my grandpa and Ivy are in a bad place.

I'm not shocked when Quincy's name pops up in my Notification Center. I debate responding now or waiting until the first outdoor practice of the season is over. Coach Barnes has been hassling me about remaining focused on track, and I know he's right. I've been distracted by my family drama, and now is the perfect time to show that I'm locked in, but the excitement I get from Quincy's text overwhelms me. I check it anyway.

> **Quincy:** Having a party next week. You should slide.
>
> **Me:** No thank you.
>
> **Quincy:** When imma see you again then? Never?
>
> **Me:** If you wanted to hang out, you could've just asked. You didn't need to make up a fake party as an excuse to see me.
>
> **Quincy:** Shut up. My party is real.
>
> **Quincy:** So?
>
> **Me:** I'll let you know after practice.

Coach Barnes has his eyes on me, and I hurriedly stuff my phone into my Nike bag. For a moment, I forget that Ivy and I aren't on speaking terms and I turn to my right like she'll be there, but she isn't. Despite the things that were said during our fight, I still miss her. My heart and mind don't care that I see her every day at school and during track. They're still grieving the loss of her. Even on a field full of my teammates with people constantly in my face, the only person I really notice is Ivy standing ten feet away from me.

The coaches split the team after the warm-up. Distance runners go with Coach Newman. Everyone else goes with Coach Barnes and Coach Parker. Our coaches herd all the sprinters and fielders to the start line on the outdoor track. Coach Barnes tells me and Jen to come to the front, along with the captains of the boys' sprinting team and the fielders.

I stand next to Jen with my arm hanging off her shoulder. A drop of rain splatters onto my skin and slides down my hand. I brush the droplet off and find myself looking at Chloe and Ivy, who are off to Jen's left side, talking about putting in more time practicing starts.

"Ah, so some of you do like each other," says Coach Parker when she notices.

"What do you mean?" a kid named Darryl asks.

"It's come to our attention that there are fractures in the group." Coach Barnes stares exactly at those people whose relationships he believes are fractured. Sprinters David and Jack, who were suspended a week ago for fighting in the hallway between passing periods. Lizzie, a shot putter, and Johnathan, our best triple jumper, who are in some weird toxic relationship and get into screaming matches every other day. The only three permanent high jumpers on the team—Felicia, Antonio, and Kate—who don't like each other for unknown reasons. And me and Ivy. "We're doing universals today because of those fractures."

I thought Coach forgot about that. I sure did.

Coach Barnes clutches his clipboard in front of him and ignores the groans and complaints from the group. "Keep an eye on your captains. If your respective captain falls behind, your squad is running an extra lap. And if more than two captains fall behind, everybody's running an extra lap."

Anthony glares at the fielders standing off to the side. "Y'all better run slow."

"If I catch anybody running slow, the entire team is running five extra laps," Coach Parker says.

"I'm scared I'm gonna pass out," Jen says. "Aaliyah, if you see me swaying, shove me forward and I'll let momentum take over."

"I'm gonna be too worried about me passing out," I say. "I can't worry about saving you too."

Coach Parker blows her whistle, and we take off running around the track surrounding the football field. I've done enough universals during my four years on the team to know exactly what to do. Run half a lap and up the steps to the smaller set of bleachers on the other side of the track, then run up and down the bleachers until you reach the opposite end. Then it's back onto the track, where we finish the lap. Pump out ten push-ups, and do it all over again.

Jen and I pull ahead of most of the sprinters and fielders by the third lap. My body doesn't hurt until lap eight. We do ten single-leg burpees like Coach Barnes says, then start the ninth lap, running a lot slower than we have been. He and Coach Parker yell at us to keep moving, keep running until they've decided we've had enough. They don't let us stop when we start gasping for air or when people start dropping like flies in the muggy air spring has brought us.

Thunder cracks in the sky, and it begins to rain as I pass by Coach Barnes, who's standing on the concrete walkway between the bleachers and the track. Everything gets kind of hazy the longer I run. My legs shake as I round the final bend, and the humidity makes breathing much harder than it should be. There's a rumbling in my stomach and ringing in my ears right before I hit the ground, spewing up what I had for breakfast this morning. I keep my eyes closed to stop the world from spinning around me, but the longer I'm on my hands and knees, the angrier I get. This practice is total crap, and so are the people who made it happen.

I get to my feet, tugging on my ears so I can hear again and blinking until the darkness disappears. I probably should be taking it easy after the fall I had, but I'm tired of running and I want this practice to end. I flag down every sprinter and fielder, stopping them before they can get back to where the coaches are. Even Ivy stops and pays attention to me because I'm co-captain of the team. She has no choice. "Hey! I know I'm not the only person who thinks this is bull crap."

"Aw, shit," says Jack. "Who made Aaliyah mad?"

"Everyone did. All this fighting and icing people out stuff has to stop." I wipe rainwater off my face, but it keeps coming, dripping into my eyes and my mouth as I talk to the group. "And I know I'm part of the problem. I've been distracted with drama of my own, but that's done. From now on, when I'm here, I'm gonna be focused on the team and nothing else. I want y'all to do the same."

"There's no way I'm being friendly with this idiot," Lizzie says, shoving Johnathan away from her.

"Cut it out! I don't care if you hate each other. Winning is what matters. Underclassmen and juniors still have time, but for us seniors, this is it. State is in May and graduation is in June, and that's the end of it. No do-overs."

And for me, these moments will be my last unless my grandpa's health doesn't improve drastically in the next few months. Since the odds of that happening are nonexistent, I need to wrap my head around that and go hard during the back half of the season because it's all I have.

"Let's go, y'all," Ivy says. "I only got, like, three more laps in me, and if one of you dumbasses pushes us into lap four, I'm beating your ass."

As unwelcome as Ivy's assistance is, it's precisely the sort of motivation the team needs. This time we run in a pack, and as soon as the coaches notice, they tell us to stop right as we make it to the three-lap cap Ivy gave.

"I hope you all remember this feeling the next time you think about fighting each other on school grounds." Coach Barnes's blue eyes pierce through every single one of us. "Go home. Rest. We'll pick up again after spring break."

I take a chance and approach Ivy after practice, hoping that because she helped me make a point, she's less upset with me. But when I sit next to her on the track, she rolls her eyes, and all that hope disappears.

"I was hoping we could talk," I say.

"Talk to your bum-ass parents, since you picked their side," she says.

I'm very aware that Auntie Yolanda must've told her about the talk I had with her and Grandpa Joe, but she doesn't know the full story. She doesn't get how messed up this all is. "That's not what happened. The way he handled things wasn't good, and Grandpa didn't get that, so yeah, I'm mad at him, but that doesn't mean I chose their side over his."

"That's not a good enough excuse."

"Um, I'm pretty sure it is."

"He saved your ass from a miserable life with your shitty parents, and now what? You're punishing him because you don't like the way he saved you? That's bullshit and you know it, Aaliyah. You should be thanking him."

"Thanking him for what? For lying to me for years? For never giving my parents a chance to make things right? Or for making me think they didn't love me?"

"They don't."

Ivy's words sting and hit on the fears I've always had when it comes to my parents. She knows how saying what she said will make me feel. We've stayed up late on so many nights talking about my parents and how disappointed I'd get during every holiday with no word from them. She consoled me when I cried on every birthday they missed. She's the one who made me feel better when I told her I believed my parents didn't care about me because if they did, they wouldn't have missed all the big moments in my life. And yet, after all that, she still said they don't love me. She wants to hurt me. Fine. I'll hurt her back.

Before I can ruin her happy the way she's ruined mine, Coach Barnes appears next to me. He squats down and looks at the both of us. "What's going on here?"

"Nothing," Ivy says. "Just having a family talk."

"Seemed a bit intense for a family talk," Coach Barnes says. "Wanna tell me about it?"

I have no interest in having a family therapy session with Coach Barnes. The only person who can make me feel better is Quincy. In my haste to get away from them, I almost run into Jen, who was hovering nearby. I mumble out an apology and grab my bag from the pile of stuff off to the side of the track and start walking aimlessly.

Ivy's words echo in my head. *They don't love me. They don't love me. They don't love me.*

8

I call Quincy and ask him to pick me up from track practice because I need to see him. I need him to prove Ivy wrong.

He pulls up next to me in the school parking lot in a car I've never seen before. His music is bumping so loud, the bass sounds distorted. He's wearing a dope Chicago Bears bomber jacket with a matching hat and leans across the center console to open the passenger-side door. He's always so effortlessly cool, and it makes me feel ten times worse because even though he's my dad, I feel like he's way too cool to want to hang around someone like me.

"Who fucked with you?" he asks.

I toss my Nike bag into Quincy's backseat and hop into the front. "My cousin."

"What'd your cousin do?"

"We were arguing and . . ." Our first real interaction was a mostly positive one, but Quincy and I haven't hit the Reveal My Deepest Fears stage yet. I don't even know if he'll keep me around long enough for me to get to that point. "She said something mean, and I'm trying not to internalize it, but it's hard when you're basically proving her right."

"The fuck did I do?"

"Do you love me? I know it's totally needy and uncool of me to ask, but I just . . . I can't help feeling like she's right about you not loving me. I mean, I had to practically force you to admit you wanted me around and even when you did, it didn't feel genuine. It was like you were saying the words because you thought that's what I wanted to hear and not because you really meant it."

"You don't know if I love you?" His tone isn't accusatory. He sounds hurt that I'd think for even a second he didn't love me. It's the closest he's gotten to sounding genuine, and it eases my anxiety a little, but it's still not enough. "Man, I thought my fucking heart was gonna explode outta my chest when Joe took you. I was broken. Wouldn't eat. Couldn't sleep. It was like he cut out a part of me and kept it for himself."

"Then why didn't you fight to keep me in your life?"

"Wanted to raise you myself, but he called my bluff and said we could take it to court. I knew I'd lose. Joe and Dee were grown. They'd already taken care of two kids and did good. But me? I was young and irresponsible and kinda stupid. No house. Didn't even have a real job at that point. No judge in their right mind would've given you to me, so I had to let it go. And Joe wasn't playing around when it came to you. He said he'd beat me six feet into the ground if I even thought about trying to be in your life after that."

"But you found me even after that."

"Lena said you hit her up, so I figured it was safe for me to come find you. I ain't think you was gonna turn me away." Quincy squirms in his seat and chooses to look out the window rather than at me. "Look, I'm not good at stuff like this—expressing myself and talking about feelings and all that. But I don't want you going around thinking I don't give a shit about you. I give a lot of shits."

"Should I assume that's your way of telling me you love me?"

He looks almost queasy as he gives a curt nod. It's not much, but for him, I think it's the equivalent of giving a long, drawn-out speech, so I don't complain. "We good?"

"Yeah." I'm glad I didn't let Ivy's harsh words and my paranoia ruin him for me. "I like your jacket, by the way."

"Oh, yeah?" Quincy pulls out of the lot much slower than he pulled in. "You a Bears fan?"

"I support all Chicago sports teams. Don't ask me anything about them though, because I don't watch the games."

Quincy laughs and I get a little giddy. He laughed at another thing I said. He really must love me to do that, because no one thinks I'm funny. "Where you trying to go?"

"So . . ."

"Don't say nothing crazy."

"It's only a little crazy. I'm kind of between homes at the moment and don't have a destination in mind."

"You homeless?"

"I don't like using that word because it implies I don't have a home to go to at all, which isn't true." I twist in my seat as trees and cars and people disappear in the rearview window. We're going in the opposite direction of where me, Ivy, and Jen live. "Where are you taking me?"

"Back to where I was when you called."

"Where's that?"

"My homies' crib."

I face forward. "Are they gonna be cool with me being there? Because I can only handle a very specific type of confrontation, and a fight with your friend who's mad at me for disturbing their peace isn't one of the types."

"It'll be good. They know you."

"What? How?"

All he says is, "We've been cool a long time."

"For how long?"

Quincy lets the wheel slide between his hands as he turns left at the light. "Since we were kids."

"You met at school?"

"Nah. The three of us lived on the same block back in the day, nosy."

"Can you blame me for wondering? You haven't talked about any of your friends before and now you drop a bomb that these two know who I am. That's massive for me."

"It's not that big a deal. They're not that special."

His nonchalance doesn't make me feel better about inter-rupting a hang out session with him and his friends, but I'm forced to pretend when he tells me we've arrived. It takes some convincing from Quincy to get me out of his car and into his friends' apartment complex once he parks. Their apartment is on the fifth floor and there are no elevators, so we have to take the stairs. I move slower than Quincy because I kind of don't want to be here and the muscles in my legs are burning from my workout. By the time I catch up, Quincy is already walking inside the apartment.

"Ay, I'm back," Quincy says.

"The fuck?" says Quincy's friend. He blows out a puff of smoke so thick it creates a cloud in the living room. "What I tell you about bringing randos to my crib?"

"Man, she ain't no rando." Quincy sits on the far end of the couch and takes the half-lit blunt his friend offers him. "This my baby girl."

Baby girl? Okay. That's sort of cute. I wave awkwardly like I'm in kindergarten trying to make my first friend. "Hi."

"Oh, shit." His friend blinks as he reaches for the remote to the sound bar and cuts the music down. "Oh, *shit*. Where the fuck did you come from?"

"School? I—" I look to Quincy for help, but he's fiddling with his lighter because it's not doing the one thing it's supposed to do—light. "Sorry. I don't know how to answer that question."

"Ay, Jaz! Guess who's here."

"Who?" Jaz half leans out of the room she's in. She doesn't see anyone but Quincy and his friend and smacks her lips. "I don't care about him, Craig."

"Fuck you, Jaz," Quincy says.

"Behind you," says Craig.

Jaz whips her head around. She stares at me, slowly moving forward with her eyes narrowed. I'm too afraid to move.

"'Liyah?" Jaz asks. "Where'd you come from?"

"That's what I was thinking," says Craig. "I don't know why she's standing over there like she don't know nobody."

"'Cause she don't know you, dumbass," Quincy says, successfully lighting up the blunt. "She ain't seen y'all since she was two. She's eighteen now."

"Eighteen?" Jaz comes at me with her arms spread and tears in her eyes. She hugs me, then pulls away so she can get another look at me. "You're all grown up, 'Liyah."

The fact that she knows my name, a nickname at that, without Quincy having to say it is wild. And he clearly didn't tell them he was going to pick me up, so my name stuck with her for sixteen years after I was gone. She cared enough about me then to remember me now and with how hectic my life has been, it's nice to have someone that's like family genuinely like me.

Craig takes the blunt from Quincy and tries to give it to me next. "You smoke?"

"Nah, she's responsible and shit," Quincy says. "'Liyah's a track star."

It's the proudest he's ever sounded when talking about me, and it's completely embarrassing. "I'm not that good."

"Don't be humble." Jaz drags me farther into the living room. She pushes me into the recliner against the wall, then sits on the couch between the guys. "Brag, girl."

"You be outside, running in the woods and all that?" Craig asks as he puts out his blunt and waves all the smoke away.

"No, I'm not on the cross-country team. I'm a sprinter. Um . . ." Bragging doesn't come naturally to me, but with Quincy and his friends expecting me to be conceited, I feel like I have to give them something. "I'm a state champ in two events. The 100-meter dash and the 4x100. That's a relay, so it's me and three other girls.

We won the last two years, and we're trying to win again this year too."

"Told y'all," Quincy says.

"Babe, remember how she was after she learned how to crawl?" Jaz asks. Then she turns to me. "We couldn't keep you still, so we blocked off whatever room you were in to make sure you didn't hurt yourself."

"Swear I thought you was gonna fall down them steps one day," Craig says.

"Nothing's really changed," I say. "I still move around too much. That's why my grandpa put me in track. He got sick of yelling at me for running around the house all the time."

"Big bad Joe still mean as hell, I see." Craig reaches behind Jaz and shoves Quincy playfully. "He had my boy running scared. My mama was on my ass that whole year before you was born 'cause Q was at our crib every day eating up all our food after school."

"She switched up once you got here," Jaz says. "I've never seen so many people fall in love with a baby the way we all did with you. Forget Q and Lena—you was *our* baby."

"Oh, no doubt," Craig says. "I had already made myself your uncle Craig before you took your first breath."

"I cried when Lena's parents took you," Jaz says. "Q never did say why though."

"'Cause it wasn't none of your business, nosy," Quincy says.

To keep the peace, I don't continue the conversation they're having. Quincy clearly doesn't want to talk about it and I'm actually enjoying being here. I don't want to mess this up. "Everybody always called me 'Liyah?"

"Yeah, you was our little 'Liyah. That was the nickname we gave you," Jaz says. "But nobody else could call you that."

I never thought about the possibility that people other than family would have memories of me as a baby. It makes sense though. I didn't exist inside of a vacuum where the only people allowed in were immediate family. Quincy and Lena had friends, and some of them must've known me then. I hope they like who I am now.

9

Quincy calls and asks if he can see me a couple of days later, since I'm still on spring break. Because of the talk we had in his car and the fact he introduced me to his friends, I'm looking forward to hanging out with him again without any baggage lingering over us.

"Is this what you do all day?" I ask after watching him for a few minutes. "You stare at an old car?"

"First off, my car ain't old," Quincy says. "It's vintage. And B, if I hadn't nearly torn my arm off at work, I'd be doing something else. Like actually fixing the car."

I check out the engine in his "vintage" car. It's all gross and dirty with what looks like a light coating of brown sludge on the parts. "Maybe we should postpone this hang out. Seems like you've got a lot of work to do."

He's quick to narrow his eyes, nonverbally letting me know he isn't pleased with my sass. "You got a lot of nerve talking shit about my car when yours looks the way it does. I'm surprised it even made it this far."

"Don't talk about her like that. She won't wanna start up and I'll be stranded."

Quincy laughs while grabbing a towel and wipes all the oil off his hands before tossing it back onto the roof of the car. "I'mma go get cleaned up real quick."

"I'll be here."

I don't go inside with him because that feels like the next step. Like entering his house is something I should only do once I've decided I want to keep him around permanently. So I lean against the hood of my car, careful to avoid all the rusted-over spots and dirt accumulated from a lack of washes. I wish I didn't have to resort to using it, but since the fight with Ivy is still going on, I'm forced to find my own way around these days.

A black Range Rover pulls into the driveway a few minutes later with Megan Thee Stallion blaring from the speakers. It's so loud that I feel the vibrations of the bass in my chest.

Lena hops out of the SUV and is halfway to her trunk when she notices me waiting by the curb. She freezes. Blinks. Then shakes her head like she's trying to see if I'm real or a figment of her vivid imagination.

I stand, frozen in place, as she slowly walks toward me. My eyes are the only part of me that move, flicking over to the house, desperately hoping Quincy shows up and whisks me away. It never occurred to me that my feelings about Quincy and Lena would flip the way they have.

Quincy, despite being vulgar and rude, has made an effort to be a part of my life. He's planning on coming to another one of my track meets and picked me up from practice the other day. He's introduced me to his closest friends and has even taken to texting me often. I feel his presence in my life.

Lena, on the other hand, hasn't done anything. And the one chance she had to do something, she couldn't even be bothered to show up or reschedule. The uninterested look I give her as she approaches me seems fitting given the circumstances.

"Aaliyah baby, what are you doing here?" Lena doesn't seem upset or happy. Just surprised. Quincy must not have told her I was coming, and I'm kind of grateful for that. I'm not ready to start a relationship with Lena yet. "You and Quincy are hanging out?"

I nod.

"Listen . . . About what happened—"

"We're good," I interrupt. I don't need some sob story about how sorry she is. If she truly wanted to see me, she would've come. She would've told me why she couldn't make it instead of standing me up. And she wouldn't have waited sixteen years to send me a freaking card.

"You get my note?" she asks.

"Yup."

She sighs. What makes her think she's earned the right to sigh about this? I'm the one who's hurting. I should be the only person sighing. "I know you said it's all good, but I wanna apologize for not showing up that day. Yo-Yo laid into me about it, but you probably already know that. She wasn't being quiet at the hospital."

All the anger and frustration seeps out of me because I get distracted by Lena's nickname for Auntie Yolanda. Yo-Yo. *Yo-Yo?* I'm losing my mind. I make a mental reminder to tease my auntie about it later. It's so weird hearing her called something so childish when she acts the way she does. Not uptight per se, but she's not exactly loose either. She's very much an Adult with a capital *A*.

Quincy comes out of the house and takes Lena's attention away from me. He stares at her like he's wondering why she's here, at her own house. "Thought you was gonna be out all day."

"Why didn't you tell me Aaliyah was coming over?" Lena asks.

"'Cause she wasn't. She's picking me up in her busted-ass car."

"My car isn't busted. She's vintage."

Quincy can't help but smile at me teasing him. He pushes my head the second he gets close enough to me. "Fuckin' smart-ass."

Lena interrupts the good vibes by reminding us of her existence. "Where are y'all going? Maybe I can meet you somewhere later."

"I don't wanna distract you from your errands," I say. "Can we go?"

"I'mma have the Uber app up in case your car breaks down," Quincy says.

"You're being dramatic. My car isn't that bad."

Quincy slides into the passenger seat of my car and hits the dashboard twice. I guess that's supposed to be my signal to drive. "This thing is a total piece of shit. I can fix it up for you at a discounted price though."

"I don't pay people to do stuff for me. If I can't do it myself, it's not gonna get done."

"I like that energy."

The fact that Quincy likes anything about me is a miracle. Though he's my birth parent, he isn't obligated to like me. He chose to like me. To me, that's better than an obligation, and it further proves that Ivy is wrong.

10

I hate parties, but I promised Jen I would help her jump Sabrina on Tommy's behalf, and she's refused to let me forget it. Even though I told her I'd go, and I'm literally living in the house the party is being thrown at, an internal debate rages inside of me the night of. It'll be too loud, too crowded, and too hot. And to make matters worse, I'll have to physically fight someone. It sounds completely exhausting.

But I suck it up because I'm doing this for Tommy. I put on something nice and head down to the basement of Jen and Tommy's house. It's about ten degrees warmer down here than it is upstairs, and like I expected, there's a bunch of people in attendance I don't know.

Like most of the guys in the basement, Tommy isn't wearing a shirt. He's in the center of the room surrounded by the friends he claims to hate. One of them tosses a beer his way for him to shotgun. He pops a hole in the can with his tooth and chugs the beer, then does a muscle man pose as his friends cheer him on. Leave it to Tommy to make dumb frat-boy antics look sexy.

A girl who looks a little older than Tommy stops in front of him, eyeing him like he's a whole meal. The moment her hand brushes against Tommy's chest, I feel my stomach sink into my toes. I don't have a right to be upset. We aren't together. I've never even admitted that I like him as more than just a friend, but my jealousy rears its ugly head anyway.

Tommy doesn't entertain her at all. He shrinks away from her and moves closer to his friends. I take a calming breath and decide to risk the possibility I may have to hang out with Tommy's friends tonight because the possibility of not being with him at all is so much worse.

I second-guess myself on the approach though, and one of his friends ends up pointing me out to him. Not to toot my own horn, but it's like the rest of the party fades when he sees me. His grin is so wide, I can practically see all his teeth, and his eyes light up like a kid on Christmas. It's the fist pump that gets me to smile. He's truly happy about my being here. He ignores his friends and the people around him and comes straight to me.

"Didn't think you'd come," he says. "You were up there forever."

"I wasn't sure if I would," I say. "This is extremely awkward for me."

"But you're here."

I take a step back. Far enough to give Tommy his space, but close enough that he can still hear me over the music without my yelling and embarrassing myself. "I guess I'm still jumping Sabrina with Jen. Is she here yet?"

He nods with his whole body. "She hasn't bothered me yet. I told Jen not to worry about it."

Thank God. I really wasn't looking forward to participating in a fight tonight. I'm still sore from the spring break practice. "I guess that means I don't need to be here then."

"Come on, don't leave." He stumbles forward into the space I just gave him. "You just got here."

"And I'm already ready to go. Tommy, I hate parties. You know that."

"Will you stay for me?"

I don't hesitate when I say "Yes."

"Let me get you a drink."

I'm not much of a drinker, but it might help me loosen up, and I'm going to need to be super loose to feel comfortable here for any stretch of time. I let Tommy fill a cup, then take it from him. The drink is sweet and doesn't taste like alcohol at all. Liquor is disgusting, and being able to taste it probably would've ruined my whole night.

He heads toward the stairs leading out of the basement but doesn't go higher than halfway. I sit on the step below him, and he moves down to sit next to me with a goofy grin on his face.

"You're here," he says.

"You said that already," I say.

"I can't believe it. I gotta be dreaming or something. Pinch me on the nipple so I can see if I wake up."

"I'm not gonna pinch your nipple. You're awake and you're confused because you're drunk."

I set the empty cup down on the step below us and hesitate with my hand in the air, because the last time I attempted to touch him without permission, he nearly fell out of his chair. Not wanting a repeat of that, I let him move into me on his own. His skin is warm to the touch and his eyes close once I make contact. He slips his arms around my waist, and soon I'm practically leaning back against the stairs hugging him. He's touchy and it's the Tommy I'm familiar with, but I know it's only happening because he's too drunk to be afraid of what I might do to him.

"I wanna kiss you," he says. "Can I do that?"

"If you want."

He lifts his head. "Do you want me to?"

I'm in the same spot I was in a couple of weeks ago when he asked the same question. Except now, I'm much more willing to disregard my grandpa's feelings about him. I nod and Tommy kisses me. I taste the beer on his tongue, and as much as I want to lose myself in the kiss, I can't, so I pull away.

Tommy tries to follow me, but I put a hand to his chest, and he stops his advances. "What's that about?" he asks.

"Are you okay with this?"

"Why wouldn't I be?"

"It's just . . . You're being different. Like you're being your old self, which I'm used to, but this isn't the self you are now. And you're drunk, so it kinda feels like the touchiness is because of that, and I'm not drunk, and I'd hate to do something that made you uncomfortable, and—" Tommy's laugh cuts me off. "What's so funny?"

"You're overthinking it."

"I wouldn't be me if I didn't."

"You know how we can fix it?"

"By getting you sobered up."

"Nope. You've gotta get as drunk as me. Be right back."

"Tommy!"

That's not at all what I was suggesting, but he's already disappeared into the crowd to get me another drink. I spend his time away second-guessing everything. It feels like I'm right. We've hooked up and hugged and brushed against each other, but these days there's always distance between us. He doesn't get close to me anymore, so the fact that he's doing it now has to be because he's drunk, right? And if that's right, it doesn't feel good to take advantage of that. I want him to feel safe with me when he's sober, but I don't know how to make that happen.

I do a quick scan of the room to see what's taking Tommy so long and end up spotting him with his ex. Freaking Sabrina. On the outside, I'm as chill and nonconfrontational as ever, but internally my anger is stewing, slowly building to a boil.

Jen is nowhere to be found, and I realize if she doesn't appear soon and things escalate, I might need to end up taking Sabrina on by myself. I stand and keep my eyes trained on them, searching for a reason to intervene.

The conversation they're having becomes heated, but it's still not enough. She hasn't done anything to him, and I don't want to come off as the crazy one in this situation. That's not a good look.

It doesn't take much longer for things to get out of hand. Sabrina is beet red as she berates Tommy, and he can barely get in a word. She doesn't seem to care that word is spreading about her very loud argument with him.

I'm still on the steps when Sabrina shoves Tommy, and I'm pushing my way through the crowd right as she slaps him in the face.

There's my reason.

Jen beats me to them because she has a sixth sense when it comes to Tommy being in trouble. She puts her entire body in front of Tommy's, even though he's got about six inches and fifty pounds on her, and shoves Sabrina back.

Sabrina recovers quickly, but I kick her in the back of her knee to throw her off balance again. She falls to the floor, clutching her leg, rage intensifying when she sees me. "Fucking bitch."

I knock whatever other expletives she planned on spitting at me right out of her big, dumb mouth with a fist to the face. I'm not an angry person and I don't fight unless I have to, but Sabrina turns me into a pissed-off brawler. Each hit hurts my hand and as I wind back for another, blood from Sabrina's nose drips down my fingers.

"Aaliyah!"

I want to hurt Sabrina. I want her to feel the same pain Tommy did all those times when she put her hands on him. I want her to be as broken physically as he is emotionally and mentally. I put all that want and wrath into every punch until, suddenly, Ivy is pulling me away from her.

"Calm down," she says.

A couple of Tommy's friends pull Sabrina to her feet. She's unsteady. Her nose looks broken and she's missing a tooth, but it could've been worse. I went easy on her, despite the strong urge I had to pummel her into the ground.

Ivy still has her hand clasped around my arm. I yank it out of her grasp.

The pure detest Jen expresses when she looks at Tommy's ex is both shocking and not. She's always been protective of Tommy, and I'm positive she would have done some damage if I hadn't jumped in to fight Sabrina myself. But she doesn't hate anyone, so when she grabs Sabrina by the collar of her shirt and says, "Touch my brother again and I'm gonna fucking kill you," no one really knows what to do.

"Holy fuck," says Tommy's best friend, Eric.

Jen stomps over to the speakers once Eric and the rest of Tommy's friends kick Sabrina out of the basement. She disconnects the Bluetooth. It gets weirdly quiet, and everyone stares at her, waiting to see what she'll say next. "Get the fuck out of my house!"

The crowd begins to disperse once Ivy joins in and tells everyone to leave before she beats their asses. Her words. Not mine.

"Aaliyah." Jen takes a minute to breathe, and when she's done, she's back to being the calm Jen we all know and love. "Go see if Tommy's okay. I need to clean before our parents get back from their trip."

I don't know when Tommy left the basement. Then again, I was more focused on breaking Sabrina's face than anything else. I take a brief second to chill in Jen's living room, away from everyone else. My hands are shaking from pain and from anger and the adrenaline rush that allowed me to punch Sabrina in the face multiple times without stopping to check for fractures. Blood is splattered on my shirt, and it coats my hand.

Breathe. Breathe. Breathe. It's over now.

11

Tommy is upstairs in his room, sitting on his bed with his head between his legs. I knock even though the door is open. Something about not knocking feels rude to me, especially in a house that's not my own.

"Is it okay if I come in?" I ask.

"Yeah," he says. "Jen's not coming?"

"She's downstairs cleaning and whatever, but I'm sure she'll be up here as soon as she's done. She put me on the make-sure-Tommy-is-okay task force in the meantime."

"It didn't hurt all that much," he says. "She's done worse."

Tommy raises his head and there's a red mark on his cheek where Sabrina slapped him. I have half a mind to track her down and beat her senseless again. She thought she could treat Tommy like a punching bag, and everything would just be cool? Nah. Eff that. I only wish I'd known about it sooner. I'm not a fighter, but I'd do it for him if it meant keeping him safe from her.

With his permission, I take a spot next to Tommy on the bed. The pain in my knuckles spreads throughout my entire hand, creeping up into my wrist. I make a fist. Nothing seems broken. Just deeply bruised. Not that that's much better, but at least I won't have to explain a hospital visit to Auntie Yolanda. "I'm not here to force you to talk about it. I know it makes you uncomfortable, but if you do wanna talk, I'll stay and listen for as long as you need me to."

The silence after I say my piece is long and not all that comfortable. I sit in it anyway, because it's better to be here quiet with him than to leave him alone after all that.

"Don't laugh," he says.

"I never would," I say.

He studies me like he's not sure if he should take me at my word. Eventually, he says, "It's fucking embarrassing. I was on the wrestling team for four years and this chick who's barely five two punked me out in front of everybody I know. It makes me feel pathetic."

"I don't think you are."

"Yeah, well, you're a better person than my friends are. I told them the whole story, and you know what they did? They fucking laughed. Right in my face and everything. The only person who got it was Jen. She was all I had after you dropped me. So I had all my friends—everybody but Jen—calling me weak and I was dating this girl who . . . She said she loved me. She told me that every day. And all I could think was, if this is love, then it fucking sucks, and I didn't want anything to do with it. But then I'd see you posting on your Insta story with fucking Daniel, and you'd tell him you loved him, and you'd touch him like he could break if you applied too much pressure, and there I was, miserable, with a girl who'd tell me she loved me and the next second, she'd be slapping me around and punching me. And the whole time I just wanted what you had with Daniel. I wanted you to talk to me like that and touch me like that. I wanted you to love me."

Tommy wipes his wet eyes with the back of his hand and hangs his head. "I thought it was happening over the summer after I broke up with Sabrina. We started hooking up and I was so geeked. It was like living in a dreamland. I couldn't wait for the day when you told me you loved me, but you never did. We barely made it a couple of months into the school year and then it was like *poof*. You were gone, and I was back to being miserable in the real world again."

"Tommy—"

"I know I'm not the kinda guy you can bring home to your grandpa. Still hurts though."

I'm sort of glad he interrupted me because I don't know what I would've said. I haven't been able to wrap my head around everything yet, but there's one thing that sticks out. "Do you love me?"

"You're amazing," he says. "How could I not?"

It's not much of an admission, but it's *something*. Obviously, I know I love him too. He's one of my best friends. I tell him everything and I look forward to spending time with him, and on the days I don't see him, I feel off. Like his presence is the one thing that keeps me happy. But is that platonic love or something more?

"You don't need to say it back. I just needed you to hear it." He notices my injured hand and gently brushes his thumb across my swollen and cracked knuckles. "Didn't think you'd actually hit her."

"An agreement's an agreement. Now that I'm thinking back on it though, Jen didn't really pull her weight." That gets a small smile out of him. "I feel like I should tell you I do love you."

"Kinda feels like there's a big-ass 'but' coming."

"I'm not where you are just yet. I mean, I like you *so* much, and I hated not talking to you for as long as I did, but my grandpa found out about us, and he went from being indifferent to hating you, and it scared me because I didn't wanna lose him over a crush."

"You like me?"

"How could I not?"

Tommy's smile is tinged with relief, and I wonder how long he's been holding on to the feelings he has for me. I think it's good that he waited until now to tell me. I don't know if I would've handled it half as well when Grandpa Joe had been active in my life. I might've tried pushing him away, and who knows what would've happened then? He could've moved on and where would that have left me? Alone and miserable with a liar for a grandfather. But I'm trying to let go of that fear. One day I hope I can feel free to tell Tommy what's been true for months. I want to be with him too.

12

The next day, Tommy makes up some crazy excuse to come with me back to my house. He's never been invited over because my grandpa said if I let him in, he'd ground me until I was ninety. It was dramatic but I listened because I didn't want to get on his bad side. I don't really care about that now.

"Are you ever gonna talk to your grandpa again?" Tommy asks.

"I would've never stopped talking to him if he had just apologized, but he was too stubborn to do that, and I can't be around him if he's gonna be a jerk about this. He was so upset about Quincy abandoning Lena and Lena abandoning me when he's the one who did the abandoning first. He's being annoying and a hypocrite, and if he's not gonna say sorry, then I need time to forgive him for that."

"How much time?"

"I don't know. It's only been like a week and a half." I put away the sweaters I'd been wearing all winter and pick out some thinner long-sleeved shirts with a couple more pairs of jeans.

"Can we not talk about this anymore? I'm starting to get irritated all over again."

Tommy doesn't question me any more after that. Instead, he walks around my room, taking everything in, touching things he really shouldn't be touching. Like my trophies and medals and the Flo-Jo and Marion Jones posters on my walls. "I like the setup. It's very you."

"I can't tell if that's a compliment or not."

"It is if you want it to be."

He approaches my memory board. I've pinned all my favorite moments over the years to the board—Grandpa Joe, Ivy, and me at Six Flags for the first time together. Me and Jen finding out that we'd be the co-captains of the track team. Tommy's one and only attempt at running cross-country. Sure, I could've kept everything in the Photos app, but I like looking at it when I wake up. It makes me happy. Or at least it used to. Now all the pictures of me and Grandpa Joe and Ivy remind me of what we no longer have.

Tommy complains whenever he comes across a picture of himself and points out one of me kissing his cheek and him smiling. "Take this down. I look like an idiot."

I ignore him because he's being ridiculous and start folding the clothes I picked out so they'll fit into my Nike bag.

"Hellooooooo," Tommy says. "Can you hear me?"

"I'm not taking the picture down," I say.

"But I don't like it."

"This isn't your room, and I told you not to come. All I'm doing is packing really quickly and leaving. That's boring."

"I'm not bored when I'm with you."

I smile and tuck the T-shirt I was folding into one of the side pockets of my bag. "That was sweet."

"I'm a sweet guy when I wanna be." Tommy is quiet and I'm sure he's waiting on me to respond, but I'm not going to gas him because of one nice comment. His breath hits the back of my neck, and he puts his hands on my waist. Only for a moment though. He's gone soon after. "You should do me a favor once we're done here. It's big. Massive, even."

"Okay?"

"I need you to suck my dick or I'll die. It's an emergency, I swear."

I let out an actual cackle like I'm a Disney villain. It's such a him thing to say.

"Aaliyah?" It's my auntie's voice, and it's coming from downstairs. Crap. Why is she here? "Is that you up there?"

I push Tommy away on instinct because there's nothing platonic about us being this close to each other, but then I think about how something that simple could potentially trigger him. I kiss his cheek. "Sorry I pushed you. But, like, stay away from me until she's gone, obviously."

Tommy sits on the edge of my bed. "I know how this is supposed to work."

"Please don't sit there," I say. "She's gonna think we were doing something inappropriate."

He moves to the other side of the room, rolling his eyes when I shake my head. "What's wrong now?"

"It's gonna look like you tried to climb out the window but didn't have time. That's sus."

Tommy dramatically falls face-first onto the floor. With his face pressed into my carpet, he mumbles, "I'm not moving again, so don't ask."

"Aaliyah?" Auntie Yolanda asks again.

I start stuffing clothes into my Nike bag haphazardly to make it seem like I was hard at work. "I'm in my room, Auntie!"

Auntie Yolanda appears not long after that. She's smiling up until she sees Tommy in the prone position on my carpet. "Hello, Tommy."

"Hi, Mrs. Sullivan."

"I'm sure you have a floor in your own home," she says. "Why are you lying on Aaliyah's?"

"Hers was closer," he says. "But, uh, I just realized I should probably keep the car warm."

"Yes, you should."

"You look great today, by the way." Tommy clambers to his feet and smiles innocently at my auntie. Then, when he turns to me, his smile morphs into the devilish one he uses right before he says something inappropriate. "Don't forget about that favor, Aaliyah. It's real important."

"What favor?" my auntie asks.

"Nothing! I'm gonna just . . ." I shoo Tommy out of the room because it's the only way to get him to move without putting my hands on him. My auntie is watching us from the doorway, so I keep going, moving farther into the hallway until I hit the stairs. "You're crazy, Tommy."

"You gonna do it?" he asks, face practically pressed up against my own.

I feel hot. I can't tell if it's anxiety from my auntie's sudden appearance or because being this close to Tommy is making me feel things. "Duh. Now go wait in the car."

"Don't take too long. I've got, like, negative gas left. It's running on fumes and little mini gas particles at this point."

"Gimme ten minutes."

Auntie Yolanda doesn't let me get in a word once I return to my room. "This fun sleepover time you've been having with your friend and boyfriend is officially over. You're coming home with me. Pack your things. I'll be downstairs."

I do what she says because what else am I going to do? Run away? No thanks. That sounds like too much work. Auntie Yolanda is in the living room, finishing up watering Grandpa's plants by the time I make it downstairs. "Not to be a stereotypical whiny teenager, but I don't wanna go to your apartment."

"And yet here you are, pouting in my face like one."

"Auntie, please. I wanna stay with Jen. She's nice to me."

"Is this about your fight with Ivy?"

"Maybe."

"Do I even want to know what this is about?"

"I'd rather not say."

If Auntie Yolanda was a meaner person, she'd have some tough words for me. But she's not mean. She's nice and has the patience of a saint. I feel bad. This fight between me and Ivy surely is stressing her out, and she doesn't need more of that. I want to tell her that Ivy and I will sort this out on our own and she doesn't need to involve herself in our drama, but that would be a lie.

"I understand you and Ivy are having issues right now, but staying with Jen and her family indefinitely isn't feasible. Eventually, you'll have to come back and live with us."

"Technically, the definition of *eventually* means an unspecified amount of time. That sounds pretty indefinite to me."

"Oh, Lord. I don't know how Dad finds the patience to deal with you."

"He's gotta dig down real deep."

Auntie Yolanda closes her eyes as she thinks. "I'll have to tell Dad about this. All of it, including Tommy being in your room while no one else was here."

"That's gonna make him hate me more."

"He doesn't hate you, Aaliyah."

"Well, if he doesn't now, then he definitely will when you snitch on me. Grandpa Joe doesn't like Tommy."

"That bothers you?"

"Yes. I want him to like Tommy."

"Because you like Tommy?"

"That's not what I said."

Auntie Yolanda gives me this look like she thinks I'm full of crap, but she's being nice about not calling me out on it. "You can stay with Jen's family until I talk to Ivy and tell her to get over whatever attitude she has with you."

I put my hands on my hips. "But that's only gonna take like two days max."

"Then I suggest you start packing tonight. I won't tell Dad about Tommy being here, but I will be talking to Tommy's parents about keeping a closer eye on you two."

I know better than to argue with my auntie since she's my de facto guardian while Grandpa Joe is in rehab, but I hate that I have to go to her apartment. It's not the same there anymore now that I don't have Ivy to talk to.

In the car, Tommy checks me out as he slowly pulls away from my house. He must not like what he sees, because he frowns right in my face like it's not rude. "What's wrong? You look sad."

"I can't stay at your place anymore because my auntie thinks we're dating and says it's inappropriate for me to be there. I'm supposed to move back in with her after she tells Ivy to stop being a jerk, but I don't wanna go back. It's gonna suck there."

Tommy does a double take and nearly crashes his car into one that's parked on the side of the road. He recovers, cursing loudly at the car like it's the car's fault he almost ran into it. "She thinks we're together?"

"Yep."

"What'd you say about it?"

"Nothing."

"You didn't correct her or anything?"

"Nope."

Tommy turns his head to the left and I think he wants me to believe he's checking for cars as he makes another turn. I catch his smile though. "Don't worry so much about living with Ivy. You can always sneak out and come over if she starts acting up. Or, you know, when you inevitably start missing me."

"Oh, it's inevitable?"

"Only a matter of time. I'm real missable."

I don't tell him he's right because I'll never hear the end of it, and I absolutely cannot deal with a smug Tommy on top of regular, ridiculous Tommy. But it does make me feel better to know I have a place to go if being around Ivy is too much to deal with. I send a text to my auntie letting her know I'll be there tomorrow. She doesn't have to know that I'm already planning my escape, and as long as I'm back before curfew, I won't get in trouble for being gone all the time.

13

During dinner, Ivy is so quiet it's kind of unsettling. She doesn't crack a single joke, doesn't smile at the corny stuff her dad says, barely talks while we watch a movie with her parents—it's like she's a different person. Because I'm sure I'm the reason why she's being so weird and I don't want to be near her anyway, I excuse myself from the movie before we're even halfway done with it and head to the bedroom.

The air mattress I've been sleeping on makes an outrageous amount of noise when I lay on it. I don't really care unless Ivy is in the room though. It's so quiet and boring these days without her and Grandpa Joe around. I never put much thought into how much of my time was eaten up by them until they weren't an option. And during those times, like now when I'm by myself, I remember how lonely I actually am.

Tommy: My balls are itching. That mean you're thinking about me?

It's such a Tommy way to start off a conversation that I smile despite feeling like I want to die. I'm still crying, and I'm still depressed, but it's a little less now that I'm talking to him.

> **Me:** I think it's supposed to be the nose.
>
> **Tommy:** Nose. Balls. Who gives a shit? Was I on your mind?
>
> **Me:** You were my next thought.
>
> **Tommy:** I had a feeling. You busy?
>
> **Me:** Does breaking down because of crippling depression and crying into my pillow count as being busy?
>
> **Tommy:** No
>
> **Me:** Then I guess I'm not busy.
>
> **Tommy:** I'm picking you up.

I have plenty of time to knock out a quick cry session and maybe a breezy fifteen-minute nap before I have to come up with an excuse as to why I'm leaving.

"What's wrong with you?" The question sounds abrasive when it comes from Ivy. I assume it's because one or both of her parents forced her to come in here. She shouldn't have bothered. I don't want to talk to her. "My mama told me to check on you. She's probably being nosy and listening in the hallway."

Called it.

"I'm fine." I burrow deeper under the covers and hope that Ivy leaves me alone the way she's been doing since Grandpa had a

223

stroke. The covers are ripped off me a moment later, exposing me to harsh light and a slight chill in the air. It takes an embarrassing amount of time to pop off the air mattress, but once I'm up, I get right in Ivy's face and snatch two of the covers back. The third is still clutched in her hand. "Leave me alone."

"Were you crying?" she asks.

"No," I say.

"Liar." She holds up the final blanket. "It's wet and your eyes are red."

I wanted to bawl my eyes out alone in a relatively peaceful way. Now I'm hot and irritated and I want to leave this apartment so I can be somewhat happy again. "So what if I was? It's not like you care."

"I care."

"When you care about somebody, you don't treat them the way you've been treating me. You talk to them. Make sure they're okay. And you don't act like a jerk all the time."

"I—"

"I don't care about you needing space or time or any of that. I would've given it to you if you'd asked. You know that. But instead of talking to me about it, you've been giving me the silent treatment and mean mugging me every second of the day. I can't do anything without you making me feel uncomfortable for existing, and I wanted to fix things, but . . . I don't know if I want that anymore."

"What?"

"Every time I bring up Quincy, you bash him and make him out to be the worst person on earth because I needed him, and he wasn't there. I need you just as much now as I needed him back then, but you disappeared. So if he's terrible for doing that, then you're just as bad. The only difference is that he's here now and you aren't because you either don't want to be or you can't. I don't want people in my life who don't wanna be there. That applies to you too." I wipe away my tears, but all it does is make my face even wetter. "I'm trying not to be mad at you, but you really hurt my feelings. You said my parents didn't love me. You knew how much that would hurt me and you said it anyway."

Auntie Yolanda pops her head in after a soft knock on the open door. She doesn't smile, probably because Ivy was right about her listening to us from the hallway. "Hi, ladies. I was going through today's mail and saw these."

The envelopes she hands us are nearly identical. One is addressed to Ivy Sullivan. The other to Aaliyah Campbell. Ivy's is from the University of Chicago. Judging by the size of the envelope, she got accepted. Mine is equally as thick and also from the University of Chicago. Since the odds of me going to college dip lower every day my grandpa is in the hospital, I don't immediately open mine.

"Wait!" Uncle William rushes into the room with none of the politeness that Auntie Yolanda had. He takes a silver knife with intricate flower designs on the handle out of a red velvet box. "Use my new letter opener."

"You're such a dork, Dad," Ivy says.

"I won't let you shame me for my love of quality letter openers," he says. "Now hurry up and open the damn thing! I can't take the suspense."

"Gimme a second." Ivy takes her dad's letter opener and slices through the paper like butter. "I'm gonna sound like a nerd, but this letter opener is nice."

"Right? *Right?*" Uncle William looks way too pleased with himself about this letter opener. Ivy was right. He is a dork. "I got it on sale. Sixty percent off."

Auntie Yolanda presses her hands together, watching as Ivy pulls out a bunch of papers and reads what the one on top says. "Well? Did you get accepted?"

"Yeah. I got in." Ivy stares at the sheet. "I got in!"

Auntie Yolanda and Uncle William erupt into cheers along with Ivy, hugging her and kissing her cheek, telling her how proud they are and how this is the first step toward a new chapter in her life. And after all the cheering and excitement, they turn to me expectantly.

"Is it cool if I hang out with Jen?" I ask.

"What about the celebration?" Uncle William asks. "I was gonna take everybody out for ice cream after you opened your letter."

"I think everyone would be a lot happier if I weren't there, and I don't have anything to celebrate either way." I toss the letter onto my air mattress. "College isn't a viable option for me right now."

You could hear a dust bunny rustling across the floor with the quiet that engulfs the room. Even Ivy looks shocked. Her shock is quickly replaced by anger. "What the hell is wrong with you? Now you're not going to school?"

"You can keep this fake caring act you're putting on," I say. "It's not necessary and all it's gonna do is piss me off even more."

"I'm sick of this self-pity thing you're doing," Ivy says. "You're—"

"Ivy, how about we give your mom and Aaliyah some time to talk?" Uncle William asks.

Ivy rolls her eyes. "Whatever."

Uncle William guides Ivy out of the room while my auntie stays with me. She gives me this look, this pitying, hurt look like she's sad I don't feel welcome around them anymore. "I think it's time we talk, Aaliyah."

"Respectfully, I'd prefer to hang out with my friend," I say.

"Sit down." It's rare for Auntie Yolanda to throw out a command as forceful as that one, so I do what she says because I don't know what she's capable of right now. "I'm listening."

The "so you better start talking" part of her sentence is heavily implied. "Things with Ivy aren't getting better, and I know you want me here with family, but the more time I spend around her, the angrier I get, and after what she said to me, I'd rather remove myself from the equation entirely, so we don't end up getting into an even worse fight."

Auntie Yolanda has massive bags under her bloodshot eyes, and her cheeks sag in a way they never have before. I feel awful about stressing her out, but I need to leave.

"It's scary how alike you and Ivy are to me and Lena," Auntie Yolanda says. "We couldn't go one day without jumping down each other's throats. But as angry as she made me—I mean, I was downright livid at times—I always felt better when she was on my side. It's too late for us, but there's still time for you and Ivy to make things right."

It's the first time she's really mentioned her relationship with Lena, and I realize I was so obsessed with figuring out the issue with my grandpa that I never asked Auntie Yolanda what happened between them. "Why don't you two talk anymore?"

"She felt like I betrayed her by taking our parents' side when they decided it would be better for you to live with them. Of course I didn't actually choose sides, but the fact I didn't pick hers was enough to justify cutting contact with me."

"Did it hurt when it hit you?"

"When what hit me?"

"That you'd never talk to your sister again."

With the cuff of her sleeve, Auntie Yolanda pats away the tears that start to fall. "Oh, the pain was unimaginable. I'd only felt hurt like that one other time, and it was when my mother died."

"I think I might be getting to that point with Ivy."

"Don't say that."

"Auntie, I made a mess of things. And I wanted to fix it all, but things kept getting more and more messed up and Ivy said some really mean things, and I was dying to go to UCLA, but I can't now because it's too far and we can't afford it anyway, even with a scholarship because Grandpa's sick and—"

"Aaliyah, breathe."

I don't know when I stopped breathing, but all of a sudden my hands are shaking, and my vision is going in and out like someone's putting a black sheet over my eyes, and I feel woozy.

"Aaliyah!"

I take in a deep, shuddering breath. Then I take three more, and by the fifth one, I'm back to being only slightly anxious instead of having a full-on panic attack. "I'm freaking out."

My auntie is next to me, rubbing soothing circles on my back, and I don't even know when she sat down, but I'm glad she's here to reel me in. "It's not your responsibility to take care of Dad. We both know he wouldn't be happy if you put your life on hold because of him."

"That's why I'm not gonna tell him."

"Before you make this choice to derail your life in some attempt to rectify the mistakes you believe you've made, I think you should know that your uncle and I have been discussing possible options for when Dad is released from the hospital. It'll be difficult to give him the care he needs between work and you and Ivy going off to school—and you are going to school. If we go by what his doctors are saying, he won't ever fully recover. He may not need to use a wheelchair forever, but he'll have trouble walking the way he used to. So, we think placing him in a care facility—"

"A care facility? What, like a nursing home? That's—no way. You can't pass him off to some strangers and hope they'll take care of him while we go on living our lives. He should be with us. We're his family."

"I understand your reluctance, but I don't see how we can give him what he needs without making major sacrifices to our daily lives."

"Let me be the one to do it then. I wanna help."

"Dammit, Aaliyah. You can't help everyone." Auntie Yolanda pinches the bridge of her nose. "Ever since you were a kid, all you've wanted to do is help people. Do you remember when you were eight or nine and Ivy fell out of that tree you two were always messing around in?"

"Yeah. She dislocated her shoulder."

"And you spent the next week researching dislocations so that if it happened again, she wouldn't have to suffer for too long because you'd know exactly what to do. But you also kept forgetting to eat because you fell down a physical therapy rabbit hole. You got so lost in your quest to help someone you loved, you neglected your own health and well-being. I don't want to see that happen again."

I stare right into her eyes with my lips curled down. There's no way my auntie did what I think she did. "Oh, my God. Did you just therapize me like one of your patients? 'Cause I feel called out right now."

"Just think about what I said, okay?"

"Fine."

Auntie Yolanda shakes her head and walks out of the room mumbling about how she doesn't know how she doesn't have a head full of gray hair. She has a point. Ivy and I push people to their stress limits without even meaning to. This fight we're having is proof of that.

14

Quincy reminds me of his party a few minutes after Auntie Yolanda leaves the room. He tells me to come through if I'm not busy, and I decide to go at the last second because even though I hate parties, I hate being in the same apartment as Ivy more.

The first thing I see when I walk into Quincy's house is Lena surrounded by a large crowd, twerking to a Flo Milli song with a drink in her hand. She's not at all what I expected, but I learned from Quincy not to go into anything with expectations anymore.

Besides, they're still young. Quincy and Lena should be thirty-four now. Or maybe her birthday is later in the year. I don't know. Either way, they aren't old, and it makes sense that they act more like this than the parents in *Family Matters*. Especially since they didn't have a kid around to force them to mature quickly.

Quincy has a thick blunt in one hand and a cup filled with a brown liquid in the other when he approaches me. His eyes are lower than normal as he offers me his blunt. "Shit. Fuck. You don't smoke."

"I kind of need my lungs to run, so . . ." I take in all the people I don't recognize. All of them are around Quincy's and Lena's age and are at varying levels of intoxication. Some are fine and are holding in-depth conversations with the other people at the party. Others are like Lena, dancing and singing at the top of their lungs, having the time of their lives. Then there are the sloppy ones. The ones who can't even stand straight because they're too drunk or high to know where they are. "Do you always have parties like this?"

"Sometimes," Quincy says. "Didn't tell Lena you was coming."

"Why not?"

"Wasn't sure if you would." It's a fair point since I wasn't sure I would either. "Glad you did though."

I don't tell him I'm glad too. I just got here and I'm not sure if I'm happy about it yet. Maybe I'll be surer after I talk to Lena. Because I know I'll have to talk to her. I've been putting off a real conversation for weeks, hoping I could only deal with Quincy, despite knowing it wasn't possible. They're in a relationship. Eventually, I'll have to be around her.

"Be right back," Quincy says.

"Where are you going?" I ask, sounding more needy than I would like.

"Refill."

Quincy finishes the drink in one gulp, then heads off through the living room, passing by Lena on the way out. He whispers something in her ear and then disappears around the corner.

Lena pushes past her friends to get to me. She has her arms outstretched but stops short of hugging me. Her excitement never wavers though. "Aaliyah baby! What are you doing here?"

"Quincy invited me. I can't stay for long though."

Her smile falls for a moment, but it's back quick enough that I think I imagined it. She's more reserved than she was when she first came up to me, and like Quincy, she finishes her drink in a single gulp. "You want something to drink? We got food too. Pizza and chips and dip and wings—"

"I'm a vegetarian," I interrupt. "And I'm not really hungry."

"Oh. Okay. Well . . ."

Lena lets her sentence trail off as she glances around the room, probably hoping she can find a way out of this awkward conversation. I know I am.

My savior comes in the form of Jaz and Craig rushing toward me from the same direction Quincy just went. Jaz is faster than Craig and pulls me into the most amazing hug. Seriously. It's like being wrapped in a warm blanket that smells like laundry detergent and vanilla body wash with a dab of perfume. "There's my baby girl. Q said he didn't know if you'd come."

"I wasn't sure if I would until an hour ago," I say.

Craig fist bumps me. "What's up? I was wondering when we'd see you again."

I catch Quincy waving at me from across the room and excuse myself to Jaz and Craig's displeasure. Lena doesn't look very happy either, probably because I welcomed a hug from Jaz while I barely ever make conversation with Lena. When I get to Quincy, he hands me a bottle of water and some celery and carrots and crackers on a plate with dip. "Here go your rabbit food."

I take the plate and water from him, kind of amazed he remembered I was a vegetarian. "Thanks."

"No worries." He takes another sip from his now-filled cup. "You play pool?"

"Like in iMessage? Yeah, I'm a killer. In real life? I'm terrible. Probably the worst in the world."

Quincy laughs. "I'll teach you. Got a table in the basement."

He leads me downstairs, and I immediately relax when I see there's no one else down here. The music is muffled through the closed door, and I know at any point, someone could burst in and send my anxiety through the roof, but this faux privacy still manages to make me feel better. "Don't you wanna be up there with your friends?"

Quincy sets his lit blunt and drink down on the bar and grabs two pool sticks. One for me. One for him. "You looked sick. Uncomfortable."

He doesn't answer my question, but he somehow manages to answer any follow-up ones I planned on asking. "You asked me to come down here because I looked sick?"

"Yup." Quincy bends over the edge of the pool table and sends the white ball flying at the multicolored balls in the center of it. The balls fly apart, and two solids go into holes on opposite ends of the table. "Could've told me you don't like parties."

"I don't like a lot of things. Parties. New situations. Or people. Or new things in general." I do my best to match Quincy's stance, adjusting when he points out that I'm holding the stick too loose. "I get anxious sometimes. I can't really control it."

"Pop out your elbow more." Quincy nudges my arm with his pool stick. "Why'd you come if you knew you were gonna be all nervous and shit?"

"Because I'm in a fight with my cousin, and you know, you asked me to, so . . ."

Quincy's eyes light up with glee and surprise and confusion, flipping between the three like a slot machine. He clears his throat and doesn't seem to notice I completely missed the white ball on my first try. "Same fight or a different one?"

"Same one. She thinks my grandpa is right and doesn't get why I want to spend time with you. I tried to make her understand, but she's intent on thinking the worst of you. Like you're this big bad that's gonna ruin my life or something. Crazy, right?"

"Huh. Yeah." He nods to the bruises on my knuckles. "What happened to your hand?"

"Got into a fight over the weekend."

"You win?"

"Duh."

Neither of us really talks after that, aside from him giving me tips on my form, and I'm okay with it. Quincy doesn't seem to mind either, which is nice. It eases the pressure of being in his home if we can just play the game. I wouldn't mind doing this more often.

By the time the party winds down, I'm 1 percent less terrible at pool. I'm not good enough to brag, and in a real game, I'd lose miserably, but I don't really care about winning anything other than track meets. And even though pool isn't a hobby I'd normally pick up, I do like playing with Quincy. If things were different, this could have been what it would've been like if my grandparents hadn't taken me, and in the midst of the chaos that is my life, it's nice to pretend like everything is normal for a moment.

"Has the music been off long?" I ask. "It's quiet upstairs."

Quincy looks up at the ceiling like it has the answer to my question. "How the fuck am I supposed to know that? I been down here with you."

"I thought maybe you noticed."

"Been too busy trying to teach the unteachable. You're trash at this. Who taught you how to play pool?"

"Nobody. Obviously. That's why I suck."

"A'ight, then what are you good at?"

"Um . . ." I hold on to the pool cue with both hands. I'm aware that I'm nowhere near as cool looking as Quincy when he does it, but I hope it's at least close. I still want him to think I'm funny and cool and fun to be around. "Avoiding all potentially awkward situations, sleeping—"

Quincy's laugh cuts me off. "I meant hobbies and shit like that."

"I don't really have time for those. Track and school keep me pretty busy." It hits me that Quincy is pressing me about this because he wants to know more about me and what I do outside of those two things. Because let's face it, that's really all I talk about when I'm with him. But I'm not really interested in anything else. "I could probably kill a plant by looking at it. That's how ungreen my thumb is. I like to swim, but I think I got banned from the YMCA for fighting with my cousin. And I'm a killer sewer but my grandpa doesn't let me do it anymore because he didn't like seeing me get hurt by the needle."

"Sewing? You're old as shit."

"I guess that's what happens when you're raised by an old man." I peep the way Quincy's jaw clenches, and I immediately start to feel bad. "Sorry. I'm sure you don't wanna hear about my grandpa all the time."

"I get it. He raised you."

I'm not a Quincy expert, but the way he said that last part sounded bitter. I place my pool stick on the table, knocking a few of the balls around, but it doesn't really matter. I was losing. "I'm gonna head out soon."

"Just like that?" Quincy asks.

"Well, what am I supposed to do? Never leave? It's two in the morning. I've been here for, like, three hours."

Quincy mumbles something that sounds like "That's not enough" and I feel my chest tighten. He crosses the basement in three long strides and starts heading upstairs. "Let me walk you out."

"I have to pee first," I say.

Quincy tells me that the main bathroom is upstairs. First door on the right. "Go ahead."

I practically run to the bathroom and burst inside after knocking twice to make sure no party stragglers were inside. Lena is sitting on the floor. I stammer out an apology that she completely ignores. Right as I'm considering holding it in until I get back to my auntie's apartment, I see the tears.

All the good Grandpa Joe instilled in me comes out. I can't think of anything comforting to say though. Lena might be my mother, but I don't know her at all. And she's clearly not okay. Nobody who's mentally sound cries on their bathroom floor. I would know. I do it all the time. "Um, should I . . . Do you want me to get Quincy?"

Lena looks up, kind of confused, like she's seeing me for the first time. She smiles, but it's more of a sad one than a happy one. "I didn't think you was ever gonna leave the basement."

"Quincy was teaching me how to play pool." I stand in the doorway clutching the doorknob, desperately trying to think of a way to make this situation less awkward. I can't come up with anything. And I still need to pee. This is a disaster. "Should I go? I should go. I'm gonna go."

"I got a question."

I freeze with my back to Lena. The universe is putting in extra work to make me feel as uncomfortable as possible. But as long as she doesn't ask me anything that'll force me to turn around, I'll be good. "Yeah?"

"Do you hate me for missing our lunch thing?" she asks. "Is that why you spend all your time with Quincy and not me?"

Crap. I turn around.

Lena's eyes are red and wet and filled with worry. "I know I fucked up, but . . ."

Great. There's a but. I'm never going to be able to pee.

"Quincy nearly lost a fucking arm, and he called me from the ER talking about how he needed surgery to repair it, and I forgot about everything except him. I didn't realize I had missed you until a couple days later, and by then I thought it was too late. Like I had missed my chance and couldn't come back from it, even if I had a good excuse."

"Okay."

"Don't tell Yo-Yo I said this, but she was right. I should've called and told you what happened."

"Yeah, you should've." As angry and hurt as I am about how Lena handled the situation, it's clear she's broken up about it, and I've never been one to keep kicking someone when they're already down. "I never hated you, by the way. I still don't."

"Then what is it? Because I'm going crazy right now trying to think of ways to fix this. I thought the note would help, but Quincy . . ." Her voice wavers and more tears fall and all I can think is that I really should've peed earlier. "He said you wanted to give it back."

She's putting this on me like it's my job to cheer her up when she hurt me. So what if I didn't want her card? Now I have to make her feel better about it? The cry she lets out makes me want to roll my eyes, but I just don't have it in me to be a jerk. I'm not built like that. "It was a nice card."

"Not nice enough apparently."

"Well, can you blame me for not wanting to take it? I hadn't heard from you in sixteen years. Not a call. Not a text. Nothing." I run down all the ways Lena has hurt me. "I thought you might try to talk to me when you were at the hospital, but you didn't want to. I saw you backing away from the room. I'm tired of being let down by you over and over again. It's the same thing every freaking time, but it's not like that with Quincy. If he says he's gonna do something, it's getting done, and that's what I need. Not your wishy-washy crap. Be reliable for once, and maybe I'll change my attitude. But if you can't do that, then I'll keep acting the same way."

"Wow. Okay." Lena applies pressure to the back of her neck, grimacing a little. "Can you sit down? My neck hurts."

I shut the door and lean against it with my legs outstretched to relieve the pressure on my bladder. "You never apologized. I didn't want a note or money or any of that. I just wanted you to say sorry."

"I'm sorry, okay? I fucked up, but I'm gonna do things differently from now on. I swear if you ever decide to let me in the way you're doing with Quincy, I'll be better."

"I guess we'll see."

"Really? That's all it takes?"

"I'm a very forgiving person. Ivy says it's one of my character flaws."

"I'mma sound biased, but I think it's a good trait to have." Sadness clouds Lena's features, and the small smile she flashes my way does nothing to convince me that she's okay. She shakes off whatever she's feeling and scoots closer to me. "I can't lie, I was hot when I heard how close you were getting to Quincy and his fathead friends. Like, the fuck? I'm your mother. I should be your favorite."

"You were jealous of them?"

"Extremely jealous. I swear I was about to fight that man 'cause he kept coming home talking 'bout how y'all was best friends and you loved him soooo much." Lena rolls her eyes. "He's so irritating. I don't know how you stand being around him."

"You're the one who's in a relationship with him. How do you do it?"

"It takes a lot of patience on my part."

"Can I ask you something?"

"Absolutely."

"What happened back then with you and him? I thought you two were broken up until I saw the picture you posted on Facebook."

Lena stares off to the side of me at the damp hand towel hanging on the rack. There's a tinge of sadness in her smile, and it makes me wonder what she's thinking about. "We broke up. Got back together. Broke up again. Moved to different states. Moved back here and reconnected. There were more breakups along the way. We've been on and off more times than I count, but we always end up together again."

"Do you love him?"

"I've never loved a man the way I love Quincy and believe me, I tried. He stresses me out more than anyone I've ever known. But I'd never wanna leave him for good."

"How long have you been together this time?"

"Three years." Lena lifts a brow, amusement tinging her expression as she taps me on the knee. "Quincy says you don't really tell him about the people you're interested in. Do you have a special person of your own or are you just focused on school for now?"

"Yeah. His name is Tommy."

"Don't be shy. Are y'all together or what?"

"It's complicated. Grandpa Joe hates him, and he was in this on-again, off-again thing with the most annoyingly toxic girl in the world up until recently, and she hates me because duh. I don't know if we're together because it hasn't really been discussed, and it might send my grandpa into cardiac arrest, but things are good with me and Tommy other than that, so I'm trying not to mess it up by making it official."

"Do you want it to be official?"

"I do," I say immediately.

"Then do it. Fuck my daddy and his feelings. He hated every boy I brought home to him no matter how respectful they were."

I don't know how or why, but talking to Lena is so natural. With Quincy, it was a little weird at first, but with her? It's like we've been in each other's lives this entire time. I wish I'd known it'd be like this. I wouldn't have iced her out for as long as I did if I had. "I didn't wanna make him mad."

"Neither did I, at first. I tried only bringing home what I thought were the most respectful boys in my school, and he still found something wrong with them. Eventually, I had to move on with my life and love who I wanted to love because there was no pleasing that man."

"You chose Quincy?"

"I did."

"And now you and Grandpa Joe don't talk. Do you not regret everything that happened?"

"All the time. I'm happy with Quincy, and I love him so much, but choosing him also meant I lost you, and I've never been able to get over that. I spent so many days hoping you were okay and wanting to see you again and thinking about the kind of person you grew into."

I kind of hate hearing about how happy she was with Quincy, even if she did think about me over the years. But thinking isn't enough. "You never came to see me. Never tried to take me back. You left, and it's nice to hear that you were thinking about me, but that's all you did. You just thought about me and didn't do anything actionable."

"I didn't know what my daddy had told you, or how you felt about me, or if you hated me for letting him and my mama take you. I was scared that if I came around, you'd reject me because I had one shot at being a good mother to you, and even though I didn't mean to, I fucked it up. I couldn't handle being a mom, and I nearly ruined you because I was too stupid to ask for help."

I haven't told Quincy that I know the truth about what happened because I don't think it really matters to him. He likes having me around now and isn't worried about the past. But Lena clearly is, and I decide to tell her so she doesn't waste time worrying that I hate her for what happened.

"My auntie and grandpa told me everything that happened not too long ago. She made sure I knew the reason why you didn't take care of me wasn't because you didn't care. You just couldn't help it. I'm not mad at you for that. But I'm not happy with the way things have gone between us, and I hate that you never tried to visit me. That's what I care about. If you put in an effort, then I will too."

Lena nods eagerly. Her hand twitches like she wants to reach out for me, but she holds herself back and I'm kind of glad. I'm not there yet with her, but maybe one day I will be.

"I will," she says. "Promise. And if you ever need a place to stay, feel free to come over. We'll always have room for you."

15

I have everything I've always wanted, yet I'm more miserable than ever before because the universe made a bunch of my wishes come true and then screwed me by taking away the two people I love most.

It's been easy avoiding Grandpa Joe during our fight. He's in the hospital and I'm busy with school and track, and even though I think about him every day, the hurt I felt has started to fade because I don't have to see him.

It's not the same with Ivy. Half of our classes are together, and we sit next to each other in most of them. Then there's track practices, meets, and invitationals. Mutual friends. Our lives are intertwined, and it was fine up until Grandpa Joe's stroke. Preferred, even. But this fight between us has festered to a dangerous level, and every attempt at talking has just made things worse.

"You look terrible," Jen says on the way out of our last class. "I'd ask if you haven't been sleeping or something, but I know that's not it."

"Quick suggestion, maybe don't immediately bring up something negative when expressing concern," I say.

"Noted. Ivy and I talked about your beef the other day."

"Since when did y'all become so close?"

"Don't change the subject. I thought we agreed you and her would squash this for the good of our relay team."

"Blame Ivy." She passes by me on her way out of the classroom, and I raise my voice so she can hear me over the crowd. Yeah, I'm instigating, but I'm sick of being the quiet one. Ivy gets to be loud and aggressive and mean, and I'm supposed to sit back and take it? Nah. "She's the one being an inconsiderate jerk who's holding on to a grudge that every other normal person has moved past."

Ivy stops in the middle of the hallway, back still to me. I can practically hear her loud thoughts. Uncle William isn't here to hold her back this time, so I brace myself for a visceral reaction. She turns on her heel and is on me in two seconds flat. I go flying into the wall, my head snaps back, connecting with the concrete blocks with a loud crack. Stars cloud my vision, but I don't let that, or the pain, stop me from whupping her butt.

I grab Ivy's shirt and, using the momentum I get from pushing off the wall, I throw her to the ground. I get in two hits. One to the stomach and another to the face before someone drags me off her.

Everything is hectic and people are shouting, and I still have no idea who grabbed me. They've got a strong hold on my waist, but I'm more focused on Ivy than whoever's behind me. She's got a busted lip, and the collar of her shirt is ripped. She could look a lot worse. I held back because as much as I hate her right now, she's still family, and I don't want to hurt her the way I hurt Sabrina.

"I'm so fucking sick of you making everything about you," Ivy shouts. "You're not the only one who's hurting, Aaliyah."

Her words drain all the anger out of me. But it's too late. Even though our fight was short, our English teacher still caught it and orders us both to go to the front office.

"I'm gonna let you go," says Jack from behind me. "Are you good?"

I shake him off me. "I'm fine."

"Coach is gonna be pissed," he says.

"I know."

It's the beginning of the week, and we've got three track meets coming up. One tonight. One on Wednesday. One Saturday. Ivy and I are going to miss the first one because there's no way we're not getting suspended. It's an automatic two-day suspension for fighting on school grounds. No exceptions.

Jen and Ivy are ahead of me, and she's got her arm looped through Ivy's. I can't tell if it's because they're so close now or if she's trying to keep Ivy from attacking me again. She doesn't need to bother. Mr. Turner hasn't let us out of his sight since the fight ended.

He tells us to hang out in the waiting room and goes into the principal's office to snitch on us. Jen takes Ivy to one side. I head to the other. I start thinking about who I'll call once I'm suspended. They won't let me leave without an adult, and since Grandpa Joe is the only person on file for me, I'll need someone else to come pick me up. Auntie Yolanda would be the most logical choice, but I refuse to sit in a car with Ivy after she attacked me the way she did. I text Quincy instead.

> **Me:** Are you busy?
>
> **Quincy:** Always. Ain't you supposed to be in school?
>
> **Me:** My cousin went Conor McGregor on me after school let out. I'm about to get suspended. I need a ride and a place to go once the principal kicks me out.
>
> **Quincy:** Omw.

There's a shift in the energy in the room once Coach Barnes storms in. He looks at Ivy. Then at me. Red in the face. Vein bulging from his forehead. Eyes all bugged out. I think he might be close to having a heart attack. "Come with me."

Coach Barnes doesn't bother knocking and walks into Principal Rodriguez's office like it's his. "I need these two in school. I don't care how you do it, but it needs to get done."

"We have a no tolerance policy—"

"I don't give a damn about the no tolerance policy, Veronica," Coach Barnes says. "These are two of my best runners. I need them to compete in our meet tonight, and they can't do that if they're suspended."

"You know that's not how it works," Mr. Turner says.

Coach Barnes jabs a finger at Mr. Turner. "Shut the hell up. This doesn't concern you."

"Calm down, Steven. I'm well aware of how important they are to the team. I walk past the trophies they've brought to the school on a daily basis, but I refuse to make an exception for them because of their status as athletes." Principal Rodriguez sits up in her chair, back rigid as a board. Here comes the punishment. "These two are the latest in a slew of incidents where physical altercations happened on school grounds, involving members of your team. I'm sorry, but I need to nip this in the bud, and the best way to do that is by making an example of Aaliyah and Ivy."

"Veronica . . ."

"They'll be serving a one-week suspension, effective immediately." Coach Barnes loses his freaking mind once Principal Rodriguez doles out our punishment. Even Mr. Turner chimes in and says it's not fair, but her mind is made up. She tells me and Ivy to go back into the waiting area and kicks Mr. Turner and Coach Barnes out of her office. Coach Barnes runs a hand down his face. He's gone from red to purple in the short time since he was kicked out.

Jen is the only one brave enough to approach him. She doesn't get too close and shoots a scared look my way. I shake my head, warning her against saying anything to him, but she doesn't listen. "You okay, Coach?"

He explodes like I knew he would. "Do I look okay?"

I get as far away from him as possible and sit on the floor with my back to the wall. It's super unprofessional, judging by the stank eye the secretary sends my way, but I don't really care about professionalism right now. I'm still trying to wrap my head around getting slapped with a one-week suspension. A full week for a fight that lasted ten seconds, all because the principal wants to make an example out of us. That's literally insane.

Coach Barnes snaps his fingers at Jen. "You. With me. We've gotta figure out who to add to the relay team while these two knuckleheads are suspended."

Jen stays back for a moment to say goodbye to Ivy, then she makes her way over to me. Nostrils flared. Lips pressed together. She's pissed. I brace myself for her wrath. "You're missing three meets at the end of the season. Everything's gonna go to shit while you're gone."

"I know," I say.

"No one on that team is good enough to replace you," she says. "We're gonna lose the relay and honestly, I'm probably gonna be the only one to win in the 100."

"What do you want me to say, Jen?"

"I don't want you to say anything. I want you and Ivy to fix your shit. It's not just affecting your relationship anymore. It's seeping out and infecting everything. It's ruining the dynamics of the team and it's fucking with our win streak." Jen gets right in my face, but I'm not mad about it because everything she's saying is true. God. I can't believe Jen is momming me right now. "I don't care how you do it, but it needs to get done, and quick. Got it?"

Coach Barnes pops his head back in. "Zhu!"

"Aaliyah?" she asks.

"Fine. Yeah. I'll try to fix things."

"No, you *will* fix things."

Jen and Coach Barnes leave soon after that. I meet Ivy's gaze across the main office, but I don't move to go to her, and she doesn't come to me. In my defense, I feel like if I got up, I'd be bum rushed by the secretary who's eyeing the two of us like she thinks we're about to start round two.

The door of the main office swings open twenty minutes later, and Quincy walks in with Uncle William right on his heels. I immediately start looking at anyone who isn't Ivy. I don't want to see her expression when she realizes I told Quincy to come get me.

"Ivy, what happened?" Uncle William asks. "I got a call saying you got into a fight. Don't tell me it was with Aaliyah."

"It was," the secretary says.

Okay. What is her deal? Is she bored or something?

Uncle William sighs. "All right, well, we'll discuss the specifics in the car. Yolanda's gonna . . . Jesus. I suggest you both prepare for a very long and loud talk with her once she gets home."

"Actually, 'Liyah's gonna be coming with me," Quincy says. "I'm taking her to my crib."

"That won't be necessary," Uncle William says. "She lives with us. She's coming home with us."

Quincy puffs out his chest and shoots a dagger of a look at Ivy. "Your kid hit my daughter. Ain't no fucking way she's going with you. Get over here, 'Liyah."

Protective Quincy is officially my favorite version of him. I push myself off the ground and head over to Quincy. I can't bring myself to look at my uncle. He's probably confused and hurt.

"It's just for a couple days until everything's not so fresh," I say. "I'll come back."

Quincy waits around long enough to listen to whatever Principal Rodriguez needs to tell him. Then he leads me out of the school and to his car, parked in the front lot.

"Suspended from school for fighting." The reprimand I'm expecting from Quincy never comes. "You more like me than I thought."

"This isn't a regular thing."

"This the second fight I'm hearing about. Sounds like a regular thing to me. Better had won too."

"It was a pretty short fight. But, like, obviously I won. She was the one with a busted lip and a ripped-up shirt."

"That's my girl."

He pulls me into a side hug that lasts for maybe a second, but the joy I feel because of it and how proud he sounds right now will keep me going for a lifetime.

16

Lena and Quincy give me some time to myself after school to unwind. It's odd that they're giving me space like this. If I were living with Grandpa Joe, there would've been an emergency family meeting called and forced apologies doled out from me and Ivy. But Lena and Quincy don't really speak to me until almost two hours after she gets home from work.

"Come in the kitchen, 'Liyah. I'm hands deep in a chicken." When Quincy said he was hands deep in a chicken, he wasn't kidding. His hands are covered with chicken crap and seasonings as he scoops out the inside of the bird. "Go through the cabinets and fridge if you hungry. Lena bought a bunch of weird healthy shit from the store on her way home."

"You did?" I ask.

"Don't sound so surprised," Lena says. "Quincy's not the only one who listens to you."

It's not that I don't think she listens to me. I was surprised she went out of her way to buy a bunch of food for me even though

I'm only staying here until I can figure something else out. "Thank you. Can I have something now? I'm starving."

"Go crazy," Quincy says. "That's all for you."

"Don't tell me that," I say, already rifling through their cupboards. "I'll eat everything up tonight and you'll have to buy more when I come back."

Lena glances at Quincy and he nods like they've had some secret conversation without using any words. She doesn't say anything right away. Just watches me pull a few granola bars from the box. "Can we talk for a minute?"

I look at her, then back at Quincy, quickly forgetting about my hunger. "Am I in trouble?"

"You're not," Lena says. "Come sit with me for a bit? Bring your food with you."

"Okay." I give one last look to Quincy, whose full focus is back on his chicken, and follow Lena into the living room. She sits on the couch, so I sit next to her with my snacks in my lap. "Is this about the fight today? Because I didn't mean to beat my cousin up, but she kinda forced me into it by hitting me first and I had to get my lick back."

"Baby, you're not in trouble. We know it wasn't you who started the fight, but I do want to talk to you about what's going on with you and your cousin. Quincy says you've been having issues with her for a while now. He thinks this fight was a long time coming and that it'll only get worse from here. I agree with him. Do you?"

I don't know. Do I? I never thought we'd get to a point where we'd be fighting in our school hallway, but we've never been in an argument for this long before either. The longest fight we've ever had was for three days because I told her "irregardless" wasn't a word. She called me annoying and told me to stop always correcting her.

"I guess I do," I say. "Every time we talk, things just get worse for us. I don't really know how to fix it."

"Maybe you don't need to."

"What do you mean?"

"I know you're still getting used to being around us and that I fucked up what should've been a good first impression, so I'll understand if you say no, but I hope you'll at least consider moving in with us."

"Oh."

"We've got an extra room, so you wouldn't have to share. Quincy says we're kind of far from your school and that your car is pretty busted—"

"Hey! She's trying her best."

"You gotta let that car rest, baby."

It helps that she managed to make me smile a little to throw me off before I start panicking. Moving in with them would be a big step, and I'm not sure if I'm ready for that. I don't really know what to say, so I don't say anything.

"Quincy says he can get you a nicer car, so you won't need to worry about yours breaking down on the way to school. And we'll buy you anything else you want. You won't have to worry about nothing when you're with us. That's a guarantee."

That all sounds nice, but I'm not sure whether I should move in with them given our family history. Choosing sides like this will definitely start a war, and I'm sick of fighting with everyone.

But I don't know if I can spend another second living with Ivy after what she did at school today, either. "Can I think about it and let you know what I decide by the weekend?"

"Yeah, of course."

17

Tommy has been more focused on school after our talk and spends most of his time at his dorm instead of at home. He invites me over the day after Lena asks me to move in with her and Quincy. I'm grateful for the chance to get away from the mess that is my life for a few hours, and because Tommy's roommate is gone, we have his room all to ourselves. On his side of the room, he's got a Chicago Bulls banner that goes across half of the wall and a signed Derrick Rose poster right next to it. His desk actually has books on it today, and one of them is even open because he was studying before I came over. Now I'm here and all I'm doing is distracting him. He doesn't seem to mind though.

"Hey, you should let me give you a facial," I say.

Tommy, visibly alarmed, says, "I don't think a girl can give a guy one of those."

"Oh, my God. I'm talking about a self-care facial, not a sexual one."

"And why should I let you give me one of those?"

"Because you like me and want me to be happy. Also, I told Lena and Quincy I was hanging out with Jen and that we'd be doing self-care stuff, so I need to pull from something real when they inevitably ask me how it went."

Tommy reluctantly lets me drag him off his bed and into the private bathroom. He sits on the toilet like I ask him to and ties a bandana around his head to keep his hair from messing up the mask. "Is this gonna hurt? 'Cause I've seen the videos, and it looks painful as shit."

"No, because I'm using a mask. Not a peel."

He grunts.

"Your skin is gonna look great. You'll love it, I promise."

"Yeah, yeah." He watches me as I take the products out of my bag, squinting at the facial cream jar like he thinks it's going to ruin his life. It's not hard to believe that he hasn't done a full facial before with his ex. Sabrina's face is always a mess. "What were you gonna tell me before I distracted you with sex?"

"Lena and Quincy asked me to move in with them."

Tommy jerks his head back. "What the fuck? Why didn't you tell me it was important?"

"Quit moving around. I don't wanna get this stuff in your eye." I dip a brush into the container holding the mask and spread it around his t-zone. "And maybe I wanted to have sex first and talk later. I kissed you, remember?"

"I must've forgot. Gimme another one."

I kiss him. It's nice having this time with him where we can just be alone without worrying about our families barging in on us and ruining the moment.

"Yeah, that does seem familiar. So, you gonna move in with them or what?"

"I don't know. What do you think I should do?"

"Well, you're always talking about how weird things are with you and Ivy. I mean, that's why you were at my house so much, right? Because she's acting like being in your presence is like this terrible, awful thing and she can't wait to get away from you."

"Don't throw it all together like that. You're gonna make me sad."

Tommy presses his lips to my stomach as an apology. "I just mean maybe some space would be good. She might drop it if you give her time to deal with whatever she's going through."

"What if she doesn't?"

"She will. You and Ivy are like familial soulmates or whatever. No matter what happens or how bad the fight is, you always end up making up sooner or later."

"It feels different this time. We've been fighting for more than a month, and she's not mad at me about something dumb. I hurt our grandpa and, honestly, if we switched places, I'd be just as mad as she is at me right now. It's not something you can get over. And, you know, she shoved me into a wall earlier this week. Am I just supposed to forget that? I could've gotten a concussion."

"Then I think you know what you've gotta do."

"Hold your head back." I put a hand in his hair, fingers gently massaging his scalp while I apply the mask to his forehead and cheeks. "I guess it couldn't hurt to stay with Quincy and Lena for a little while."

"Only go if you think they're gonna treat you right. I don't wanna have to go over there and start acting out because they hurt you."

"And what would you do?"

"I don't know. Something reckless." Tommy checks out his face in the mirror. It's covered with a white cream and makes him look like Michael Myers. He doesn't complain, so I assume he's okay with it. "You think they'll be able to handle having you there full-time?"

"I'm pretty self-sufficient at this point. It shouldn't be an issue."

"You've still got needs. Like emotionally. And they've gotta buy you food and shit. Make sure they're home if you need 'em. No crazy parties when you're trying to sleep before a big meet. You think they can change their lives to make you comfortable? Because if not, it wouldn't be worth it, you know?"

With Tommy listing things out, I realize I may be more high-maintenance than I thought. And if Lena and Quincy cracked when I was a baby, there's no telling how they'll react when I have actual real-world problems. "If it doesn't work out, I guess I can go back to staying at your house until my auntie forces me to come live with her again."

"They don't hate me like your grandpa, so I can sneak over sometimes to make sure you're good."

"He'll like you one day. I'll make sure of it."

"Don't even stress." Tommy boops me on the nose with the brush. "Already got a plan for that."

I don't think Tommy will do anything bad. I'm mostly just curious as to what he could possibly say to get on my grandpa's good side. It's not easy. I'm not even on his good side right now, and I'm related to him. "Should I be worried?"

"Nah, I got this. Now sit. It's my turn." Tommy starts brushing at random parts of my face with some areas having more of the mask on them than others. He clearly has no idea what he's doing, but he's making a genuine effort and that's enough for me. "Damn, Aaliyah. Your pores are fucking massive."

"Shut up. They are not."

"To be honest, I don't even what a pore is."

"They're little holes that release oil and sweat." I take his hand and guide it and the brush toward my nose. "Start here. Work your way out, up, then down."

For the first time in a while, Tommy seems completely at peace. He's got this cute little grin as he spreads the mask on my face, and the longer I look up at him, the wider it gets. I ask him why he's looking at me like that. I'm expecting him to make a crude or ridiculous joke, but he just says, "Thanks."

"For what?"

"For being different."

Anything I could think to say in response would come off as pretentious and maybe a little conceited. The truth is, it's not hard to be different from his ex and it's not like it's a goal of mine. I'm just being me. And with how much I question whether the people in my life want to be around me, I'm thankful every day that he's so open about liking who I am.

18

Uncle William is the only one home when I go back to the apartment to pack, and I'm glad that he is. Of the three, he's the least likely to flip out and the most likely to call in reinforcements once he loses control of a situation. That'll give me time to get out before Ivy or her mom show up.

"Hey there," Uncle William says from his spot on the couch. "Finally decided to face the music, huh?"

Before I came here, I told myself that I wouldn't lie. Now that I'm here though, telling the truth isn't so easy. I mean, how do you nicely tell someone, "I love you, but I hate living with you"? "Um, not exactly."

Uncle William follows me to Ivy's bedroom. He leans against the door frame, watching me pack up some of the clothes I brought from my house. "Everything all right?"

"Not exactly."

"Talk to me. Maybe I can help."

"You're not gonna like it."

"If you're worried about Yolanda being upset with you about the fight, I should tell you she isn't. We both know Ivy started it, and we made it clear that kind of behavior will not be tolerated. We also told her she needed to apologize the next time she saw you."

"I appreciate you both doing that, but I did kinda instigate the fight, and either way, it's . . ." *Come on, Aaliyah. Don't punk out now. Say what's real.* "It's too late because I'm moving out."

Uncle William pretends to fall and runs into the door by accident because he's dramatic. "Please don't say you're trying to move back in with Tommy and his family. That's all I'll hear about for the next month."

I stuff a few pairs of jeans into my bag, trying to fold them as small as possible to fit the maximum amount of clothes into it. I take a breath. I'm kind of scared of what he'll say when I tell him where I'm moving to. He doesn't have any strong feelings about either of my parents, but he may get upset on Auntie Yolanda's behalf. "Lena asked me to move in with her and Quincy."

"God, that's worse!" Uncle William throws his arms up, cursing as his hand smacks the top of the doorframe. "Damn it. Why would you tell me that?"

"Because you asked!"

"I didn't know that's the answer you'd give. I wish it was Tommy's family. That'd cause less chaos." Uncle William pats his front and back pockets. "Where'd I put my phone? I need to call Yolanda."

And here come the reinforcements. "You're calling her right now? She's at work."

"You can't tell me something like that and expect me to keep it close to the chest. She'd kill you for thinking it was a good idea, and then she'd kill *me* for not telling her the moment I found out. And as much as I love you and want to help however I can, I like being alive more."

The second Uncle William leaves to find his phone, I start throwing clothes into my bag as quickly as possible. Auntie Yolanda isn't a violent person, and she hardly ever yells, but there's a zero percent chance she's going to let me leave this place once she finds out where I'm going.

As I tiptoe down the hall, I keep an eye and ear out for my uncle. But he isn't in either of the main areas, so he must've found his phone in the bedroom. Because I don't want to come off as completely disrespectful, I type up a text to my uncle on the elevator ride down to the first floor.

> **Me:** Sorry I left without saying goodbye, but I didn't want to get held hostage by you and my auntie. Love youuuuuu. Don't be mad.

Then I send a bunch of orange heart emojis to soften him up.

> **Uncle William:** You suck.

I send him a GIF of a penguin running because what's cuter than a penguin waddling around? He texts me back a GIF of Nene Leakes saying "Proceed with caution" that is most definitely a threat, and I immediately shut off my phone because nothing good will come from having it on.

PART FOUR
APRIL

1

Tommy calls me while I'm getting ready for bed. It's past ten and I should be asleep, but the few bits of serotonin I have left increase exponentially at the thought of talking to him. That thought overrides the logical part of my brain that's telling me to let it ring, so I'm not a zombie at my invitational tomorrow. I answer the call.

"Look out your window." Confused but intrigued, I open the window and stick my head out. Tommy is standing by the tree closest to the house. He grins and holds up an arm like he's a prize. "Sneak me in."

"Can you scale the side of a house?" I ask.

"Normally, yeah, but I fell out of a car last night while I was drunk, and the doctor said I tore some ligaments or whatever in my shoulder, so I can't use my right arm. What are my other options?"

"Front door. Shouldn't your arm be in a sling or something?"

"Probably."

He doesn't seem too worried about not using a sling for his arm, so I drop it. I tell him to meet me in front of the house in fifteen minutes to give me enough time to butter up one of my parents.

Quincy is nowhere to be found, but Lena is curled up on the couch with the lights dimmed. The volume on the TV is low and the multicolored images reflect off her skin. And she's wearing glasses. Since when does she wear glasses?

"You look like you're up to no good," Lena says.

"Oh, yeah? Did your fancy little spectacles examine my body language?"

"Spectacles?" Lena's laugh is beautiful. It's light and airy and it kind of twinkles the way Tinkerbell's fairy dust does. I think she might actually be magic. "You're too much."

"In a good way?" I ask nervously.

"Of course."

"Cool. So, hey." I hurry over to the couch and sit on the cushion next to her with my arm resting on the back of the sofa. She mimics my position, and it sort of feels like we're at a sleepover telling each other secrets. "I have to tell you something, and I need you to be chill about it."

I don't have the same fear with her that I had with Grandpa Joe about this. It's freeing to ask if Tommy can visit without worrying about being fussed at.

"Tommy's outside," I say.

"It's ten o'clock."

"I'm aware of that. Can he come in?"

"I don't think you know how this is supposed to work, Aaliyah baby. You have to sneak the boy in without me knowing. Don't tell me what you're going to do. That defeats the purpose of the whole sneaking aspect."

"Well, I was gonna have him scale the side of the house, but that wasn't a real option, so I'm here because letting him come in through the front door is easiest. And I didn't wanna, like, disrespect you or your rules or anything because I'm starting to like living here, and I don't want you to kick me out. This way is better for everyone, don't you think?"

"If you say so."

"I do say so. So?"

She shakes her head. Her gaze drifts down and she blows out a heavy sigh. "I'm sorry. Every time you talk, I'm reminded of how well my daddy raised you and how you probably wouldn't have turned out half as good if you'd grown up with us. It's hard to admit, but with you living with us now, I realize I was never gonna be good enough because I don't know how to be. I would've ruined you."

"You're being too hard on yourself," I say.

Lena waves away anything else I wanted to say. The negative thoughts she has about herself and her abilities as a mother are valid. I think lots of parents feel that way. I want to tell her it's okay to not be perfect. That all I ever wanted was her in my life—flaws and all. But I don't think she'll believe it. "Go. Tell Tommy he can come inside."

"I can tell him we can hang out some other time," I say. "I don't wanna leave when you're . . ."

Any word I could possibly use will come out horribly, so I end it there.

"I'll be okay."

I'm kind of worried about her. It doesn't seem like she's doing very well with me being around more. Like my presence is a reminder of how much she's messed up over the years and it's breaking her heart into smaller pieces day by day. I'm not sure how to help, or if I'd only make things worse by bringing up what I noticed. I decide to just go by her word and hang out with Tommy like I'm supposed to. As soon as I open the front door, Tommy jogs toward me, grinning like he won the lottery. His smile gets even sweeter when he sees Lena. It's odd. He never really seemed to care much about her one way or the other, and now he's shaking her hand and acting like she's the queen of England all because, unlike my grandpa, she actually let him into her house. "Hey, Mrs. Aaliyah's mom."

"Hi," she says.

I tell Tommy I'll meet him upstairs in my room because I want to say good night to Lena, but really, I don't feel comfortable leaving her when she's so obviously going through some kind of mental issue. But I'm not sure how I should comfort her since this relationship is so new, so I come up with a quick way to make her feel better and hold up a hand.

Lena stares at it. "What are you doing?"

"Giving you a high five." When Lena doesn't react, I grab her hand and slap it together with mine. "You might not think you're doing a good job, but I do. You're trying. Right now, that's all I need. And maybe you won't believe me when I say it, but I think you're awesome."

"You're sweet," she says. "But you're only saying that because you don't know about all the mistakes I've made."

I don't know how to respond to that. Maybe those mistakes are making her afraid. I have the same fear. Everything is superficial in our relationship, and I don't necessarily like it, but I'm terrified of revealing anything too real. I would never say this to Lena—not because I don't want to hurt her—but because she's already let me go twice. Once as a baby and again in the hospital. I'm trying to get over it, but there are still times when I want to lock away all the worst parts of myself, so she'll never have to deal with the real me. I can't do that though. I need to trust her. I need to be honest.

"You're not a bad mother," I say. "You're flawed, same as me and everyone else on earth. There's nothing wrong with that. Sometimes people forget that making mistakes doesn't make you a terrible person if you have the right intent. You do."

Lena doesn't say anything, but she hugs me on the way to her room. I hold on to her a little longer than I should. I want to remember how incredible it was to hug my mom for the first time in my life.

2

A few minutes go by before I realize I forgot to ask Lena what the appropriate time for Tommy to leave would be. He stays in my room while I head to Lena's room down the hall. I raise a fist to knock but stop when I hear Quincy talking.

"Why'd you let that boy in here this late?" Quincy asks.

I immediately lower my hand. If Quincy isn't happy about Tommy being here so late, asking when he should leave could backfire. Maybe I should just let them come to me when they feel like enough time has passed.

"My daddy would never let a boy come over at any time of the day," Lena says. "I'm using this to try to sweeten her up before we break—"

"We're not breaking shit. She don't need to know."

"And if she finds out one day? She'll hate us forever."

"She won't find out if you keep your mouth shut. Just be cool. The only other people that know are my folks, and I got a plan for that."

It's an odd conversation and I can't make sense of it without context. What doesn't Quincy want to tell me? I thought I'd learned everything from Grandpa Joe and Auntie Yolanda, but maybe they only know their part and are just as oblivious to the full picture as I am? I need to figure out what that is.

I knock on the door and poke my head around it when Lena tells me to come in. They both look nervous, as if they think I overheard them. I did, but I don't want them knowing that, so I play it off. "How long is Tommy allowed to stay here tonight?"

Lena visibly relaxes. Quincy crosses his arms over his chest and says, "Y'all got three minutes."

"That's crazy," I say.

"Now it's two," he says.

"By the time I make it back—"

"One."

I turn to Lena because Quincy is being ridiculous and I'm not in the mood to deal with his nonsense tonight. He's hiding something from me. I mean, they both are, but at least she wants to tell me the truth. He's content with keeping me in the dark for a lifetime. "How long for real?"

"An hour," she says.

"Cool."

Quincy yells behind me that I need to keep the door open, and I tell him I will. Not because of any kind of respect I have for him or his house—because again, he's lying to me—but because when I talk to Tommy about it, I want to make sure I can see them coming.

Back in my room, and to Tommy's disappointment, the door stays wide open. I sit right in front of the door in a chair I grabbed from the living room while he sits on the bed.

"What's the deal with the awkward seating arrangements?" Tommy asks. "You pissed at me or something?"

I didn't think about how paranoid acting this way could make him. He probably had to deal with rapid mood changes and weird behavior from Sabrina all the time, and even though I know he knows I'm not like her, there has to be some residual fear left over from that relationship. I'll need to get better about that. Instead of trying to persuade him, I give him a quick kiss and sit back down. The worry doesn't leave him, but the color in his face comes back, so he doesn't look quite as sick anymore. "I'm trying to make sure they can't eavesdrop," I say. "I heard something weird while they were in their room."

"Damn it," he says. "I was hoping I wouldn't have anything to report back."

His comment tears my attention away from the door. "Report back to who? About what?"

"Jen asked me to check in with you because she said Ivy said that her mom said she was worried about you living here, and since you weren't answering your phone, she thought something might've happened."

"How could something have happened? I just got here."

"I was told it was because they don't have the best track record when it comes to you. Joe apparently freaked out when they told him about you moving in." Tommy quickly adds, "He's all right. Just upset, but your aunt talked him down. It probably would've been easier if you returned her calls."

The fact that even during our biggest fight ever, my grandpa still has it in him to care about my well-being means a lot to me. And neither of them seems to hate me for the decision I made. They're just worried about me. "I was afraid of what she'd say if I talked to her. I thought she might be mad and try to force me to move back in."

"I mean, she still might."

"Well, I wouldn't need to be here if Ivy hadn't hit me."

"Don't worry, I can fix this. You and Lena seem pretty tight. How about I report back everything is chill here, so they're less freaked and won't try to drag you back to Ivy before you're ready? In exchange, you've gotta tell me about the weird thing you overheard."

"Only if you promise not to tell anyone. That includes Jen."

"But we tell each other everything."

"I'm not ready for anyone to know yet. It could be nothing."

"You obviously think it's something. Spill."

"Promise you won't tell Jen."

Tommy rolls his eyes and puts a hand to his chest. "I promise I won't tell Jen until you tell me it's okay."

I don't necessarily want to worry him because it really could be nothing, but maybe I should worry. If it wasn't bad, they would've told me. Right?

"I accidentally snooped on them, and they're hiding something from me. I'm not sure what it is. Lena seems to want to tell me, but Quincy is against it, so it must be bad, right? I mean, the only reason she let you come in tonight is because she thinks it'll sweeten me up. Maybe it's the paranoia in me talking, but that sounds catastrophic. Why else would I need sweetening?"

"What could be worse than your grandpa disowning Lena at her time of need?"

"It doesn't have to be about him. It could be something unrelated."

"Maybe they tried to give you up for adoption before your grandparents took you, but they couldn't go through with it and now they're embarrassed and scared to admit it."

I guess it fits. Quincy's parents would probably know about something like that, and it would be pretty bad, but bad enough for them to believe I'd hate them forever if I knew? I doubt that. "I already know they weren't the best parents. I'm kinda over that now."

"Plot twist. Quincy's not your real dad. They secretly did a blood test and just found out, and now they don't know what to do because this whole time he's been acting like your dad when he really isn't."

"Tommy, if you're not gonna be serious—"

"This is me being serious."

I ignore him because his ideas are going to get crazier and crazier, and it'll cause me to spiral with all the possibilities. I need to focus on what's real. "Quincy said his parents know. I could try to talk to them."

"Do you have their number?"

"No."

"Luckily, I'm here and can help you with that." He checks the hallway to make sure they aren't listening, then leans forward, all excited. "So, here's what you're gonna do. Hang out with Quincy one on one and sweeten *him* up. Ask him about his family once

you've been hanging for a bit. It's important you don't act suspicious because if he thinks you've got ulterior motives, he's not
gonna want to give you the number. Pretend like you just wanna
get to know his parents better—because you're missing your
grandma Dee—he'll feel like shit about keeping them from you.
Once he gives you the number, ask about the secret, and *boom*.
You've got your answer."

"That's surprisingly not a bad plan."

"What'd I tell ya? I'm the king of plans."

Tommy's ego aside, he's right about one thing. The best way
to learn is to go around Quincy and speak with someone who has
no stake in this. One of his parents would be the best person to go
to, but to do that, I need a way to contact them, and he's the only
person who can give that to me.

3

I wait a few days before enacting Tommy's plan. If I were to ask the very next day, that might come off as suspicious. But three days later? Well, that's just a coincidence. I tell Quincy on Saturday night I want to spend some time with him, and he lights up. If I weren't suspicious of him and his motives, this could turn out to be another nice moment for us, but I'm on a mission. I can't let myself become distracted.

Quincy goes over to his fridge and shows off all the groceries inside. He starts pulling out food items with this satisfied look on his face. "Check this out. Got you more of your rabbit food, so I can start making special meals for you."

"That was nice of you," I say.

"Ay, what can I say? I'm a considerate dude. Wanna help me out? I can teach you a thing or two."

"Sure." Despite my best efforts to pretend like it's no big deal, I can't help the excitement buzzing through me and start grinning like a total dork. Usually Grandpa Joe ends up doing all the cooking himself because, in his words, I "don't know what I'm doing." To his credit, I never did, but he didn't need to point it out. "What do you want me to do?"

"Clean the veggies and chop 'em up. I'll get the pot boiling and make the sauce for the lasagna." Because I must look awfully pitiful chopping up all the different kinds of peppers he's laid out, he shows me how. He puts the tip of the knife to the cutting board and rolls it back, letting it smoothly slice the green bell pepper into a thin sliver. "Tip to heel every time. Go slow, so you don't chop your finger off."

I do what he says, and things go a lot better. Grandpa Joe should've explained it like this instead of yelling because I didn't read his mind. "How'd you learn how to cook?"

"My pops worked as a chef for thirty years. Moms was gifted. Learned what she could from her grandma and all the stuff my dad showed her, then she taught me everything she knew." He nods at the fridge while he stirs the red sauce in the skillet. "Get yourself something to drink if you want. No beers though. I don't need Lena yelling at me about getting you drunk."

I can't believe Tommy's plan is actually working. This is the first time Quincy has mentioned his side of the family, and it didn't really take all that much effort to get it out of him. I decide not to press the topic just yet, and quickly come up with a way to tiptoe through this without him becoming suspicious. "She cares that much about me drinking?"

"Yeah. She said she didn't want you turning into an alcoholic like the ones on my side."

"There's alcoholics on your side?"

"Just about everybody." Quincy must not see the irony in the situation when he asks me to hand him a glass so he can pour out some whiskey from a bottle. He takes a sip, then turns the oven on to preheat. "Was kinda hoping Lena's genes overpowered mine when it came to you."

"Were . . . or are . . . your parents alcoholics too?"

"They were, but they got sober."

I do my best to act casual and lean against the countertop like Quincy. Him sipping on his whiskey, me sipping on my water. I rack my brain, trying to figure out a way to slip in that I want to speak with his parents without him becoming suspicious as to why. "Are you close with your mom and dad?"

"We used to be."

"What happened that you aren't anymore?"

Quincy narrows his eyes. "Why do you wanna know, nosy?"

Be cool, Aaliyah. You can do this. Just follow Tommy's plan. "I don't know. I guess I'm just fascinated by the fact your mom is still alive. Grandma Dee has been gone for a while now, and I'm starting to forget what she sounds like. It'd be nice to have some memories with your mom since I won't be making any more with Lena's."

He sighs. When he finishes his drink in a single gulp and immediately pours another glass, I know he's stressed. He always does that when he's stressed.

"It's okay if you can't talk to her right now. If you give me her number, I can call her myself."

"Nah, it's all right. If you really wanna meet her, I can arrange that."

I tell him it's no rush, but secretly I'm hoping he does rush. This is my opportunity to kill two birds with one giant stone—I'll finally be able to speak with my grandmother and find out what Quincy and Lena are hiding from me. I just have to wait for Quincy to arrange it.

4

Grandpa Joe is the first one to crack after more than a month of us both being stubborn. He tells Auntie Yolanda he wants to see me, and I go to his rehab center the first chance I get. As disappointed in him as I was, I can't deny how much I've missed him, and he clearly has missed me too.

He's nowhere near as grumpy as he usually is. He smiles when I walk into his room and even though his words are still slurred, I can understand most of what he's saying. "C'mere, kiddo. Got something to show ya."

"He's been practicing since your last visit," the nurse says.

I take my usual spot in the chair next to his bed. "Let's see."

Grandpa Joe's nurse picks up the pop can on his dinner tray and hands it to him. He grabs the cup with both hands. Then he goes a step further and drinks using the straw. No mess. No pop dripping down his shirt after spilling from his slack jaw. He beams at me. "Not bad, huh?"

I lose my freaking mind, yet all I can do is lay my head in his lap and cry. After everything he's gone through, after watching him silently cry, unable to move or speak because of the stroke, I can't hold it in anymore. I didn't think he'd ever get to this point again. I hoped, God I hoped, but I wasn't sure.

Grandpa Joe rubs my back. "Let's walk. Might help calm you down."

As much progress as Grandpa Joe has made since early February, he still has a long way to go. He tries to act like our walk around the unit of his rehab center doesn't tire him out, but it's obvious it does. He's moving slower than he was when we started, and he has a tight grip on my arm for support. Rather than letting me direct the conversation to his health status, he brings up Tommy of all people.

"That Thomas boy came to see me."

"He did *what*?"

"Showed up outta the blue. Came to me like a man and broke it all down. Cursed too much though. I didn't like that."

I'm genuinely terrified. I can't tell if my grandpa likes the fact that Tommy came to see him or if he's upset. Does he like Tommy now? Does he hate him more?

"Yolanda told me what you said about him," Grandpa Joe continues. "You want me to like him 'cause you like him. He told me the same thing."

"I tried so hard to stay away from him."

"Why?"

"Because I didn't wanna lose you. We had so many rough patches this year. Too many, in my opinion, and I didn't wanna upset you by continuing to do things I know you didn't like. I had already pushed it too far with Lena. Being with Tommy started to feel like it could be the last straw."

"Didn't mean to make you feel like that. Like you had to be unhappy to make me happy."

"I want things to be okay with us."

"We'll be good. Date him if you want."

"But I thought you didn't like him."

"Don't. But you do and that's fine with me."

It's like the pressure that's been weighing me down these past couple months has been lifted. Grandpa Joe's blessing means so much to me, and the fact that he's given it after despising Tommy for the better part of a year? Man, that's everything. "And it's the same for my parents?"

"Guess it has to be. How's your mother?"

I keep hold of his arm as I help him walk in circles around the unit. "She's okay. I mean, I'm assuming she is. I don't really know her or Quincy well enough to determine when they're good and when they're not."

Grandpa Joe's breathing is a little too ragged for me, so I cut our walk short and take him back to his room to let him rest. "He treating you right? Gonna mess him up if he ain't."

"Everything's . . ." The word *fine* is on the tip of my lips, but I can't bring myself to get it out. The truth is, everything isn't fine. It's obvious they're hiding something from me and hoping I'm too stupid to figure out what it is. But if I tell Grandpa Joe that, it'll just make him upset and mess up all the progress he's made. I refuse to be the reason why he gets sick a second time. "Everything's okay. It was awkward in the beginning, but he's warmed up to me. I kinda like being around him now. He's a mechanic like you were. I haven't asked him to help me with my car though. Feels weird, since that's a me-and-you thing."

"I'm all right with him fixing your car."

"Since when do you want Quincy to help me with stuff?"

"Want you to be safe. Even if he's the one making it happen." Grandpa Joe grunts and moans as I help him back into bed. He's able to do a lot more to support his weight, enough so I don't call the nurse in to help. She comes in anyway to reset the alarms they've put on his bed because, apparently, he thinks he can do everything for himself now that he's mobile and keeps getting up to use the bathroom in the middle of the night. "Thought about what you said, though, and you're right. I shouldn't have thrown Lena to the wolves like that. She was too young. Wasn't right of me."

It's as much of an apology as I'm going to get from Grandpa Joe. He's the kind of guy who's insufferable when he's right and downright rude when he's not. He'll tell you to "go to hell" before he apologizes, which makes the talk we had very special. Knowing how much it took for him to even get the words out is enough for me, so I give him what he's hoping for. Forgiveness.

5

Unsurprisingly, Tommy gives Jen the address to my parents' place, and she gives it to Ivy, who gives it to Auntie Yolanda. Ivy and my auntie show up a couple of days after I see Grandpa Joe, intent on doing a wellness check even though Tommy told them I was fine. I guess I'm not surprised they didn't believe him, but it kind of sucks that they showed up when I had plans to question Quincy about setting up a meeting with his mom.

The tension in the air is palpable when Auntie Yolanda and Ivy storm into Lena's house like evil space cops in those Star Wars movies. Normal Aaliyah would be stumbling over her words and talking nonstop to lighten the mood, but I don't want any attention on me right now. Quincy slipped down into the basement sometime during their arrival, and I wish I'd gone with him because I don't want to be up here either.

"Aaliyah," Auntie Yolanda says.

"Hey, Auntie," I say back.

"We need to talk," she says.

I'm not sure if she's talking to me or Lena or if she means we should all talk together. Her gaze stays on Lena while Ivy hangs back behind her mom, and I use it as an excuse to dip before things get hectic. "This feels like a stay-out-of-grown-folks'-business type of situation, so I'mma go to my room."

No one tells me to stay. In fact, neither of them looks my way. I doubt they even heard a word I said, which is fine. I'm perfectly happy to be ignored. I feel immediate relief when I'm alone and pick up my phone to send a text to Tommy.

> **Me:** Ivy and my auntie just showed up. A WWE match might be starting soon. I had to hide. Come save me!
>
> **Tommy:** fuuuuuuuuuuuck gimme like 30 mins

I notice Ivy hovering in the hallway outside my room. She turns her head when I look at her like it wasn't totally obvious she was just staring at me. I sigh because I know if things between us are going to be fixed, it'll be up to me to fix them. "Are you gonna come in here or stand in the hallway like a weirdo until it's time for you to leave?"

She strolls inside and starts walking around like everything's normal. Like we aren't chest deep in the worst fight of our lives and our entire relationship isn't being held together by that thread the Fates use in Greek Mythology. "This is a wack room."

There's nothing on the walls, compared to my actual room that has pictures and posters all over it. I barely have any clothes hung up in the closet because most of my things are still at home. The room is bare for a reason. "It's temporary. The room is supposed to be wack."

"You sure? Because it's starting to seem pretty permanent. You're living in their fucking house, Aaliyah. How is any of this temporary?"

I could argue with her, and scream, and start another fight, and put the nail in the coffin when it comes to us and our relationship. Or I could be the bigger person. I could see things from her side even though she's been refusing to see them from mine for months. It's what Grandpa Joe would want me to do. It's what he did for me and him, and I'll always love him for that because he saved us.

"I've been thinking about you lately," I say.

"Have you?" she asks in an almost hopeful way.

"No. Not really."

"Fuck you, Aaliyah."

"I mean, I'm here because of you, so you were always in the back of my mind. But I tried not to think of you consciously because it was easier to deal with everything if I kept you off my mind as much as possible. And I was doing . . . not okay, but I was trying to get better after what happened, and now you're here and . . . I don't feel good about it, because I don't know if you're gonna start being an a-hole to me again."

All the anger and sadness and guilt I've been holding in for months comes pouring out of me in the form of a word vomit, and I know I sound crazed, but I can't stop talking. Not until Ivy really knows how I've been feeling since the moment I realized I was at fault for Grandpa Joe's stroke. Because it was my fault no matter what people say. I should've been there for him, and I wasn't.

"After you started punishing me, I didn't have anybody to talk to. Not really. Because everyone I know knows you and they all kept saying the same thing—that everything would be fine between us soon enough. But then the days turned into weeks, then months, and nothing was fine. It was so much worse than before. I was drowning, Ivy, and you were the one person I thought would save me. You were the only one who could do it and you just..." I inhale a shaky breath and wipe away the thick, hot tears streaming down my cheeks. It's no use though. They keep coming. "You abandoned me. I've been so lonely and sad and anxious without you around to set me straight. I only went to my parents because I felt like I didn't have anyone else to rely on. It's nice being around people who actually like me and yeah, things are weird and complicated, and feelings have gotten hurt, but we're all trying to work through it."

I plop down on my bed, completely exhausted after doing absolutely nothing. "I was tired of being alone, and I had to do something to keep me going, otherwise I'd be right back to how your mom found me after Grandpa's stroke. Confused and unclean and depressed to the point of obvious concern. So I'm sorry you're upset, but I did what I had to do. I won't apologize for that, and I shouldn't have to."

"I knew what I was doing, and I knew how it would make you feel," Ivy says matter-of- factly. "I just didn't care."

"That's not making me feel any better."

"Sorry. I'm still trying to get out of the 'be an asshole to you' phase I've been stuck in." Ivy sits next to me, and instead of keeping her distance the way she has been since our grandpa's stroke, she's close enough that I can feel the heat from her body on mine. "Grandpa yelled at me the other day and said I wasn't being fair to you. Then he told me the story about what happened. About how he was the reason why you weren't being taken care of when you were with your parents and how he disowned Lena when she needed him the most."

"And?"

"That was a pretty fucked up thing for him to do."

"It was."

"I shouldn't have said that Lena and Quincy didn't love you."

"No, you shouldn't have."

"I was hurting just as much as you, Aaliyah, and you never asked how I was. Not even once. Everything was all about you, and I felt like since you didn't give a shit about me, then I shouldn't give a shit about you either. And yeah, that was probably the wrong way to handle it, but it's what made me feel better."

Ivy's confession makes me feel like crap. As cruel as she was, she was right to be mad at me. I let her down just as badly as she let me down because I wasn't there for her. "Are you okay?"

"No." Ivy hangs her head. Her breathing comes out ragged and heavy, shoulders shuddering like all that anger she's had brewing inside her is traveling through her body right now. "I fucking *hated* you and I didn't know how to deal with those feelings because I'd never felt them toward you before. The whole time it seemed like you didn't care that our world was falling apart. You didn't listen when we told you to drop the thing with Lena, and what happened? It nearly broke you into pieces, and Grandpa had a stroke. Then you started hanging with Quincy even though you know how Grandpa felt about him, and it just felt like you were setting yourself up for another disappointment, and I just . . . I couldn't help you through it again. I was still exhausted from the last time. I couldn't sit by while you refused to listen to reason, and I couldn't let you hurt Grandpa again."

I don't know what Ivy wants me to say. I feel like anything I could come up with wouldn't be good enough. Obviously, if I'd known then what would happen, I wouldn't have tried to meet with my parents. If I could go back and do things differently, I would. But life doesn't work that way.

"Still, it wasn't right of me to treat you the way I did, no matter how mad I was," she says. "I'm *so* sorry. Can you forgive me?"

"Of course." I pull Ivy into a tight hug, and she doesn't complain or anything when I mumble, "I missed you," into her shoulder.

"God, you're such a sap." There's the Ivy I know. But when she leans away, she wipes away a few tears. She totally missed me back. "I still don't like that you're here, but Grandpa says he's okay with it, so I have to be too."

I refrain from telling her what I told Tommy a few days ago. She'd go running to her mom and Grandpa Joe before I even knew what Quincy and Lena were hiding. But after all the lies I was told by my grandpa, and all the secrets Quincy and Lena have been keeping from me since I reconnected with them, I've realized something—Ivy is the one person in my life who has always been straight with me. Even if I didn't want to hear what she said, she's never been dishonest, and in a world full of liars, I need someone like her on my side.

"I think you should know that I'm sorry for ignoring your feelings. I should've checked in to see how you were doing, but I was so stuck on the fact that I nearly killed our grandpa, I lost perspective for a while."

"Aaliyah, come on. You didn't almost kill him. He's never taken care of himself the way he should, and he gets mad about everything. Eventually, something else would've pissed him off and he would've gone through the same thing. And FYI, you shouldn't be hard on yourself because you saved his life that night. It doesn't matter that you weren't there leading up to it. It just matters that you were there to help him when he really needed it."

I never once thought of it like that. The doctor said the same thing that night at the ER. I remember that vaguely in my mind, but I never took it to heart because I was too busy blaming myself for not being there for my grandpa. He's alive because I was there when it counted. Hearing Ivy say that after what we've been through means so much more to me.

Since everything between me and Ivy is okay now, I text Tommy and tell him he doesn't have to come. I don't need him to rescue me anymore.

6

After months of drama and headaches, everything in my life has come together. I finally have everything I've always wanted—a relationship with my parents, and Grandpa Joe and Ivy on my side despite some understandable resistance. Tommy and I are . . . something. But the one thing I thought was a given, I can no longer have, and that's on me.

I talked with Coach Barnes about it. Had him call the coaches at UCLA and tell them that I can't come to their school anymore. I know it's what's right. I can't be that far from Grandpa Joe.

When he was only kind of sick, I told myself that he'd be okay with me over there and him here because he was healthy enough and I knew I'd see him on the holidays. But now? With what happened to him and the part I had in it? I wouldn't be able to live with myself if I left him here. The thought of not going to UCLA still kills me though. Instead of my parents, it'll be my biggest *What if?*

Coach Barnes approaches me and pulls up his pants as he squats in front of me. "Time to go home, Campbell. Meet's over."

I'm aware of that, and yet I'm still sitting in the middle of the track field by myself in spite of it. As spectators and participants of the meet slowly file out of the field area, I spot Tommy waiting for me on the track. Of course he'd still be here. He's always here. For a good while, he was the only person I could count on.

"Still thinking about UCLA?" Coach Barnes asks.

"I'm bummed about it," I say.

"Losing UCLA isn't the end of the world, kid. Might seem like it is now, but eventually you'll see that things went the way they were meant to. I lost out on going to LSU after I tore my hamstring. Had to take some time off and never got back to what I was, but it opened the door for me to become a coach, and that's what I really love."

"Where am I supposed to go if it's not UCLA?"

"University of Chicago is still interested."

I scoff. "That's a D3 school."

"You'd be a good fit there, and with Sullivan and Zhu already committed to the school, you wouldn't have to start over. You girls have four years of chemistry built in and ready to go for the relays. I'm not saying you've gotta go. Just consider it. It'd be a shame for somebody with your talent to drop the sport, even if you can't go to your dream school."

I nod and he pats me on the shoulder before leaving me in the middle of the field, but I'm still upset. My dream is falling apart, and I had a hand in that. Despite what Auntie Yolanda says, I know that if I hadn't been so stubborn and stayed away from Grandpa Joe, I would've been there when he started having trouble. I could've seen the signs. I could've helped him. Forced him to see reason and go to the doctor. They might've been able to catch the stroke before it even happened, and I'd still be planning on starting a new life in California. Instead, I'm here, contemplating going to a D3 school.

Tommy bounds across the field once Coach Barnes leaves, checking over his shoulder as he comes closer. "He yelling at you about something again?"

"Coach Barnes doesn't yell. He speaks loudly and with passion, and no. He told me I should give the University of Chicago a shot since I'm not going to UCLA anymore."

"That'd be sick." He sits in the grass next to me, knee brushing against my own. "Imagine you still running with Ivy and Jen. Me cheering you on from the stands. It might not be UCLA, but at the end of the day, it doesn't matter what school you're at. You're gonna kill it wherever you decide to go."

"It's not about that. It's about my college plans falling apart before I had a chance to actualize them, and I know what you're gonna say. It's not that bad. I still have options, but even if my grandpa didn't need me, I don't know if I wanna go to a school that's not UCLA."

"But you love competing. You're not gonna feel good if you skip out on running next year."

"You think I should commit to the University of Chicago?"

"I don't think anything. Jen told me that as your guy, I've gotta step up and do something to stop you from making a huge mistake. I told her I didn't wanna do that 'cause you can make your own decisions, so she said she'd give me twenty bucks if I said what she told me to."

Of course Jen bribed him to talk to me about college. She loves forcing Tommy to get into my business. "As my guy?"

"Yeah." He glances over at me nervously. "I know we haven't talked about it, but I figure . . . I mean, you beat the shit out of somebody for me. That's gotta mean something, right?"

"I think it does. Are you comfortable with us making things official?"

Tommy doesn't answer right away, and I think that means that he isn't. Not fully anyway. It makes sense. Even though Sabrina hasn't attempted to contact him since I gave her a two-piece, he's still dealing with the trauma that comes with being in an abusive relationship. His brain is still in fight-or-flight mode, and it doesn't matter how nice I am or how I gently I touch him; he's been trained by Sabrina to think that something bad is always around the corner. It takes time to get over that, and it's been nowhere near enough time for him.

"I trust you and I wanna be with you in an official kind of way," he says carefully. "But I'm scared. Can we take it slow?"

"Of course. You tell me what you wanna do, and we can do it."

"Wanna get some food? You can ask me all about the University of Chicago and decide on if you'll go based on how awesome I make it sound."

I don't see myself going to the University of Chicago, but I'll gladly listen to him talk about it if it means I get to spend time with him. "Sure, Tommy."

He pops up from his spot and holds out his hand for me to grab. He's a lot more relaxed now that he knows I'm cool with taking things slow, and I feel good knowing that I'm not making him uncomfortable by pressuring him into something he doesn't want. He wants to be with me. We make each other happy. That's really all that matters.

7

It's been a couple weeks since I asked if I could meet Quincy's family. He hasn't made much of an effort to contact them and only talks about them when I bring them up. I wouldn't normally push, but as more days go by, the urge grows stronger, and Tommy takes it upon himself like six times a day to tell me to quit being a chicken.

I'm not afraid of Quincy. If I were, I wouldn't have agreed to live in his house. I *am* worried he's suspicious about my motivations and is putting off contacting his mom to keep me from learning something, though I can't tell whether that's a normal fear or my anxiety making my thoughts less rational again. I get another text, this time from Ivy asking me if I'm good, and I ignore it like all the others tonight. I'm on a mission to get some kind of contact info for Quincy's mom. I'll worry about responding to all the calls and texts I've missed later.

Quincy is on the other side of the pool table, lining up his stick to sink a striped yellow ball into a side pocket. "You're getting better."

"I have a good teacher," I say.

Quincy doesn't say anything in response, but he smiles. He knocks the ball in with ease and does a lap around the table, scanning it to find his next shot.

"Um, can I ask you something?"

"Don't gotta ask if you can ask a question. Just ask."

"Right. Sorry. I just, um, wanted to make sure you were okay with me asking a question. I don't wanna bug you too much, but the more I think about it, the more excited I get. So I guess I was wondering if you'd had a chance to call your mom yet. I'll be getting busy soon because of finals and State, and I'd rather meet her while I've got free time."

"Haven't."

His response is so short and dismissive that I wonder if he's mad at me, but that can't be right. I haven't done anything to him. I figure maybe he's in a bad mood or something and take a soft approach. "Oh. Okay. Well, do you know when you'll be able to do it?"

"I'll do it when I do it."

It's not really the answer I was hoping for, and I'm a little lost for words. He's being weird, and it's not his usual weirdness either. I can handle that type of weird, but this? This is something else. "You don't even have to do anything. Gimme her number. I told you I can call her myself."

Quincy tosses his pool stick on the table and leaves the basement. I don't immediately follow him because I'm shocked he's acting like this. What the heck is wrong with him? He's being a jerk for no reason. Instead of leaving it alone the way he clearly wants me to, I storm upstairs and find him in the kitchen downing a glass of Hennessy like it's water. He doesn't speak to me. He barely even looks at me.

"What's wrong with you?" I ask. "I just wanna meet my grandma. I don't know why you're turning it into this big, awful thing that can't be mentioned. You're the one who said I could talk to her. If you didn't want me to, you shouldn't have let me get my hopes up."

"I only told you what you wanted to hear," he mutters.

I see red. I never curse, even though there are times when I really want to, because I always feel like I can get my point across without being disrespectful. But right now? Oh, I'm ready to blow up. I take a deep, calming breath and do my best to remember my manners. "I really hope you're not saying you told me I could meet her to appease me."

"Appease? The fuck does that mean?"

"You lied to me so I'd leave you alone. Not cool, Quincy. Extremely not cool."

"I ain't apologizing for it."

"I don't care about an apology. I want an explanation. Why'd you lie?"

Quincy pours himself another drink and gulps that one down too. He slams the glass on the countertop, sending the remaining liquid splashing across his hand. A crack slices through the glass until it shatters. He ignores the blood dripping down his hand and pain I'm sure he's feeling and glares at me. "Fuck it. You wanna get into it, then let's get into it. I don't want you meeting her at all. You're my fucking daughter. Not hers. And I ain't letting her swoop in so she can poison you against me the way Joe tried to do."

"Oh, my God. Selfishness is the excuse you're going with? Really? You can't hold your mom hostage because you're afraid she might tell me something negative about you."

"Yes, the fuck I can."

"I want her number."

"No."

It's rare that I'm angry to the point of wanting to hit something, but Quincy is bringing it out of me slowly but surely. I walk right up to him, shooting a death glare his way. "Give it to me."

"No fucking way," says Quincy, pointing a thick finger at me.

On instinct, I slap his hand the same way I would if I were fighting with Ivy. "Don't put your hand in my face. It's rude."

"Ay, watch who you slapping." Quincy grabs both of my hands, smearing blood on them, and holds on tight when I try to yank them back. I push all my weight forward, bumping into him hard enough that he lets go of me. He matches the acceleration of my rage, nostrils flared, and lunges at me with that same finger pointed at my face. "You're a spoiled-ass brat, you know that? Don't come at me 'cause you didn't get what you wanted. That's not how the world works."

"How are you turning this around on me? You lied!"

"People lie every day. Get the fuck over it."

"Hey! *Hey!*" Lena comes flying in from out of nowhere and puts herself between me and Quincy. She looks at him, then at me. Neither of us offers an explanation for what happened. "What the hell is wrong with y'all?"

Being around him is only going to aggravate me, so I storm out of the kitchen and slam my bedroom door behind me. It's something I'd never do at Grandpa Joe's house, but I wouldn't have gotten into a screaming match with him either.

8

I can't even rest in my room because of how livid I am. Quincy thinks blatantly lying to me is going to fly. Well, it ain't. I know why he's really being like this, and I'm no longer believing his lies. I spend the next twenty minutes pacing while ignoring the texts and calls from my friends and family coming through on my phone.

I don't want to talk to anyone, but with where I'm currently living, I know if I don't respond to the messages, I'm going to have a lot of people barging into the house to make sure I'm okay.

My phone is under the bed and the screen is cracked because I'm an idiot and chucked it at the hardwood floor with all my strength. I wipe off bits of glass, straining to read the names displayed on the screen between the cracks.

Tommy. Jen. Ivy. Auntie Yolanda. Uncle William.

The flow of worry from the time of the first text until this very moment is obvious. Tommy tried texting me this morning because he wanted to hang out. When I don't respond, Jen sends an "Are you okay?" text. She talks to Ivy, who talks to her parents, and now I have five worried people blowing up my phone at eleven o'clock at night. I have a decision to make. Who should I respond to?

I cut on my music to drown out the shouting coming from the kitchen and stare at my phone. Jen and Tommy are both terrible choices. They'll immediately clock that something's wrong, and if I tell them I got into a fight with Quincy, they're going to arrange a ridiculous hang out session to "protect me." But I know if I tell Uncle William or Auntie Yolanda, they're going to remove me from the house. Willingly or unwillingly. I settle on Ivy because I think I can convince her to keep what happened a secret.

Me: Quit blowing up my phone. I'm fine.

Like I knew she would, Ivy FaceTimes me almost immediately after the text is delivered. She stares at me through the screen, eyes narrowing at whatever it is she's seeing that she doesn't like. "Which one of your goofy-ass parents made you mad?"

"I'm not mad," I say.

"Just because we didn't talk for a while doesn't mean I can't still tell when you're lying."

"Fine. I'm mad, but I can't tell you why."

"Why not?"

"Because you're gonna tell your parents, and I don't want them to know. They're gonna turn it into a whole thing, and I want a break from things tonight."

Suddenly, I'm looking at the carpet in Ivy's apartment. She's back a minute later with the pictures lining the walls of her bedroom behind her and her AirPods in her ear. "What happened?"

"Me and Quincy got into a fight. He said some things, and I said some things, and then Lena showed up and had to jump in the middle of it. The whole thing was messy."

"Did he put his hands on you?"

"Not in the way you're probably thinking."

"Aaliyah—"

"Calm down. I'm fine."

"I'm coming over. Don't fall asleep."

I end the call and jump onto the bed when there's a knock on my door. Lena comes in after I tell her it's okay. And thankfully, she's alone. "I'm not apologizing," I say. "I was right to be mad at him."

"I didn't come in here to make you apologize. I wanna help you see things from his point of view. We know this—you living with us—is temporary. You're gonna have your bags packed, ready to move back in with my daddy, the second he leaves the hospital. That's a hard thought for us to hold on to, and it was even harder when we told you you could stay here, knowing you'd be gone soon."

I settle back into the pillows propped up against the head-board. "You're saying it like you won't ever see me again. I'll still be around."

"It won't be the same."

"I don't know what you want me to do. As much as I like being with you here, it still isn't my house. I don't belong here. I'm a guest. And I don't mean to hurt your feelings by saying that. It's just how I feel."

"That's the problem. We don't want you to feel that way." Lena pops a leg up and tucks it under her thigh. "We want you to stay here with us."

"You think I'll want to stay here after what Quincy did? He lied right to my face, and he's still trying to keep me away from his mom on purpose. It's mean and it's not fair. I'm not living here full-time if he's gonna keep lying to me."

"He's never gonna tell you this—too much pride—but he's afraid of losing you again. The thought of never seeing you again scares the shit out of him, so when you asked about his mom, all he could think of is you being taken away by my parents and poisoned against us. He doesn't want the same thing to happen with his."

This must be about the secret. What else could cause Quincy to react the way he did? And now here Lena is trying to clean up the mess and soften me up like she said she would. Well, it won't work. I won't let them trick me into believing everything is fine when it's clearly not.

"I don't care how he feels," I say. "It's not right of him to keep me from my grandma the way Grandpa Joe kept me away from you. I don't want another eighteen years to go by with me not knowing her."

Lena looks hesitant, twisting her lips as she glances between me and the door. It's like she's wrestling with her thoughts and doesn't know if she should support me or Quincy. "I'll see if I can convince him to give you the number."

As Lena is leaving, I sense a sadness settling over her. But this time, I can't bring myself to care. "Neither of you can lie to me anymore. This is it. Your last chance to tell me everything is today."

Lena doesn't look at me when she says "Okay."

9

Ivy must've gone 150 mph the entire way here, because she makes it to Quincy and Lena's house faster than what should be humanly possible. She's waiting for me at the front door and bumps me out of the way in her rush to put eyes on Quincy, who's sulking in his recliner in the living room. Lena chewed him out a second time after she was done talking to me, so he's had an attitude ever since.

Quincy meets my eye and purses his lips, nonverbally voicing his displeasure with me. I return the look, and he goes back to watching TV. No one speaks to Ivy, and Ivy doesn't speak to them. This is a disaster. No wonder I'm still miserable. We're supposed to be family, and everyone hates one another.

To keep the peace, I don't let Ivy stay in the main section of the house for too long. Lena's and Quincy's tempers seem to rival Ivy's, and with the three of them in the same enclosed space together, the blowout would be colossal. I make sure Ivy is in my room with the door closed, then meet up with Lena in the kitchen. "Thanks for letting her come over."

"I didn't have much of a choice," Lena says.

"Are you mad? You seem mad."

Lena tosses her dishrag into the soapy water and turns around to face me. She might not actually be mad, but she's certainly not happy. "I don't get it. Weren't you crying about her being a dick to you like a second ago? Didn't she attack you and get you suspended from school? Now y'all are besties again?"

"We made up."

"She made you cry."

"Everyone I know has made me cry, including you and Quincy. It's not that serious."

"It's serious to me. She treated you like shit for months." Lena points in the direction of my room, jabbing her finger at the air. "She's the reason why you had to come live with us. She made you miserable."

"That's how we are. We fight a lot and sometimes it gets ugly, but then we talk it out and everything goes back to normal."

"I don't like it."

"You're my mom. Of course you don't like it." I stand next to her at the sink and drop a hand on her shoulder, a grin threatening to overtake the sort of grumpy expression I've been sporting since the fight with Quincy. "And as your daughter, it's my job to ignore whatever you say if I don't like it."

"Is that what you do with my daddy?"

"I'm here with you right now, aren't I?"

She looks over my shoulder and keeps her eyes trained on the hallway. "I'm gonna give you the number, but you can't tell him I did."

"I won't say a word."

Lena sends a text with a contact called Mama Shirley with a purple heart emoji. Her next text just says I'm sorry, and now I'm extremely concerned as to what I'm going to find out from Quincy's mom. I want to question Lena, but what would I say? "I eavesdropped on you when you were talking about a deep, dark secret, and I wanna know what it is"? Yeah, right.

Instead, I ask, "Are you okay?"

"Trying to be," she replies.

"What are y'all in here whispering about?" Quincy asks.

I'm back to being grumpy. Quincy matches my irritation in his own way, choosing to drink excessively instead of using healthy coping techniques. He's blocking my path out of the kitchen, and all it does is anger me more. I could be nice about it. Say excuse me and make myself small enough to scoot past him, but I don't want to be polite because he's pissing me off.

"I'll be in my room," I say.

Quincy has plenty of time to move out of the way. He doesn't though, because he's annoying. I approach him and he slowly turns his body sideways to give me room. He kicks out his foot at the last second and trips me, and I retaliate with a quick pop on his shoulder. He tries popping me back, but Lena rushes forward and knocks his hand away.

"Both of y'all need to cut that shit out now," she says.

Quincy chugs the rest of his drink and goes to get a refill. "She started it."

"Shut up," Lena says. "Go, Aaliyah."

In my room, Ivy is reclining on my bed like it's hers. She makes room for me and puts her phone down, which definitely makes me feel like I'm a priority to her. It's nice to feel that way again. "What took so long?"

"Lena wanted to give me a word of caution about you, and Quincy wouldn't get out of my way." I lie on my stomach facing Ivy with a pillow clutched in my arms. "Other than the fight earlier, it's not so bad living here. They let me take as many naps as I want, and there's always food to eat."

"You're easy to please."

"I'm a simple girl."

"What did y'all fight about?"

"I don't wanna get into it."

"Well, I've gotta say something. My mama is already suspicious 'cause of how quick I left the apartment. She knows it was because something happened to you over here and she's already planning on talking to Grandpa Joe about you moving back in with us."

"Aw, man. You told her that?"

"I had to give her something. She wasn't gonna let me leave if I didn't."

"You didn't have to come."

"Yes, I did."

Arguing with Ivy when we just got good again is a horrible idea, so I don't bother. If she thought she needed to be here, then she was going to come, and nothing would've stopped her.

"Aaliyah, tell me what happened."

Ivy's stern but soft side only comes out in dire times. The fact that she's using it now means she's actually worried about me. She already thinks the worst of my parents, and with the news of my fight with Quincy lingering over us, she's probably thinking something horrible happened, and I'm too scared to tell her about it. I guess I kind of am. Not because of what I think Quincy will do to me, but because of what she might do to Quincy. I decide to give her something—not the whole story, just enough to ease her worries.

I hold up my phone with Lena's texts displayed on the screen and show Ivy. "This is the reason for me and Quincy's fight. He and Lena are hiding something from me, so I figured I'd be able to learn more from his mom, but he refused to give me her number. Lena just did and told me not to tell him."

"And she said she was sorry?"

"Yeah."

Ivy settles back against the headboard with her arms crossed. She asks to see the text a couple more times, then falls back into silence as she mulls it all over. After a couple of minutes have passed, she says, "That's bad."

"I know. I'm kinda scared of what his mom will tell me."

"Call her."

"Ivy, I just said I was scared."

"Quit being a chicken and make the call."

I'm so happy I have Ivy back in my life properly. She doesn't let me go back and forth on whether I should call and when and what I should say. She just tells me to do it, and that's the kind of pressure I need. She stays right by my side when I make the call and gives me a thumbs-up when I leave a successful voicemail, asking if Shirley will call me back and explaining who I am to her. Then she talks me down when my nerves start to spike after I hang up.

The rest of the night is filled with her trying to keep my mind off of what Shirley will say if she returns my call. She tells me vague things about her crush, and it makes me hate how much I've missed in Ivy's life over the past few months. But then I remember the alternative is not knowing at all, and I choose to be grateful I'm finding out now and won't have to spend the rest of my life wondering.

10

randpa Joe summons me to his rehab facility the next day. Ivy delivers the message while I'm in the middle of smashing some pancakes Lena made for breakfast. She went crazy in the kitchen. Fluffy pancakes, waffles, the freshest, juiciest fruit I've ever tasted, biscuits, and bacon and sausage for her and Quincy. Ivy leaves without eating, so I take her portions and add them to my second plate. I thank Lena for breakfast and quickly get dressed. As I'm about to leave the house, Quincy jumps in the way and blocks my path again.

"What's your problem, dude?" I ask.

"I ain't no dude," he says. "I'm your father."

"Fine. What's your problem, Father Quincy?"

Quincy cracks a little, but the smile doesn't last. He folds his arms across his chest and stares down at me. "Where you going?"

"To see my grandpa, nosy." I slip past him quick enough that he doesn't have a chance to move over and block me. He trails me as I walk toward my car parked by the curb. "And quit following me."

"Don't walk through my grass."

I stomp the rest of the way as payback for him bugging me, hop into my car, and prepare to drive off, but Quincy taps on my passenger-side window to get me to roll it down. "Yes, Quincy?"

"You doing something later?"

"Probably not. Why?"

"I'mma be chilling with Jaz and Craig all day. They been asking about you."

"Is that an invitation?"

He shrugs. "Guess so."

"Our fight is over then?"

"If you want it to be."

The *no* is already prepped and ready to go because I've still got an attitude with him. Then I think about what I could potentially gain from a visit with Quincy's friends. Since I haven't heard from Shirley, this could be a great opportunity to dig for more information while I wait for her call. "I'll meet you there."

Quincy pats the roof of my car and backs away, but he doesn't go inside yet. I asked him once why he always waits until I've driven off before going back into the house and he said, "You never know what could happen." He isn't all bad. That's something I need to remember in the future when he inevitably gets on my nerves again.

I pop the driver's-side door open and stand with half my body still in the vehicle. "Thanks for fixing my car, by the way. I really appreciate it."

He nods, then I'm gone. I take my sweet time getting to my grandpa's rehab facility. Not because I don't want to see him, but because I know he heard about my fight with Quincy and he's going to talk trash about him nonstop. This is going to be a long visit.

Auntie Yolanda is on the phone outside Grandpa's room, talking a mile a minute to someone I'm assuming is Lena because she mentions me. I manage to dip into his room without her seeing me, though I almost wish I'd taken a second to wave or something, because the tension in the air is unbearable.

My grandpa is shaking as I sit in the seat by him. The bed is actually rocking with every vibration, and I swear I see anger waves coming off him when the light from outside hits him just right.

"So, you're mad . . ."

"I sure the hell am. I told you—"

"Maybe don't get yourself all worked up while you're in recovery. I'm okay, see?" I show myself off, patting my arms, chest, stomach, and legs so he'll know I'm not lying. Then I sit back in the chair and take my grandpa's hand in mine. "Calm down. You're gonna hurt yourself."

"Can't be calm when you're in danger."

"I'm not in danger. Quincy and I had a fight, but we squashed it before I came here."

Grandpa Joe grunts. "Bet ya he did that so you wouldn't come in here spilling your guts and making him look bad. Manipulate. That's all he does."

"Grandpa—"

"Don't make no excuses for that boy. I known him longer. I know what he's like." Grandpa Joe turns into a grumbling mess and starts moving around in his bed. Because he's still a fall risk, his bed alarms go off immediately. "Where's my clothes? Nurse!"

"Grandpa, what are you doing?"

"Getting out of here. You coming back home with me. You'll be safe there. Nurse!"

His nurse flies into the room and rounds the bed so she's on his other side. "Is everything all right, Joe?"

"He's trying to leave."

Yeah, I snitched. But he's going to ruin all his progress if he discharges himself before his doctors say it's okay, so I feel like snitching in this instance isn't a bad thing.

"I'm going home," Grandpa Joe says.

"Dad, sit down," Auntie Yolanda says from the doorway with her phone still up to her ear. "Your doctor hasn't cleared you yet."

Grandpa Joe refuses to be reasonable, and soon enough, three more nurses who aren't assigned to him plus his doctor are in the room trying to calm him down. I end up being escorted out by security because he keeps yelling my name, and it becomes clear to everyone that I'm the reason he's agitated.

I'm still outside Grandpa's room when Auntie Yolanda joins me. She's no longer on the phone and forces out a smile, but I have a feeling she's about to say something I might not want to hear, so I speak up first.

"Why'd you tell him about the thing between me and Quincy?" I ask. "He's in there freaking out over nothing."

"Is it nothing?" Auntie Yolanda asks. "Because according to Ivy, it didn't seem like nothing."

"She was being dramatic. And Grandpa Joe didn't need to know about it."

"He's your guardian. If something's wrong when it comes to you, he deserves to be told."

Auntie Yolanda shuts down my protests with a shake of her head. "I think, just to give him some peace of mind, it's best if you sleep at our place tonight. I already ran it by Lena, so you don't have to worry about her being upset."

Even though his door is closed now, I can still hear Grandpa Joe shouting as his medical team attempts to calm him down. That's the main reason I agree to go home with my auntie after I'm done spending time with Quincy and his friends. For obvious reasons, though, I don't tell Grandpa Joe or Auntie Yolanda that that's why I can't go straight to her apartment.

11

It's been a few days since I left a message with Quincy's mom asking her to call me back. But just like when I reached out to Lena at the beginning of the year, thoughts of Shirley ignoring me plague my mind. And the confusion and anxiety I have about the secret only makes it that much worse. To ease my mind, I decide on another approach.

The only reason why I agreed to spend time with Quincy and his friends on a Friday night is because of the opportunity it presents me with. Craig and Quincy are often so distracted with each other and the copious amounts of weed they smoke that it should be easy to get Jaz alone for long enough to ask her about what Quincy is hiding from me.

Craig lets me and Quincy into the apartment after I spend almost two minutes knocking on the door. His scowl switches to a large grin when he sees it's me. He hugs me and daps up Quincy. "I was wondering when I'd see you again."

He sees Quincy all the time, so I assume he's talking to me. "I was just here the other day."

"Yeah, but you had to leave all early 'cause of your track meet." Craig makes his way through the living room and collapses onto the far end of the couch. "How'd that end up going?"

"I came in first in all my events." Normally I'd love to have a conversation about the meet and all the fun I had when I won, but today I'm on a mission. "Is Jaz here?"

"Yeah, she's in her room," Craig says, pulling a Backwood out of the package to roll. "Go say hi if you want. She ain't doing nothing but watching TV."

Since I have permission, I head to the back of the apartment where Jaz's room is. The door is open and she's lying in bed with the remote in her hand. I almost feel bad about interrupting her peace. Almost. But my desire for the truth overpowers how uncomfortable I feel at disturbing her right now. I knock lightly on the door and wave. "Hey, uh, sorry to bother you when you're getting in some relaxation time. Craig said it was cool if I said hi."

"More than." Jaz hops out of bed and hugs me like she hasn't seen me in years. "How'd your meet go?"

I smile when she brings my track meet up without me having to mention it. She and Craig are good like that. They care about my track meets because I do. They remember the things I tell them even if I haven't seen them in a while. "It was good. I almost broke a school record with my relay team."

"Of course you did. You're a track star."

Jaz's smile is so unbelievably sweet and genuine that just the sight of it calms me. Not enough that I'm not still worried about the radio silence from Quincy's mom, but I'm a little less anxious in Jaz's presence.

"Quincy says you'll be running at UCLA next year. You should hear the way he talks about you when he's with me and Craig. He's so proud of you."

I wish this news had come before the issues with Quincy popped up. The me before our fight would've loved to hear about how he bragged to his friends about me. But the me now couldn't care less. "I'm actually not going to UCLA anymore."

Her smile falters a bit. "Mind telling me why? He said it was your dream school."

"It was. I mean, it still is, but it's just not a viable option." I hang my head. The realization that I'll be giving up on something that I truly love doing hits even harder now because I'm only a few months out from the fall semester starting and I have no real plans. "My grandpa is sick, and he's gonna need someone to take care of him while he recovers."

"You don't seem happy about it."

"I'm okay. It's just, running is my favorite thing to do. I love competing, and it sucks that I won't be able to do it because I was too stubborn to listen to what people were telling me."

Jaz pats the spot next to her and I sit on the edge of her bed. "What do you mean?"

"For years, my grandpa told me not to bother with Quincy or Lena and I didn't listen. We got into a fight and because of that, I wasn't really around for a while. If I had been there, I would've noticed the symptoms of his stroke and could've gotten him help sooner. Now he's stuck in rehab and all my plans are falling apart."

"Well, I don't know Joe all that well, but if he cares for you the way I think he does, he probably won't be happy about you throwing your life away and blaming yourself for what happened to him, right?"

"He'll be pissed."

"That means you're not doing the right thing, baby."

"I don't know what else to do. My auntie was talking about putting him in a nursing home. All the places around us suck. They don't take care of their patients like they're supposed to, and I'm not gonna continue on with my life while he's miserable. That's not right either."

"I think there's a solution to this that you're not seeing yet. If I were you, I wouldn't give up. You applied to other schools, didn't you?"

"Yeah. The other schools should be sending letters out soon, and I found out not too long ago that I got accepted to the University of Chicago."

"That's right around the corner, and I'm sure they have a track team. You can make your own schedule in college, so you'd still have some flexibility to help your grandpa. It's something to think about."

Jaz sounds so optimistic about it that some of it bleeds over into me. The University of Chicago seems doable the way she's explaining it. Maybe I don't have to completely give up on college. It'll be hard. I might have emotional breakdowns throughout the year from the stress of it all, but maybe I could make it work.

"If I can't convince you, then maybe Quincy can. Come on. Let's go talk to him about it."

"I'd rather not."

Jaz is already at the threshold, but my words stop her from leaving the room. She spins on her heel and watches me for a moment before shutting the door. "What's going on?"

"I don't know. It could be nothing."

"You obviously think it's something."

"He and Lena are keeping something from me. I called his mom because I thought she could tell me what it is, but she hasn't hit me back yet, and it's stressing me out."

"I'm not sure how much Quincy's mom would know." Jaz returns to her bed and sits next to me. "They don't talk much anymore."

"Why not?"

"Their problems started back when Lena's parents took you. Shirley wanted to keep in touch, but Quincy refused to give her and his dad your contact info. He felt like if he couldn't see you, then neither could they, and Lena stuck by him like she always does. It took a few years before they moved on from that. Then one day, Quincy stopped bringing them up and wouldn't respond if me or Craig asked about them."

"He never hinted at the reason why they stopped talking?"

Jaz shakes her head. "Craig and I planned on asking Lena, but she disappeared on us for a long time, and we sort of forgot about it. I figured they'd broken up, until Quincy told Craig that they were looking at apartments together. I still don't really know what happened."

"Aren't you curious about it?"

"I used to be. But I learned a long time ago that if Quincy doesn't wanna talk about something, it won't get talked about, so it's best to leave it alone."

I check my phone like it'll have a missed call from Quincy's mom in the Notification Center that I didn't see. Of course there's nothing there, and maybe there never will be. Maybe she forgot about me and all my voicemail did was bring up bad memories. Maybe his mom isn't interested in talking to me after all these years. "I can't just leave it, Jaz. I have to know the truth."

"Shirley's never been much of a phone person. I doubt she's changed since I knew her."

"Do you know where she lives?"

"Her and Quincy's dad owned their house back in the day. They might still be there."

Jaz provides me with the last known address of Quincy's mom. I already promised Auntie Yolanda I'd go to her apartment immediately after leaving Jaz and Craig. And tomorrow is the last track meet of the season, so I won't have time to go to the address now. But if I don't hear back after this weekend, I may have to pay Shirley a visit sometime next week. Hopefully she hasn't moved.

Thanks to Jaz, I got a lot more information than I ever anticipated getting. Between the fight with Quincy and his parents and Lena's random disappearance, the picture I have is even less clear now. What happened all those years ago? And why does Quincy refuse to talk about it? Could it be that bad? Could it change the way people view him, and that's why he's so determined to keep it a secret? And what part does Lena play in it all?

12

I spend the rest of the night after I leave Jaz and Craig's place worrying about whether Shirley will call me back and what she'll say if she does. Or if she never calls, that I'll be forced to go to the address Jaz gave me. What happens if she hasn't lived there in years? Then what will I do? Try to forget about it like Jaz? I don't know if I can.

By the time morning rolls around, I'm dead tired from lack of sleep. I'm aware that I can't afford to miss the last track meet of the season, especially with the qualifying meet right around the corner, so I drink a Pepsi on the ride with Ivy to the host school. It's nowhere near enough caffeine, but it's all I'm allowed to drink. Grandpa Joe banned me from having energy drinks years ago because he said they're bad for my heart, and I never questioned him on it.

Ivy and I kill it in our individual events and spend the time before our relay together on the small visitor bleachers across the field from where the rest of our team is. She's watching me more than she's watching the boys run their 4x200-meter relay. I don't complain because it's been a while since she's looked at me with concern.

"Aaliyah, I'm sorry, but you look like shit," Ivy says.

"Hey, guess what. Just 'cause we're cool doesn't mean you get to start doing this crap again."

"I'm simply being honest."

"You can keep your honesty. I know how I look." I'm fully aware I look a mess today after the sleepless night I had and that I'll only look worse as the day goes on. The only good thing about it is that Tommy won't be here to see me in my current state. "I was too busy spiraling to get proper sleep."

"Yeah, and it was annoying. Just call her again if you wanna talk to her so bad."

"I'm not gonna call her twice in less than a week. She'll think I'm crazy."

Ivy rolls her eyes and snatches my phone from me. She holds it out of reach as I try to grab it back, then elbows me in the gut and claims it's an accident. She's got plenty of time to locate Shirley's number while I'm doubled over in pain. By the time she hands me back my phone, Shirley has already answered the call.

"Hello?"

I freeze. Everything I had planned on saying to Shirley left my brain the moment she said hello. I wanted this, and now when I'm faced with an opportunity to speak to her, I can't think of a dang thing to say. What is wrong with me?

This time Ivy for sure elbows me on purpose and says, "Say something, girl."

"Um, hi." I clear my throat. "Is this Shirley? Shirley Matthews?"

"It is," she says. "May I ask who's calling?"

She sounds so nice compared to Quincy. I guess I expected her to sound like him. Super rude with a hint of a Chicago accent. But the voice on the other end is sweet like sugar and a little Southern like my grandma. Is she from the South or does she just sound like that? "Sorry. My name is Aaliyah Campbell. I'm Quincy's daughter. Your granddaughter. Um, I left a message, but I don't think you got it."

There's a brief pause, then she says in the same pleasant tone, "Oh, honey, I check my voicemails once a year, if that. I'm glad you called again."

"Yeah?"

"Of course. I've gotta say, I'm happy to hear from you, but I'm shocked you're calling. Last I heard from Quincy, he said you were off somewhere with Lena's parents and he hadn't spoken to you."

"We recently reconnected." It's odd speaking with Shirley. The only grandmother I've ever known was Lena's mom. I never thought I would be talking to one of Quincy's parents. Ever. This moment feels almost surreal in a way. "Quincy doesn't really talk about you. I had to get your number from Lena."

"That boy loves acting like we don't exist. I can't say that I blame him. In his mind, we should've been around more. Helped him and Lena take care of you because her parents refused to." Shirley sighs and I can't help but think how even her sighs sound lovely. "I hope you believe me when I say we tried our hardest to do right by you, but Quincy's father got sick, and I had to spend so much time and energy helping him that you three slipped through the cracks. I always blamed myself for not doing more."

"But if you did everything you could—"

"Oh, we certainly tried that first year. Bought you all the diapers, and food, and toys you could ever need. Eventually it became too much with his father's medical bills on top of that. Next thing we knew, you were gone. I always wondered how you were doing."

"I've been good. My grandparents treated me well."

"Oh, Quincy's father is going to be so happy when he hears that. We worried so much about you, but we never knew who to call, and with Quincy refusing to talk to us, we just had to settle with hoping nothing bad had happened to you."

She sounds relieved. Like she thought the worst had happened to me all those years we were separated, and she's only now okay because I've told her that I'm all right. I can't believe Quincy let his pride keep him from providing her with information about me. Even if he didn't know how I was then, he knows how I am now, and he didn't bother to tell either of his parents that I was back in his life. How could he think that was okay?

Ivy bumps me with her shoulder and points to the track. It's almost time for our relay to start. I know I have to go, but I still have so much I want to say to Shirley, and I have even more questions to ask. I hold up a finger to tell Ivy that I'll join her, Jen, and Chloe in a minute. There's still one more question I need to ask.

"If it's all right with you, we'd love for you to join us for dinner sometime," Shirley says. "I'll fix you up something good."

"I'd love that." A home-cooked meal sounds real nice, and from my own grandmother at that. Tears well up in my eyes. It's been so long since I had one of those that I'm starting to forget what it was like. "I don't mean to cut our talk short, but I have an event starting soon and I need to get back."

"Oh, of course, honey, don't let me hold you. I hope to hear from you again soon."

"I'll definitely call when I'm free." This is it. My chance to find out the truth. I hope she can give me what I need, but if she can't, that's all right too. It was nice to talk to her either way. Hear her voice and learn a little more about the part she played all those years ago. "I just have one more quick question and then I'll let you go. Jaz told me you and Quincy had another falling out after I'd already been taken. Can you tell me why?"

"Well, in short, it was because of your brother."

I blink rapidly, caught off guard. It takes a few more seconds before I register her words. "My brother?"

"Yes. Quincy expected us to take on the bulk of care for him because, in his words, he and Lena were 'too busy for a kid.' When we refused, he cut contact again. It wasn't right of us, but at the time—I mean, they'd just lost you not long before that and now here they were doing the same thing all over again. We had to stick to our guns. Let them know that their behavior was unacceptable and that was the only way we knew how."

My chest feels tight. Suddenly, it's hard to breathe.

"I know you said you have to go, but I'd love to speak with him if he's there with you. Make sure he's okay too. He's what—a few years younger than you, right? And you must be at least sixteen or seventeen. Or maybe a little older. I get my dates all mixed up." Shirley laughs. "Sometimes I forget my own age."

This can't be right. Grandpa Joe would've told me if I had a brother. Unless he also didn't know. Shirley did say he was younger than me. If that's true, maybe nobody knew.

"Of course he's more than welcome to come over for dinner," she continues.

The words I wanted to say get lodged in my throat. My lips are stuck together like they've been glued, and I feel like tape is under my butt, keeping me in place. I have to move. I have to say something.

"I don't know anything about having a brother," I croak out.

It's quiet for a moment. Then Quincy's mom says, "Oh, my. I had heard through the grapevine he was taken and just assumed . . ."

I don't want to believe Lena and Quincy had another kid. They wouldn't have kept something like that from me. But then I remember how Quincy lied about setting up this meeting. How he refused to give me his mom's information because of his own insecurities. How Lena apologized when she gave me Shirley's number. Jaz telling me about Lena's mysterious disappearance after I was taken. The second fallout Quincy had with his parents. It all leads to me having a secret brother. "I'm sorry, I need to get ready for my race."

I end the call abruptly. This isn't something I can handle right now. Maybe not ever.

13

"**C**ampbell! Focus up."

My relay has started, and I have no idea how I missed the gun going off. The first leg is already coming up quick on the second. Chloe holds out her hand carrying the baton as she gets closer to Jen. The exchange is flawless. Jen hits top speed seconds into her leg, leaving the other girls behind, struggling to keep up. She passes the baton to Ivy, who's a little slower, but we have a good lead thanks to Jen and Chloe.

I miss part of Ivy's run because I can't seem to focus on anything outside of Lena and Quincy's son. My brother. My brother. My brother.

It doesn't seem real, no matter how many times I repeat the words in my head. Coach Barnes tells me to get on the track when I'm slow to join the girls from the other school. I need to focus on the race. Not my brother. Not Quincy. Not Lena.

Ivy is already in the hand-off zone, so I start running with my hand outstretched behind me. As I tighten my grip around the baton, it slips through my sweaty fingers, and I drop it.

The baton clatters to the ground, and so does my dignity. I've never dropped the baton in a race. Ever. By the time I recover, we've lost our lead, and I cross the line in third place. *Third*. We might as well have lost.

Coach Barnes does his best to hide his anger, which means he's bright red, but he doesn't show any outward expression otherwise. He doesn't speak either. Probably because he knows he'd let out a stream of curses if he did.

Me, on the other hand? I go crazy. All the anger and confusion and sadness I'd tried to keep under control reaches a boiling point. I don't congratulate the other team. I barely look at Ivy and Jen and Chloe when they ask if I'm okay. I chuck the baton at the ground and stomp off the track, ignoring my teammates' shouts for me to come back.

Coach Barnes's voice is the one that cuts through the fog in my head. He runs in front of me, and I'm taken back by how red his face is. The vein in his neck pulses like it's about to pop. He doesn't look good. I think he might need to go to the hospital. "Once the meet ends, I want you back on the track. You owe me ten laps. One for dropping the baton and nine for throwing the damn thing."

"No," I say. "I'm leaving."

"You're not done competing."

The rest of whatever he's saying is lost on me because I'm not paying attention anymore. There's only one thing on my mind, and it definitely isn't this stupid track meet. I don't care how much trouble I'll get in for leaving. I can't stay here, so I walk over to my car and leave.

The rage building inside me is directed at two people. Lena and Quincy. I gave them so many opportunities to tell me the truth. To tell me everything. And yeah, maybe I would've been upset, but maybe I could've gotten over it—maybe not this week or month or even this year—but eventually, I would've let all the hurt and anger that came from them telling me the truth fade away. We could've started over again. Really got the fresh start we should've had months ago. Instead, they kept something massive from me, and I can't forgive them for that.

I'm so upset that I drop my keys onto the floor of my car, but I don't bother picking them up. I ring their doorbell, finger jamming down on the button with enough force to snap it. When pressing a button isn't enough to satisfy me, I start pounding my fist on the hardwood.

"Quincy!" *Bang. Bang. Bang.* "Lena! Open the door!"

The door flies open. Lena's irritated expression doesn't disappear when she sees it's me. "Girl, why are you banging on my door like you the police? And where the hell is your key?"

"You had another kid." I shove past her and stomp through the kitchen and living room, looking for Quincy. A large part of me wants it to not be true. I want there to have been a mix-up. Quincy's mom got it wrong. Bedroom. Bathroom. Still no Quincy. Basement. Yes. The question is on my lips, threatening to spill out, when I see Quincy standing over his pool table. "You had another kid? You didn't think that was important information for me to know?"

Lena walks around me and goes to stand beside Quincy. She can't even look at me.

"Who the hell told you we had another kid?" Quincy asks.

"Is it true?" I ask. Neither of them says anything. "You had him a few years after my grandparents took me. He was adopted instead of being sent to live with family like I was."

"How did you—"

It's not a no. "Oh, my God. How could you not tell me?"

"We didn't want you to know how badly we failed," Lena says. "We were embarrassed."

"I don't care how embarrassed you were," I say. "You stuff it down and say what needs to be said. You don't sit on the truth like cowards."

"A'ight, look, we fucked up like everybody else in the world," Quincy says. "Let's squash it."

"Like I could ever trust you again," I say. "How many other kids did you have? Am I gonna get a visit from an eight-year-old at college? Do y'all have a toddler living with Quincy's cousin? How many? Tell me."

"It's just you and him," Lena says, reaching for me. "We're sorry."

I slap her hand away and glare at her through tears. "Don't touch me."

"Aaliyah baby—"

"Don't call me that," I say. "You should've told me about my brother. It wasn't right of you to keep that from me. After everything, I deserved to know that. But this entire time you've only ever admitted to things when you have no choice. I'm sick of that. I'm sick of things being this way."

"Then we'll switch up," Quincy says. "Tell you everything. The full story."

I laugh bitterly because they still don't get it. They won't ever get it. "It's the same thing with you two every time. You lie, and then I find out the truth and you tell me that's the last lie you'll tell me. And then a few weeks later, *boom*. Another freaking lie."

"Aaliyah baby—"

"I'm not your baby," I interrupt, chest heaving harder by the second. "Two kids. You had two kids, and you messed up with both of them. You treated us both like dirt and then you lost us and what? You thought it was cool to come back into my life after Grandpa Joe took care of all the hard stuff? Is that your thing? Are you gonna do it with my brother too? Ignore him for sixteen years and then pop up out of nowhere like everything's cool?"

"That isn't what we were trying to do," Lena continues. It's all she says because the intensity of my glare sends whatever other bull crap she was going to say right back into her mouth.

"How about you calm down and we'll sort this shit out when you do," Quincy says.

"Don't tell me to calm down when you've been lying to me this entire time. You were never gonna tell me, were you?"

"We . . . we . . ." Lena trails off, eyes wide as she looks at Quincy for help, but he says nothing.

I leave the basement before she tries to spin this in some way to make me feel bad for them. They aren't going to trick me into forgiving them again. As I walk through their house, Lena attempts to appeal to me one more time.

"Aaliyah baby—"

I spin on my heel, completely sick of her garbage caring-mother act. "I'm not your fucking baby!"

Lena's mouth drops. She looks to Quincy again for help, but he's as speechless as she is. Even 1 can't believe what came out of my mouth. But the anger and hurt 1 feel is real and needed to be expressed in a way that could only be accomplished by cursing. They lost me because they weren't ready to be parents, and instead of taking the time to learn from that experience, they turned around and had another kid and lost him too. Grandpa Joe was wrong to abandon Lena when she needed him, but he was right about my parents being unreliable. 1 don't need people like them in my life.

14

I'm forced to temporarily forget about Lena and Quincy and all our problems for the next three weeks because it's May, which means State is around the corner. It's easy because I haven't told anyone about my brother, mostly because I want to be the one to tell Grandpa Joe and this family has a habit of telling him things that I don't want him to know just yet.

After pushing myself through the brutal punishment Coach Barnes doled out to me for being unprofessional at our final meet of the season, I'm in incredible shape and easily earn a spot at State in the qualifying round, along with my teammates.

State is at the Eastern Illinois University O'Brien Stadium this year, and the crowd is packed with the friends and family of the athletes on the track. I keep to myself during all the events before mine, with my music blasting in my AirPods. It's abnormal for me. Usually, I'd be watching my teammates compete and would be cheering them on, but I'm not feeling up to it. Even though Shirley made feel a bit better when she called earlier to wish me good luck, I'm still pretty bummed out because Grandpa Joe isn't here yet.

I know I shouldn't let his absence affect me at this point. He's missed every meet I've had this year, but with him on the mend, I thought this would be the one he made it to. It's important. This is the final competition of my high school career, and after everything that's happened, I need Grandpa Joe on my side for this last win.

Jen comes over to where I'm sitting off to the side of the bleachers and gestures for me to remove my AirPods. "You're not talking to anyone, and it's starting to worry some people on the team."

"Some people or Ivy?"

"Ivy. And me. Everything okay?"

I push my AirPods back into their slots and shut the case. The roar of the crowd is much louder than it was when I had my music on. I almost wish I hadn't taken my earbuds out. The noise is as much of a distraction as Jen's questions. "Not really."

"Talk to me."

"I think I'm nervous." It's not exactly what's wrong, but I don't wanna go into the real reasons why I'm upset. Thinking about my grandpa missing out on this meet any more than I already have is just going to ruin my concentration, and I need to lock in. "It's our last high school meet. After this, everything will change, and if we lose, there's no coming back next year to try to redeem ourselves. This is it."

"It's been freaking me out too. Ivy had to calm me down on FaceTime last night."

I look at her curiously. Because of our fight, I hadn't been clued into Ivy's personal life, and I didn't want to talk about her when I was with Jen for obvious reasons. But this? Them talking all the time and helping each other when I'm not around isn't normal. "You and my cousin are close now. Is something going on I should know about?"

"Something like what?"

"*Something.*"

"That's a question for Ivy. Not me."

It's a weird thing to say. If nothing is going on, then the answer should be a resounding no. But she's being weird, which means the true answer is yes. I drop my AirPods case onto the turf and lean back on my hands, staring out at the track as a few boys competing in the 4x800-meter relay run past. "She's crushing on you, isn't she?"

"She's not *not* crushing on me."

"Is it reciprocated?"

Jen's pinky brushes up against mine, and despite all the shouting and cheering from the stands and the other athletes, things feel weirdly peaceful for once. I think that might be the Jen effect. "It couldn't be while you two weren't cool. I felt like you might see it as a betrayal if I picked a side, even though I never actually chose you or her."

"And now?"

"I like her."

"Why didn't you just tell me? I know why she didn't, but we've never not been cool. You could've said something, and you didn't."

"Ivy wanted to keep it a secret. She said you were gonna keep bugging us about not breaking up until after State, so we didn't ruin our relay flow."

"I mean, that's common sense. The only reason the team didn't fall apart when me and Ivy weren't talking is because she switched with you. There's only so much switching we can do before we run out of options."

"Well, I figured it doesn't matter anymore because track is over after the weekend. Are you cool with us being together?"

"Of course I am."

Jen grins and pulls me to my feet, dragging me over to where the rest of our relay team is waiting. It sort of feels like she started this conversation so she could come clean about her relationship with Ivy. I'm okay with that. At least she told me instead of letting me figure it out on my own like some people. But I can't think about Lena and Quincy right now. I need to focus on the race.

I drop my AirPods in my bag and remind my team of the order before our relay starts. Chloe. Ivy. Jen. Me. After that, I keep my head down and don't say another word as the girls get into position. As the anchor, I'm on the side of the track closest to the crowd. Like usual, Tommy is here to support us. Even his and Jen's parents called off work so they could be here. There are only three people missing. Grandpa Joe and Ivy's parents.

Tommy waves from the crowd when he sees me watching, then he unfolds the large sign he was carrying with him. It says DO BETTER THAN LAST TIME.

I love how much of a goof he is. He makes it easier for me not to take life too seriously.

Coach Barnes has his stopwatch out with his thumb hovering over the start button. "We need a good start, Watts! Come on, just like you and Sullivan practiced."

Chloe nods at our coach and sinks down. Fingertips on the track. Feet on the blocks. Head tucked down.

"Ready."

As I glance at the crowd of people entering the track with snacks from the concession stand, I spot Uncle William. Then I see Auntie Yolanda. And finally, Grandpa Joe in his wheelchair. I smile for the first time today. He made it. I get a burst of energy that I don't know I would've had if he hadn't shown up when he did. Now I just need to channel it into a win.

"Set."

Chloe and the rest of the runners in her leg push themselves up. The guy holding the starter pistol aims it in the air and pulls the trigger. After near constant practice with Ivy on the blocks for the past three weeks, Chloe's start is flawless. She rounds the bend neck and neck with a girl from Whitney Young. The handoff to Ivy is seamless, and Ivy inches her way to a slight lead on the straightaway.

Jen starts running slower than her normal speed, so she doesn't leave Ivy in the dust, but takes off like a rocket the moment the baton is in her hand. She's a bullet on the bend, and I can hear the excited screams from the crowd as she pulls ahead of the girls in her leg.

I stay slightly bent over with my eyes on Jen until she crosses into the handoff zone. Eyes forward. Run. My takeoff is faster than it would've been if Ivy had still been the third leg because I know Jen will catch me. I extend my arm behind me and hold on tight when Jen puts the baton in my hand.

Coach Barnes is off to the side, running next to me, jumping, and punching the air all in one fluid motion. "Go, Campbell! Go!"

The anchor for Whitney Young matches my pace initially, but she's no competition for me. I pump my arms and move forward. Forward. Forward. Soon she's no longer next to me and is only in my peripheral, trailing by at least a second. I don't let myself get comfortable though. I push through the pain and the suffocating humidity and all the fear I had about dropping the baton again and dart across the finish line, still in first place.

Grandpa Joe is the first person I look for, but Coach Barnes is the first one I see. He's shouting something, struggling to be heard over the roaring crowd as he and the other coaches lose their minds. I make out only one word—record.

We broke a record. *We broke a record.*

Baton still in hand, I meet Jen halfway and leap into her arms screaming. Ivy and Chloe sprint across the grass, and together, Jen and I tell them the news. We're a twisted-up mess of arms and legs and tears, and I think I might pass out from the excitement.

Ivy makes it to our family first. She kisses Grandpa Joe on his cheek like ten times and even though he makes a face like he hates it, I know he's going to think about that moment often and smile. Ivy's engulfed in her parents' arms by the time I separate myself from Jen and Chloe.

I run to Grandpa Joe and fall into his lap with tears in my eyes. The fact that he's even here when he could barely speak or walk four months ago is a miracle, and I can't stop my emotions from getting the best of me.

"Look at me, kiddo."

I ignore the people around us trying to congratulate me and focus on my grandpa. I'm so geeked right now. I can't keep the smile off my face for long because he's here.

"Gotta go to college," Grandpa Joe says. "Never seen you happier than when you run."

"But—"

"Already worked everything out. Yolanda and William's lease is up in August. They're moving into the house to take care of me since we got the room."

Auntie Yolanda comes to the rescue again. She's done so much for us over the years, and now she's putting her life on the back burner to help out Grandpa Joe even more than she already has. The woman is truly an angel.

"I'm switching over to the night shift at work," Uncle William says. "That way somebody's always home with Joe during the week."

"You and Ivy can help on breaks and weekends as long as it doesn't interfere with school and track," Auntie Yolanda says. "It'll be tough, but I think we can make this work if we all chip in."

I wrap up my uncle and auntie in the tightest hug I can muster. As grateful as I am for Auntie Yolanda, I know none of this would be possible if she hadn't married the coolest dude in the world. Uncle William is willing to uproot his life and change his schedule to help us. That deserves to be acknowledged.

With my auntie and uncle helping Grandpa Joe, I'll have time to attend college and run like I wanted to. No, I won't be going to my dream school, but running somewhere is better than running nowhere.

I don't say it out loud, and I hate that I'm even thinking it, but I'm glad I don't have to give up on running yet. Without it, I'd be as lost as I was after Grandpa Joe had his stroke. But thanks to my family, I can help my grandpa as he continues to recuperate and still do what I love.

15

Going back to Lena and Quincy only a few weeks after our last confrontation probably isn't the smartest thing to do, but I've never made good decisions when it comes to them. I hang around outside their house for over an hour because I can't gather the nerve to walk up to their front door and ring the bell.

I already know what I want to say. If they truly do care about me, they'll do what I ask without question. But as much as I hope they'll do right by me, I don't know that they will. They care about me in the shallowest way possible. Their caring lacks real depth. It's surface-level and nowhere close to the way Grandpa Joe cares for me.

And maybe it's because they don't know me the way he does. We didn't spend enough time together for them to care about me on a deeper level. But I also feel like that's total crap. They're my parents. There shouldn't have been a need for it to get to a deeper level. It should've been there from the jump. They shouldn't have to get to know me before they could care about me and my feelings.

I stand tall and ring their doorbell. No one knows I'm here. I held the secret about my brother close to the chest because once one person knew, everyone would, and Grandpa Joe physically isn't healthy enough to hear this news yet.

Lena is the one who answers the door. She freezes, eyes widening at the sight of me. "Aaliyah b—I mean, Aaliyah. We didn't think we'd see you again."

And they didn't make an effort to reach out in the three weeks since I confronted them about the existence of my brother either. That isn't lost on me. Even during our worst arguments, Grandpa Joe eventually made an effort because his love for me and the need to have me in his life overpowered his anger.

It didn't always have to be me reaching out to him. He's not perfect and he's made a lot of mistakes, but he's done his best to own up to them. It took him a bit longer after our fight about Lena, but eventually, he came to terms with his fault in that, and we were able to move past it. That's what I want from Lena and Quincy. Effort. I'm here now to see if they can give me that.

"Who's at the door?" Quincy asks.

"It's Aaliyah, baby," Lena says.

"Aaliyah? Our Aaliyah?"

"How many Aaliyahs do you know, Quincy?"

Quincy comes running from wherever he was in the house with a smug smile on his face. "Told you she wouldn't be mad forever."

Lena invites me into the house, and the three of us walk into the living room together. Quincy sits on the couch with Lena. I sit on the loveseat. Neither of them speaks, so I take the initiative and kick off what's hopefully going to be a good conversation.

"I know you think me coming here today means I'm not mad anymore, but that's not true. I'm still upset, and I have a right to be. That doesn't mean I should've yelled at you the way I did. I think the news just came at the wrong time, you know? I had finally started to feel comfortable around you. I'd started to trust you. And then . . ." I make an explosion sound with my mouth. "I didn't know how to deal with the news about my brother, and instead of talking about it, I let my emotions get the best of me. So I'm really sorry for screaming at you the way I did. It was super not chill of me."

"Ay, it's all water under the bridge now," Quincy says. "We can move past it."

There's the Quincy I've gotten to know over the past few months. He's all nonchalant like this is something we can just "move past" instead of recognizing that it's a massive problem we need to resolve.

Because it's clear they won't apologize on their own, I say, "You never called to say sorry. Three weeks went by, and I never even got a text explaining your side of things. That hurt."

"Didn't think you wanted to hear from us after the way you left," Quincy says.

"You're supposed to push anyway. My grandpa pushed and because of that, we were able to make it through one of the worst arguments we've ever had."

Quincy rises from his spot on the couch, all pissed off because I dared to mention my grandpa around him. "Man, fuck Joe. He poisoned you against us."

"No, you did that," I say. "Despite everything he said about the two of you, I was still willing to give you a chance, and you

345

ruined it. This is on you. Both of you. Don't blame him for your mistakes."

"You're right, and we're gonna spend every possible moment making it up to you," Lena says. "We'll learn to be better. We promise. Right, Quincy?"

They still don't seem to understand the reason why I'm here. I thought it would be obvious. Apparently it isn't, so I need to spell it out for them. "I want an apology for keeping my brother a secret and for going three weeks without trying to make things right. It's gotta be a real one from both of you, and you've gotta mean it. That's what I want. It's nonnegotiable."

"Might as well ask for a billion dollars while you at it," Quincy says.

It's not a surprise that Quincy is against giving me the apology I deserve. He seems like the kind of guy who's never apologized for anything a day in his life. But Lena isn't like that, and if I have to cut him out and only deal with her from now on, then so be it.

Except Lena isn't looking at me. She keeps her focus on Quincy and instead of forming her own opinions and apologizing, she waits until he shakes his head. Her eyes don't meet mine again.

A lack of an apology from Lena is more disappointing than not getting one from Quincy because that's just how he is. But her? I thought she cared about me. And maybe she does, but it's clear she cares about Quincy just a little more.

"I think it'll be better for everyone if we don't see each other anymore," I say.

Quincy rolls his eyes. "Quit being dramatic. So we didn't tell you we had another kid. Who fucking cares? It ain't like he was living with us this whole time and we tried to hide him from you. He's not ours anymore."

"You had a responsibility to tell me about him, whether he lived with you or not," I say.

Quincy's response is nothing but a grunt. He's perched on the arm of the couch with his arms crossed and a stank expression on his face. That lets me know I'm right for cutting him off. He won't change.

I keep my head high, so they don't misinterpret my sadness for weakness. "If you won't apologize, then this conversation is over."

Quincy stands, nods at me, and disappears somewhere into the house, leaving me with a version of Lena I've never seen before. The realization that this is it for us must've settled in, because she has tears in her eyes and keeps shaking her head.

Honestly, I'm not sure what to do, but I feel bad leaving her the way Quincy just did. I cross the room and squat in front of her, and she wraps her arms around me tight, sobbing into my neck. I don't know how I end up comforting her when I'm the one who was hurt, but I'm not mean enough to turn her away. I let her hold on to me as tight as she wants because this is the last time I'll ever see her. I won't invite her to see me off to college or to any of my college track meets. No birthdays or holidays will be spent together. She won't be there for any of it because I don't want her to be. This moment is all we'll have, so I let the moment last because I think I need it too.

EPILOGUE
SEPTEMBER

Before I know it, it's moving day. I'm nervous about starting this new chapter in my life. I'll be, hopefully, making new friends and learning new things and experiencing all the exciting college moments Tommy has told me about, and the best part is, I won't need to do any of it on my own. Ivy, Jen, and Tommy will be with me every step of the way. It's the biggest reason why I chose to attend the University of Chicago versus another in-state school.

Because all first- and second-year students attending the University of Chicago have to live on campus, Ivy and I pack up our belongings and stuff everything into the back of our cars with a lot of help from Tommy.

He takes a brief break and sits on the curb, a cold bottle of water clutched in his hand and a scowl on his face. After helping Jen move into our dorm earlier, and now us, he's tired and super aggy. "You three have too much shit."

"Quit talking so much," Ivy says. "We need you to have all your strength so you can help when we get to the dorm."

Tommy side-eyes her and grumbles that we're taking advantage of him as he follows her back into my house. He's not wrong. But it's not like Grandpa Joe can help us while he's stuck in a wheelchair, and Ivy's dad won't be back in town until next week. So it's up to Tommy to help us do the work of, like, three dudes by himself. I'll help, of course, and so will Auntie Yolanda. Ivy, not so much. She's not lazy per se, but she's definitely a pro at wiggling her way out of doing any real work.

I carry my Nike bag and backpack filled with new school supplies out of the house and attempt to squeeze them both into the trunk of Ivy's car. It's a tight fit, but I make it work. After a quick survey of the quiet block, I take a breath and sit on Tommy's recently vacated spot on the curb. This isn't how I expected move-in day to go back when I started to seriously panic about what the college experience would be like for me. It's better than I could've hoped for because I'm not alone. I'll be going to a school that's close, with the people I care about. If I start to stumble, the ones I trust will be there to pick me up. And while the track-and-field program at University of Chicago isn't on the same level as UCLA, they have a great coaching staff and amazing athletes on the roster.

I do still have worries. Even though Grandpa Joe is on the mend and I'll only be thirty minutes away, leaving him is hard for me. I keep imagining the worst things happening to him while I'm gone. He could pass out and hurt himself. Have another stroke.

Die from a heart attack. With the amount of health issues he has, the possibilities are endless.

Grandpa Joe rolls up to the curb with a pair of thick black sunglasses on. He told me the sun has felt extra bright since his stroke, so I bought them for him. With his money, of course. I'm not rich.

"I'll be all right, kiddo," he says.

"How'd you know I was thinking about you?" I ask.

"Ivy told me I'm all you've been talking about lately. Don't know how many times I've gotta tell you that I'm the grandpa. I'm 'posed to be worried about you. Not the other way around."

"It can be both ways."

"No, the hell it can't."

I don't bother arguing with him because I know I won't win. He's still stubborn. Maybe more so since his stroke, but it's easier to talk to him about the hard stuff now. I don't know if he would've changed if everything hadn't happened the way it did. It's the one good thing that came out of the disaster that was my short attempt at forming a relationship with my parents, and it's why I feel comfortable telling him the truth about why I no longer want them around.

Part of me wanted Quincy and Lena to ignore what I said and continue to push for a relationship with me out of their love for me. I wanted them to care enough about me to show up, even if I told them not to. I wanted them to say, "Forget what you want. We're what you need." Just once I wanted them to be decent to me. To be honest with me no matter how hard it was. To apologize when they were in the wrong instead of trying to brush past their fault in the whole thing. But they're incapable of doing that, and I'm slowly learning to be okay with it.

"Grandpa, I have something to tell you about Quincy and Lena, and I need to know that you're okay to hear it."

Grandpa Joe takes a few deep, calming breaths like I showed him. He won't admit that he might have just as much anxiety as me, but after missing three months of my life, he's more receptive to taking care of himself now. "I can hear it."

I believe him. It takes me some time to tell him because as much as I trust he can handle the news, I know it still has the potential to break him. It nearly destroyed me, and I don't have the health problems my grandpa does. But no one else is around, so this is the perfect time to reveal the truth. "I finally understand what you meant when you said they were no good. Not necessarily as people, but as parents. They're not like you. They can't handle it when things get hard. They don't change. And they lie, not to protect their child, but because they're scared to look bad and don't want to have the tough talks that every parent has to have. That's why I forgave you and not them because when push came to shove, they kept lying, but you took responsibility and made an effort to be different."

"They're lucky I can't walk. I'd march over there and whup both of their asses right now if I could."

He knows the risks of letting his temper get the best of him. His doctors are always telling him about how he needs to be calmer in his daily life. He's usually better about not allowing himself to get all worked up, but Quincy and Lena are such a sensitive topic that it's hard for him to regulate his emotions.

"Grandpa, come on."

"I'm calm. Tell me."

"I found out something when I was staying with Quincy and Lena." Just remembering the conversation I had with Quincy's mother is almost too much to handle. I put my head in my hands as all the pain I felt and shock and anger comes rushing back. "They had another kid. A boy. Quincy's mom assumed he was with us because he was taken from them like I was. I don't have a name or an age or anything really. I just know that he exists, and he's out there somewhere."

I let Grandpa Joe sit with the revelation. He'll no doubt have questions that I won't be able to answer, but at least we can navigate this together now that he knows. It was hard keeping this secret from him for so long, and maybe it wasn't right to hide it, but I needed to know he was ready to hear it without it torpedoing all the progress he's made since he had the stroke. Over the last four months, he's proven he can handle receiving news he doesn't like, and that's why I've decided to bring this up to him now.

Tommy exits the house with a bunch of bags hanging off him. He shoots a questioning look at me when he sees my grandpa staring out into the street as cars drive by. He's quick to move on when I mouth that I have it under control.

I don't need to see Grandpa Joe's eyes to know he's upset. A tear slides down his cheek, and I end up having to stand to check on him because he hasn't moved or said anything since I dropped the news about my brother. I can quickly tell it's nothing like it was before. His face is fine, and he holds on to my hand when I rest it on the arm of his wheelchair. I ask him if he's okay even though I already know the answer.

"Would've took him if I'd known," he says finally.

"They wanted him to stay a secret, so he did."

Grandpa Joe asks if I can find him. It's a question I knew he'd ask, and I wish I had a better answer for him. I tell him the truth. I don't know if I can, and I don't know if I even want to. I'm sure my brother has a nice family that loves him and takes care of him. I'm not sure if I want to wreck the peace he's built for however long he's been alive. It's not fair of me to do that to him. To force myself into his life when he may not want me in it. I've had enough of trying to force myself into the lives of people who only want me there some of the time.

My whole life I just wanted to feel wanted. I wanted to feel like I was enough. That I was loved. But I had that. I had it in Auntie Yolanda and Uncle William, who supported me not just monetarily but emotionally, and took me in when I had nowhere else to go. I had it in Ivy, who cared so much about me and pushed me to want more for myself and the people in my life. I had it in Jen and her parents, who let me live in their house for free at a time when everything was falling apart. And I had it in Tommy, who, despite going through something horrible with Sabrina, still had it in him to be my rock during the worst time of my life. I have all the family and love I need and always have. I just couldn't see it until now.

ACKNOWLEDGMENTS

If *I Could Go Back* was inspired by the unexpected death of my grandfather, Willie, in August 2019. I'll never forget when I got the call. I was working an overnight shift at Amazon and was finally allowed to use my phone on a break. I checked my messages and saw that my sister had been blowing me up. When I called her back and she told me the news, I couldn't breathe. It felt like the walls were closing in on me. I got so weak that I couldn't stand. I didn't say much and hung up the phone and I broke down and cried right there in the middle of the breakroom. I could barely get out the words "My grandpa is dead" when I was asked what was wrong. They could have had me work through it. Told me to suck it up and move on, but they didn't. I was allowed to leave work. A coworker walked me to my car, and I sat in the driver's seat for a while just bawling my eyes out. I was alone and broken and I didn't know what to do or who to talk to. So, I wrote. I wrote a book about a man who stepped up and took care of his granddaughter and protected her. I wrote a book about a girl who loves her grandpa more than anyone else in the world. And most importantly, I wrote a book about a grandfather who went through a horrible medical crisis and *lived*. Unfortunately, my grandfather will never read this book. He won't know that it was inspired by the man that he was and the love I have for him. I miss you *so* much, Grandpa.

Thank you to my agent, Sam Farkas, for taking a chance on me. I knew from the first moment we spoke that you would be the perfect person to champion me and my stories. There were no other choices for me. It was always only you. You're the person I trust the most when it comes to the books and characters I create, and I can't wait to continue on this journey with you by my side.

Thank you to my editor, Ashley Hearn, for seeing something great in this story and guiding me in the right direction. The changes you suggested made this story even stronger than it was and I couldn't imagine working on this with anyone else.

Mom. I love you with my whole heart. Without you, none of this would be possible. Your strength has inspired me and allowed me to push myself to be the best version of me. Watching you grow and not only meet your goals but exceed them has been such a joy. All I've ever wanted was to make something of myself in the hopes that you'd be proud of me. I hope you are now.

To Grandma Cheryle, what can I say? You were my rock and my safe place at a time when I desperately needed it, and I will always be grateful to you for that. I could put together a string of words to say how much you mean to me, but it wouldn't suffice. So, I'll just say—thank you. Thank you for taking care of me while my mom was working her way through school. Thank you for the laughs we've shared over the years. Thank you for being there for me when I needed you. And thank you for encouraging me to read as a child. This book wouldn't exist without you.

To my younger sister, Taylor, our five-year age gap doesn't mean a thing. You are my best friend. I have more fun with you than I do with anyone else. I laugh more with you. I'm excited about life because of you. Most of the pictures and videos saved on my phone have you in them. Sometimes I go back through the memories we've made together and start laughing all over again. You've grown into an amazing woman. I love you.

Alaysia. Girl. You already know what it is. I'm so glad I met you. Thank you for all the FaceTimes and the good times we've had and for helping me in more ways than just with my writing. You're my writing bestie and I value you as a true friend.

Laurie Dennison, you're an angel. I'm forever indebted to you for taking on my book during Pitch Wars and for mentoring me. I wouldn't have gotten my agent without you. Thank you for everything and I wish you nothing but the best.

And to Jamee . . . Well, I could go on for pages about how impactful you were in my life. None of the books I've written would have been written if it weren't for you encouraging me to write them. I'll always love you for that and for so much more.

To everyone who has helped me in any way with my books over the years—the No Drama Zone that has drama sometimes; Mykel, who read the first book I ever wrote and has been one of my best friends since 2013; the lovely and extremely busy Liz, whom I don't talk to nearly enough; Amaan, who helped me come up with the title *If I Could Go Back*; Khalil, for our brainstorming sessions while working at Amazon; and Veronica (Vi), for using your incredible talent to create stickers and bookmarks for this book—you're all so incredible and were so helpful to me during this entire process. Thank you!

Lastly, thank you to you, the reader who picked up this book and decided it was worth your time. I hope you enjoy it and love the story and the characters as much as I do.

ABOUT THE
AUTHOR

BRIANA JOHNSON is a young adult author and Chicago native. She spent her twenties living everywhere except Chicago, but has returned to the Windy City because everywhere else is too expensive. She currently lives on the North Side with her sister. A graduate of the University of Maryland Global Campus with a degree in computer networking and cybersecurity, Briana travels the U.S. as a systems analyst. When she isn't writing or working, she enjoys seeing all the beauty the world has to offer. *If I Could Go Back* is her debut novel.

⟡𝕏 @WikipediaBri